The Brensham Trilogy

The Blue Field

John Moore was born in Gloucestershire in 1907 and educated at Malvern College. As he himself said, his half-hearted efforts in school and in business were always overshadowed by his keen love of nature study and his irrepressible passion for writing. He spent several years hitch-hiking round the world, writing freelance articles and short stories about his travels, including 'Tiger, Tiger' and 'The Octopus'. Many of his novels are set around Tewkesbury, where he lived for a major part of his life, and with books such as *Portrait of Elmbury*, *Brensham Village* and *The Blue Field* he made his name as an unrivalled chronicler of the English countryside. He died in 1967.

Also available in the Brensham Trilogy

Portrait of Elmbury
Brensham Village

The Brensham Trilogy

The Blue Field

John Moore

Pan Books London and Sydney

First published 1946 by Wm Collins Sons & Company Ltd
This edition published 1971 by Pan Books Ltd,
Cavaye Place, London SW10 9PG
3rd printing 1976

ISBN 0 330 02870 7
Printed in Great Britain by
Richard Clay (The Chaucer Press) Ltd, Bungay, Suffolk

To

COMPTON MACKENZIE

in affectionate regard

CONTENTS

AUTHOR'S NOTE

This book is a successor and companion-piece to *Brensham Village*, which in its turn continued the account of people and happenings in England's 'Middle West' begun in *Portrait of Elmbury*. Some of the same characters appear in all three books; and *The Blue Field* carries the story up to the present day. I should like to emphasize once again that 'Brensham' is not a particular village but a synthesis of villages; into which I have imported certain characters, real and imaginary, whenever it suited my purpose to do so.

JOHN MOORE

April 1948

PART ONE

LANDSCAPE WITH FIGURES

Poetry and Sprouts – Crack-brained Brensham – My People – The Top of the Hill – The Blue Field – The Two Potterers – The Ploughgirl – Frolick Virgins – Young Corydon – Letter from a Liberator – 'The Pastoral Loves of Daphnis and Chloe' – The Wild Old Man – Carnivorous Cider – Mr Hart, Wainwright – Goodman Delver – The Poacher – The Trophy – 'A Foolish Thing Was but a Toy' – Old Adam – The Ruin of Orris – O Fortunatos Nimium – 'It will have blood, they say; blood will have blood' – Ups and Downs – Liberty 'All – Fermented Happiness – Pru – Our MP – Mrs Halliday – The Irreconcilable

Poetry and Sprouts

MY PEOPLE have poetry in their hearts and dreams in their heads – and, for much of the time, what feels like half the West Midlands on their boots. They are a quick, imaginative, even a passionate people, but they also grow excellent asparagus, fat Victoria plums, and the best brussels sprouts in England. For many months, therefore, they slop about through the rich dark mud of their little farms, holdings and market-gardens, ploughing, mucking, spraying, grafting, pruning, sprout-picking, and so on. At times they are circumscribed by large and lesser floods, and at others the hoar frost on the sprout-tops makes their hands so cold that I have seen the men, as well as the land girls, crying with the pain of it. Nevertheless they sing songs and dream dreams; though you might not have suspected them of it if you had leaned with me over the gate of William Hart's Nine-acre Piece, as he called it, on a typical November day and watched the gumbooted bumpkins (for so they would have seemed to you) at work in the half-flooded fields.

At such a season the prospect which confronts you is gloomy in the extreme. Over the gate lies a black morass, in which yesterday's rain has made a chain of little lakes and upon which as like as not today's rain drips softly with a hissing sound rather like the noise made by an old and disillusioned ostler grooming a horse. The brussels sprouts, melancholy of aspect, rise up out of the mud and are reflected in the dirty water; their yellowing outer leaves, torn off by the winds or the sprout-pickers, sail idly upon the brown lagoons. Of all the crops cultivated by man, sprouts make the dreariest landscape; and I believe the English are the only nation which spends its labours upon growing and tending them, which cherishes and takes pride in them, and which eventually eats them with relish. It is an addiction which we share with the caterpillars of the large white butterfly, and with certain sorts of blight.

The sprout-pickers, one to each row, bend low over the plants, heads down, behinds in the air, in the traditional attitude of ostriches, and when they have finished one plant they straighten themselves painfully and hobble to the next. There are men, women, and even a few children as well, for whole families take a hand when the tight-folded buds, as hard as walnuts and almost the same size, are ripe for picking and worth ten shillings a pot. So you would have seen in old William's field not only his regular workmen and his quota of land girls but also a few of his relations and neighbours, putting in a day's work either because they needed the money or because William had lent *them* some labour when they were picking their plums or their peas.

At sprout-picking time we get into the way of recognizing people by their behinds: and from William's gate I should have been able to point out to you the neat and rounded bottoms of Mimi and Meg, the landlord's daughters from the Horse and Harrow Inn, the corduroy trousers of Briggs the blacksmith (for sprout-picking is sometimes more profitable than waiting for horses to shoe), the often-patched breeks of Jaky Jones the odd-job-man, the blue ones of Dai Roberts Postman (if he had finished delivering the letters), the camouflaged paratroops' jacket of George Daniels who dropped into Normandy on D-Day and has never worn anything else since, and the enormous, elliptical and inexplicably sombre behind of Count Pniack, the Polish soldier who married Mimi during the war and fathered the twins whose light-blonde heads exactly match the yellow of the floating sprout leaves. Somewhere about we should probably have seen a pram, in which two illegitimate children belonging to William Hart's youngest daughter, like Spartan brats exposed in the Apothetae, slept peacefully despite the cold rain; while their mother Pru, surely the naughtiest girl in Brensham, picked sprouts in proximity to the most personable young man she could find. In addition to all these there would have been about half a dozen land girls, with coloured handkerchiefs tied turban-fashion over their hair in the forlorn hope, I suppose, of preserving the wave in it until the village dance on Saturday night. Even though they were working a quarter of a mile away, and all bent industriously over their task, old William could have told you which was which without a moment's hesitation. Susan, Margie, Lisbeth, Betsy, Wistaria (believe it or not!) and Ive: 'I knows 'em by their little backsides, you see.'

And his leathery, apple-cheeked face, framed in the wild white beard, would have creased into the multitudinous grin which heralded his belly-rumbling laughter.

There was always a great deal of noise and laughter going on round William. Being crippled with arthritis, he could not work with the pickers, but stood by the spring-balance which was hung on an improvised tripod at the gate; and as he weighed the bags and kept the tally of them he maintained a ceaseless flow of banter and tomfoolery, teasing, chaffing, giving everybody nicknames – 'Old P silent', for instance, for Mimi's husband, because that was how the Pole tried to explain the pronunciation of his difficult name. Somehow it always seemed warmer in the part of the field where William was, as if he were a kind of human brazier, giving out a benevolent glow. Indeed, now I come to think of it, he did remind one of a brazier because the weather, aided perhaps by the home-made wine which he drank in tumblerfuls, had burned his face a deep fire-red. It shone like a little sun through the white mist of his beard, among the lustreless lagoons, the skeleton sprouts and the wan yellow leaves; but outside the range of that radiance the chilly dampness lay all about, it came down with the fine rain and struck upwards from the dark brown mud in which the feet of the pickers went *slosh*, *squelch*, *slosh*, *squelch* as they carried the bulging white bags to the weighing-place by the gate.

No, indeed, if you looked at Brensham in wintertime you wouldn't suspect us of poetry, you wouldn't credit us with dreams.

Cracked-brained Brensham

In April, of course, the scene is very different. Then our countryside seems made for poets to live in, though its brief loveliness would surely break their hearts. On the first fine day, when the chiff-chaff announces his arrival and the Brimstone butterfly comes out of hibernation, the plum blossom draws a diaphanous lace curtain over the vale; and next weekend the trippers come tearing down from Birmingham and the Black Country to admire the orchards in full bloom. 'Why, it's a dreamland!' I have heard them exclaim. Thereafter in turn the pear, the cherry and the apple burst out – and it is truly a bursting-out, as startling and violent as the explosion of a bomb, touched off by the south wind and the sunshine. It doesn't last long; the petals are generally falling when the cuckoo comes; but by then the young leaves have begun to unfold, and somehow the orchards seem to expand and spread themselves as the foliage gets thicker. Soon this green tide covers up the unlovely market-gardens, hides the seedling sprout-plants, and flows over the spring onions, carrots, radishes and potatoes which grow between the tree rows; so that by June the orchards have made a little forest round about the long straggling village of Brensham, and the second wave of tourists finds us embosked in an unexpected Arden.

Our crooked village street acts as a sort of trap, a lobster pot for tourists; slowed down by the bottlenecks and the sharp corners, they pause to look about them; and most of them are struck at once by something slightly unusual in the appearance of Brensham village, something which I can only describe as an *antic* appearance. For one thing it has never properly sorted itself out from the orchards, green leaf and brown thatch are everywhere intermingled, the plum and pear and apple trees lean crookedly over the street and you can stretch up your hand to pick a juicy Victoria as you walk along the pavement. For another, the half-timbered cottages which seem to grow up among the trees are likewise gibbous and asymmetrical as if one saw them in a distorting mirror. Suburbanites who are used to box-shaped houses, with the walls all plumb and the corners all right-angles, have difficulty in adjusting their eyes to our mis-shapen dwellings which bulge and lean and overhang as if they were about to collapse, and look as if they were rough-hewn out of some black-and-white matrix rather than built with a proper regard to stresses and strains. In fact, they settled themselves comfortably into these curious shapes three or four hundred years ago, soon after they were put up, and have scarcely shifted since; and they will probably still be standing when an atom bomb has reduced the suburbs to brick-dust, for they are the sort of tumbledown houses which never tumble down.

Because of this antic look, Brensham's ancient nickname suits it rather well. It is a nickname of which we are secretly proud: people call us crack-brained Brensham; and if you ask them why, in the neighbouring villages and in the market town of Elmbury, they will shake their heads and say that we are like that, 'tis a crack-brained place with crack-brained folks in it, allus was and allus will be till Kingdom Come. They will even tell you that it was Shakespeare himself who gave us the name; but I'm afraid there's no evidence for that. He is certainly supposed to have made up a rhyme about some other villages not far away: piping Pebworth, dancing Marston, haunted Hillbro', drunken Bidford, and so on; and crack-brained Brensham would have fitted into the rhyme very nice by – but it isn't there.

Anyhow, whoever invented it, the epithet is tagged on to Brensham for ever now; ours is the village where any extravagant thing may happen, and we are the unpredictable people of whom nobody knows what we're likely to do next. We are the subject of all sorts of tales and legends and proverbs and sayings at which old men in pubs have chuckled for hundreds of years and some of which are supposed to exemplify our extreme innocence and stupidity: we are the village, for instance, which 'mucked the church spire to make it grow'. But in others our alleged simplicity becomes mixed with a sort of wild and wayward fancy: we 'hurdled the cuckoo to keep it always spring'. Who wouldn't want to do that, in Brensham at blossom-time? A sublime folly indeed.

I don't know anything about the origin of these legends, but at any rate it is true that we possess the tallest church spire in three counties, and there's a little, square, willow-girt field next to our cricket-ground, to which the spring comes early with stitchwort and ladysmocks, and which is shown on the Ordnance Map as Cuckoo Pen.

Even the tall church spire, by the way, is slightly out of true; not startlingly so, but just enough to puzzle visitors, who cock their heads sideways to look at it and ask themselves: 'Is that spire straight or am I seeing crooked?' And there is another peculiarity about the church, which is dedicated, rather unconventionally, to Saint Mary Magdalene: the outside of its west wall bears traces of a coat of whitewash spattered all over with round marks each about the size of an orange. These marks are a source of great bewilderment to visiting archaeologists; but the explanation is really quite simple. Previous generations of crack-brained Brenshamites were in the habit of playing a game of their own invention – it somewhat resembled fives – against the west wall of the church, which they whitewashed annually for this purpose until some reforming clergyman decided that the practice was unseemly and had it stopped.

The village pubs, too, have unusual characteristics. The Adam and Eve bears two naked figures on its hanging sign, painted by an extremely uninhibited artist and displayed by a landlord who has no puritanical notions about fig leaves. The Trumpet, not to be outdone, shows the head of a bright-eyed, cherry-lipped, come-hither-looking minx on its sign, which strikes you as irrelevant until you learn that the name of the inn is locally corrupted to 'The Strumpet'. Lastly there is the Horse and Harrow (which Brensham calls the Horse Narrow) with its leaded windows over which the shaggy thatch comes down like beetling eyebrows and with an elder-shrub growing absurdly out of its chimney and forming a tuft of twigs like a feather in its cap. Beside the Horse and Harrow stands a large Blenheim apple tree; and the building and the tree seem to lean together, 'like a pair of drunks', says Joe Trentfield the landlord, 'when you can't tell which one is propping up t'other.'

I must not forget to mention Mrs Doan's Post Office and General Stores, which is remarkable chiefly because of the strange assortment of goods displayed in its window and upon its shelves. Most of these goods are extremely old-fashioned – there are curious Victorian hair-curlers stuck on cards decorated with engravings of curious Victorian hairstyles, there are boxes of lead soldiers belonging to armies and regiments long disbanded – 'Montenegrin Infantry' and 'Serbian Hussars', there are babies' rattles painted in red, white and blue to celebrate the jubilee of Queen Victoria, and milk jugs bearing the legend 'Mafeking', and framed pictures of the Coronation of King Edward the Seventh. There is even a 'line' in frilly bloomers, discreetly stored away on a top shelf. And every year in early February Mrs Doan fetches down from an attic or store-room a boxful of nineteenth-century Valentines, printed about 1880, which she hopefully lays out upon her counter.*

* These Victorian Valentines are not, as you might suppose, pretty-pretty or simpering, but are mocking and mischievous, taunting the young women for whom they were destined with possessing long noses or spots on their faces, or accusing the young men of being idle boasters,

Mrs Doan's mother, who had the shop before her, must I think have been possessed by a sort of *folie de grandeur* before she died; instead of ordering goods by the dozen she suddenly took to ordering them by the gross. And Mrs Doan has never troubled to replace the unsaleable lines, professing the belief that 'Folks would come back to them in the end.' Now, at long last, her faith is justified. Fashion has come full-circle, and the hairstyle shown on the copper-plate card advertising curlers begins to look startlingly modern. Summer visitors buy the Mafeking jugs as quaint curiosities; and even the frilly bloomers, we are told, are coming into favour again. As for the Valentines, they were discovered last year by the land girls from the hostel down the road, and since there are about two dozen land girls, each of whom at any given time is sure to be in love with six young men, Mrs Doan must have sold a whole gross of them. With renewed confidence she declares 'Folks will always come back to things, if only you've got the patience to wait long enough.'

Another old-fashioned thing which Mrs Doan deals in is peppermint – not the mildly-flavoured stuff which you buy in ordinary shops, but an aromatic concoction which will cure your cold (and very nearly blow your head off) if you pour a few drops of it into boiling water and sniff it before you go to bed. Mrs Doan distils this spirit, according to her mother's recipe, in the wash-house at the back of her shop; and the whole village know when she is doing so, for the strong sweet smell tickles your nostrils though you are fifty yards away.

---

bar-loungers and cads. The rhymes are as rude as the pictures. One goes like this:

> You advertise your charms in a very noisy way,
> Resolved to have a sweetheart, if it's ever to be done,
> But after all your mighty efforts, *there seems a strange delay*,
> And while other girls have Lovers, alas you've nary none!

Mrs Doan, as her mother did before her, also looks after the Post Office and telephone exchange, so she knows everything that goes on in the village. In her mother's day, it is said, the Post Office business was conducted entirely *coram populo*, so that the gossips would take a walk down to the Post Office 'just to have a read at the telegrams, my dear'. Nowadays only the telephone calls are regarded as public property, and Mrs Doan's daughter has more than once saved the landlords of the local pubs from getting into trouble by ringing them up to say 'Somebody's just phoned the policeman to tell him you're keeping open after hours. Thought you'd better know. Ta-ta.'

The lower part of the village – between the Post Office and the church – still bears the scars of war; for early in 1945 a homing Lancaster, winged over Germany, fiery-tailed like a comet, ploughed its way through the churchyard, knocked down the three poplars at the edge of the Rectory garden, and finally blew up, bombs and all, on the patch of green where our boys used to play football. The explosion splintered the doors and windows of a score of cottages, added another two or three degrees to the inclination of the church spire, and threw a shower of burning wreckage upon all the thatched roofs within range. The dry thatch quickly caught fire, and soon half Brensham was burning; and because the road from Elmbury was blocked by the blazing tail of the bomber the fire engines took forty minutes to get through. By the time they arrived the old men, the women and the children of Brensham had pulled the thatch off their cottages, pitchforked the crackling straw into their gardens, hacked away the smouldering timbers, and saved every building except one cottage and an old barn. For weeks afterwards there was hardly a man in the village who did not wear bandages on his hands.

Now, three years later, the marks of the explosion have

almost disappeared. You can still see the jagged stumps of the poplar trees and the deep furrow across the churchyard; and the new thatch shows white against the brown where Jaky Jones the odd-job-man did the longest odd-job of his career – for he worked on the roofs for eighteen months and began to feel as much at home up there, he said, as an old tom-cat. But the crater, which was eight feet deep, has filled with water, so that we now have a pond on the village green, where five ducks go puddling and marsh-marigolds open golden chalices to the April rain.

As Brensham's scars heal, so does the memory of that flaming midnight fade from its people's minds. You might think that the affair would already have become a famous legend to be told and retold in the pubs to the summer visitors: The Night When Half Brensham Was Afire. But instead the unpredictable village has bundled away its Bomb into the limbo of its long history to be half-remembered for a while and then forgotten as the Wars of the Roses are forgotten, and Cromwell's Roundheads riding to Worcester fight, and the goings and comings of soldiers hunting the beaten King, the beacons of Trafalgar and Waterloo and the burning ricks of 1830, and even, in time, the bonfires of V-Day. If you should ask the company in the Horse and Harrow why there is now a pond on the green where no pond was before they will answer briefly 'An aerioplane done it,' adding perhaps the additional information that 'we calls it Bomb Pond'. In a hundred years' time, I shouldn't mind betting, they'll still call it Bomb Pond; but if they are asked why they'll say that nobody knows, rightly, but it has allus been called so.

Beyond the church, at the bottom of the Rectory lawn, runs the river, Shakespeare's Avon winding its way down to the Severn between flat meadows and osier-beds: margined with loosestrife, lily-padded, perch-haunted, meandering.

This is the ultimate objective of most of our summer visitors. Many of them are anglers, who line the banks on Saturdays and Sundays patiently watching their painted floats and whooping with joy whenever they pull out a tiddler. Their needs are catered for by Jaky Jones the odd-job-man whose cottage at the end of Ferry Lane bears on its garden gate in summer the horrifying invitation:

LOBWORMS, FAT MAGGOTS, WARSP-
GRUBS IN SEASON, TEAS.

Other visitors hire motor-launches from Elmbury, four miles downstream, and infuriate the fishermen by chugging up and down the narrow river, with their ladies browning themselves on the half-deck and looking as languid as Cleopatra in her barge, while the boat's wash frightens the fishes and drowns the floats, and its bilge-water covers the surface of the river with a rainbow film of oil. The humbler brethren of these superior mariners take out rowing-boats and canoes which they cannot manage, upset themselves, and are profitably rescued by our villagers; while the dry-bobs, as it were, picnic in the meadows by the ferry, spoil the mowing-grass with their love-games, and amaze the aged ferryman with their exiguous sunsuits. Sooner or later they all find their way to one or other of the village pubs where they promptly catch the antic spirit of the place and drink pint-mugs of our rough local cider, which sends them away singing and acts later as a potent purge.

Meanwhile the more decorous sort sketch the quaint church or take rubbings of its Memorial Brasses; study the flora of the riverside or hunt for bee-orchids on Brensham Hill; photograph the Oldest Inhabitant and ask him questions about our Folk-lore, which he obligingly invents for their benefit; or go foraging down the leafy lanes where at almost every gateway chubby-faced and cheeky children offer bundles of 'sparrow grass', chips of strawberries, and baskets of yellow and purple plums each in their season. By the end of September there is not a fruit-grower in the district who does not believe himself to be rich, forgetting that the bundles of pound-notes are his squirrel's hoard which must last him through the long winter.

As the days shorten, the stream of buses and cars dwindles and dries up. At weekends in October there are still a few devoted anglers to be found beside the river; but these become fewer, until one Sunday afternoon when the floods are rising the last of them turns up his coat collar and trudges reluctantly away, glancing over his shoulder as if he were defeated Canute, while the eddying water seeps over the withered sedges.

Then the oakwoods on Brensham Hill fall into a brown study, and stripped of their leaves the orchards in the vale become as drab as a monk's habit. Brown too is the floodwater lying on the meadows, and dark sepia like the old thatch on the cottages is the ubiquitous mud. Only here and there do you see a scrap or splash of colour left over from September like the tattered relics of a carnival: a few late Laxtons and Worcester Pearmains cling to the apple boughs and are brighter than robins' breasts in a winter hedge, a patch of tawny asparagus-tops smoulders like a squitch-fire and an isolated half-acre of red cabbage shows an iridescent gleam of purplish-bronze rather like the gleam on flakes of iodine when they catch the light. But soon even these colours fade, and we are left with a landscape of residual brown-and-green, like an Old Master upon which the varnish has become opaque; and against this landscape the figures of our hobbledehoys move to and fro among the sprout plants, as slow and plodding as cart-horses and, you might think, as stolid.

My People

And indeed they have a deceptive air of stolidity. Dwelling as they do in a countryside of sharp contrasts, of backbreaking mud and heartbreaking beauty, sprouts in December and apple blossom in May, they know that all things are transient, both the good and the bad. Because their little livelihoods are bound up with the changes and chances of English weather, at the mercy of hooligan winds, inexorable floods and unsparing frosts, they have acquired, I think, a philosophic acceptance of fate. They know alike the treason of false springs and the blessed benison of summer. They know that bountiful seasons are often followed by frugal ones, and that the worst drought is sometimes succeeded by the worst flood. They know that the apple blossom is as brief as young love, and that the longest winter melts at last into the sweetest spring. They do not, therefore, tend to lose their heads when good luck comes their way nor their hope when the world goes ill for them. They have learned to take things in their stride, be they May frosts or falling aeroplanes or, for that matter, world wars.

In the 1914 war Brensham parish sent about thirty-five men into the forces. In 1939 there were fewer young men available, because some of the potential fathers had been killed in the previous holocaust and others, during the agricultural slump, had drifted to jobs in the towns. Nevertheless the village managed to scrape together twenty-eight, which was about a fifth of the whole male population; and this time a score of young women joined up as well. They went off, these farmers' sons and market-gardeners' daughters, these clodhopping labourers, these poachers and odd-jobmen, in no fervent nor even enthusiastic fashion but in exactly the mood of Francis Feeble whose Cotswold blood for all I know may run in their veins. 'By my troth, I care not; a man can die but once; we owe God a death; an't be my destiny, so; an't be not, so; no man's too good to serve his Prince; and let it go which way it will, he that dies this year is quit for the next.'

Thus unheroically the men of Brensham went to war. They who perhaps till then had caught but a glimpse of the flat sea on Bank Holiday at Weston-super-Mare now sailed across the stormy oceans; they whose previous notion of adventure was to go by cheap ticket to Birmingham to watch the Albion play football now bought Birmingham-made Buddhas in Eastern bazaars; they who had cursed the winter floods of Brensham thirsted in waterless deserts; and the poachers who had learned on our hillside the quick and silent way of killing a rabbit now learned quick and silent ways of killing men. Some of our farmers' boys flew as tail-gunners through the fiery night above Berlin; others, like George Daniels, were dropped out of aeroplanes into strange countries with tommy-guns in their hands. They talked by signs to Greek peasants about crops and to French peasants about cows. They gave chocolates to Italian children and cigarettes to German girls. They sat in foreign cafés and ate foreign dishes and sang the choruses of foreign songs with a broad rustic accent and got drunk on foreign wine. They discovered the profound truth which makes a mock of wars, that all girls say much the same thing when they are in a soldier's arms and that the men of opposing nations all look much the same when they are lying dead. And when at last the extraordinary adventure was ended they came home – nineteen out of the twenty-eight came home – and bundled away the memory of the war in much the same way as their fathers and mothers bundled away the memory of Brensham's Bomb, and slipped back as if they had never left it into the rhythm and routine of Brensham's life, Saturday afternoon cricket, and darts in the pub in the evening, apple-spraying and plum-picking, the brief beauty of April, the leafy pleasaunce of summer, haysel and harvest, the long labours of winter, mud and sprouts and cold hands.

You might indeed be forgiven for thinking them stolid! Yet, I who know them and have grown up among them – I have seen Bottom, Quince, Snug, Flute, and Starveling walking in their shoes, I have seen them quickened by the same strange fancy which played about the heads of that weaver and his crew in the magic 'Wood not far from Athens'. For they are still at heart the people who hurdled the cuckoo to keep it always spring, the crack-brained incalculable people in whose hearts the secret poetry burns as bright as their late scarlet apples clinging obstinately to the trees; the cap-over-the-windmill people, no strangers to love and laughter and moderate in neither; fierce in defence of their little liberties; much given to singing and drinking; and possessed of a certain unpredictable wildness of the spirit which rises in them from time to time like a sudden wind. On the rare occasions when this happens they become, for a space, the most intractable, disorderly, turbulent people in the world.

I am going to tell you the story of a man of Brensham who was so wild and intractable and turbulent that he failed, in the end, to come to terms with our orderly world (or perhaps one could say that our orderly world failed to come to terms with him). And I shall tell you too of a time at midwinter in the dull wet colourless season of sprouts, when suddenly the wild grey-gooseweather came blowing down from the north and with it came I know not whence this boisterous wind of the spirit gusting through the hearts of Brensham folk. But first, before I come to that part of my story, I must describe some of the events which preceded it; and it will be well if we take a closer look at the structure and pattern of the crack-brained village straggling among its orchards between the river and the hill. For that will serve both as an introduction to the characters and a prologue to the play; let us follow, then, the good advice of Bottom the weaver:

Quince: Is all our company here?

Bottom: You were best to call them generally, man by man, according to the scrip.

The Top of the Hill

We'll begin at the top of Brensham Hill because from there you will get a good idea of the kind of country in which our village is set. This is the land which has made and moulded us. Look north, south, east and west, and you shall see as it were the four corner-stones of our character: the ancient foundations of our way of thinking and living, our wisdom, folly, manners, customs, humours, what you will.

Look north, then, where the Avon snakes down from Stratford through the Evesham Vale. With the aid of glasses on a very clear day you can just make out the red-brick ordinary-looking small town which people in Patagonia and Pekin have heard of, though perhaps they couldn't name anywhere else in England save London. Shakespeare seems very close when you walk on Brensham Hill. He had friends in this neighbourhood, but a day's good tramp from his home, and just across the river lived one who witnessed his will. You will find yourself wondering, when you see a very old tree, whether he sat in the shade of it; or when you come to a pub, whether he drank there. Now and then on some old labourer's lips a country word or a turn of phrase brings him closer still. For example, we have a word which schoolboys use for the crackly dry stems of the hemlock and the hedge-parsley: 'kecksies', a local word which is heard, I think, nowhere else in England; but Shakespeare puts it into the mouth of the Duke of Burgundy in *Henry the Fifth*:

> 'Nothing teems
> But hateful docks, rough thistles, *kecksies*, burs . . .'

So, you see, he spoke our speech and thought our thoughts. These our woods and fields, our lanes and rivers, served him as a backcloth for Arden or Athens, Burgundy or Illyria.

Look south, downstream, to the old town of Elmbury standing at the junction of Avon and Severn. Just below the junction is the battlefield called the Bloody Meadow in which the Red Rose went down and the White Rose triumphed on a May day in 1471. By chance a deep-red flower called cranes-bill grows profusely in this meadow; at times it almost covers it; and if you look through strong glasses from the top of Brensham Hill at this patch of English earth on a summer day you will see the dreadful stain upon it, you will see it drenched in Lancastrian blood. After the battle the routed army streamed into Elmbury Abbey for sanctuary, and the young Prince Edward who fell that day is buried there. With him lie the great lords who helped to shape the fortunes of England for three centuries, the makers and unmakers of Kings whose mighty names thunder through the chronicles of Hall and Stow and Holinshed: the Despencers and the De Clares and the Warwicks and the Beauchamps, and that false, fleeting, perjur'd Clarence who met his inglorious end in a butt of Malmsey wine. These old stones and bones give us, I think, a sense of the past: not a knowledge of history (for there are few men in Brensham who could tell you the date of Elmbury's battle nor which side won it) but an acceptance of history, which is much the same thing as a sense of proportion. It accounts, perhaps, for our attitude to the Brensham Bomb and to a couple of wars in a lifetime; but it is not a conscious attitude, it is simply a piece of our background with which we have grown so familiar that we forget it is there – just as when we go to church at Elmbury we forget the Lords of Old Time who lie all round us and keep us silent company.

And now look east to the strong Cotswolds where rugged shepherds have watched their flocks since 1350. The winds blow cold there, and at night the stars in their courses wheel slowly across an immense sky. The men from being much alone grow taciturn, and their long stride takes a queer rhythm from the slopes of the whaleback hills. Brensham, seven hundred feet high, is itself an outlier of the Cotswolds; so thence, perhaps comes our hillmen's lope, and thence the trick of being silent when we have nothing to say.

Lastly, look west to the Malverns and beyond them to the mountains of Wales. It's not very far across the Severn and the Wye to the dark shut-in valleys and the cold slate villages and the savage Fforest Fawr; it's certainly not too far for a man to go courting if he had a mind to – so if an anthropologist came to Brensham and started to measure our heads he'd discover a fine puzzling mixture of long ones and short ones and betwixts and betweens. And he'd find if he could look inside the heads a compound and amalgamation of Welsh wildness and English sedateness, Border magic and Cotswold common-sense. For though we live in a fat and fruitful vale, yet we have a sense of looking out on to the wide waste-lands and the mysterious mountains. That's where our occasional turbulence comes from, and the fancy that tried to pen the cuckoo, and our love of singing.

The Blue Field

Now on a day in late July, if you had stood on Brensham Hill and looked down the furzy slope towards the village, you might have seen a remarkable spectacle. In the middle of William Hart's farm, which occupied about a hundred and fifty acres along the skirt of the hill, a seven-acre field had suddenly become tinctured with the colour of Mediterranean skies. It happened almost in a night. One day there was a faint azure mist upon the field, like smoke from a squitch-fire. Next morning when the sun came up a cerulean carpet covered it; and we almost caught our breath at the sight of this miracle, for although our farmers with their seasonal rotations paint the land in many colours, blue is not one of them, blue stands as it were beyond the agricultural spectrum, and this particular shade of blue, so clear and pure that it made one think of eyes or skies, was something that we had never seen in our countryside before.

Moreover it made an extraordinary contrast with the rest of the hillside; for there was no other bright colour to share the sunlight with it. In other years, as a rule, there is purple clover or pink sainfoin or luteous charlock; but the authorities had caused most of the hill to be ploughed up for corn. So the familiar pattern was one of ash-blond oats and rust-coloured barley rippling in the wind like the fur of a marmalade cat, with the foaming green of the orchards making a hem to the skirt of the hill. Now, between the orchards and the corn, appeared this astonishing lagoon of blue which caught and held the eye so that within an hour the whole neighbourhood was talking about it. 'Have you seen old William's field of linseed?' people said. 'It does your heart good to look at it; but Lord, I wouldn't be in his shoes when the trouble starts!'

The Two Potterers

It was Mr Chorlton, the retired prep-school master, who first suggested to me there might be serious trouble. Being nearly seventy and very lame, he plays a smaller part than he used to in our village life; but from his garden gate the old philosopher observes and comments as shrewdly as he ever did, and acts as a sort of Greek chorus to our little comedies and tragedies.

'I am wondering,' he said, as he gazed up the hill at the marvellous flaxfield – for linseed is a form of flax – 'whether perhaps it is the kind of trivial gesture which begins big rows: an absurd but memorable *casus belli*, like Jenkin's ear.'

I had gone to have tea with Mr Chorlton and his old friend, Sir Gerald Hope-Kingley, in whose house he lived; for his own cottage, halfway between Brensham and Elmbury, had been destroyed by the flaming tail of that Lancaster which fell out of the sky in 1945. All his worldly possessions had been burned with it: his precious library, his collection of eighteenth-century first editions, his cabinet of butterflies which represented a lifetime's hobby, and his small cellar of wine. Yet the loss of so many cherished things did not break him as we all thought it would; he shrugged his shoulders and smiled and told us that he felt strangely free. 'It is interesting to discover, when all is taken from one, how little one really needs,' he said soon after it happened. 'Out of those two thousand books, I have only bothered to replace three: Shakespeare, Plato, and the Old Testament. As for butterflies, I shall probably get more pleasure out of watching them at the flowers than looking at them in my cabinet. And as for the wine, I shall strive to acquire a new taste for Government Port. The only thing I want is a roof over my head; like Diogenes, I am looking for a tub!'

A few weeks later Sir Gerald, whom we had all given up for dead, returned from a Japanese prison camp in Burma, and immediately invited Mr Chorlton to go and live with him. He was a hydraulic engineer who had retired to Brensham some years before the war for the avowed purpose of Pottering About in the Garden. He had pottered happily and unsuccessfully with Alpines, sweet-peas, cacti, lilies, Aquaria, bird-watching and nature photography until the war came, when His Majesty's Government requested his services and he pottered off to Burma for the purpose, we understood, of destroying some complicated waterworks which had taken him three years to build. He blew them up in about three minutes, but his incurable habit of pottering got him caught by the Japs, and he spent the next two years devising an ingenious still, under the floor of his hut, for the purpose of making alcohol out of mangoes. It didn't work very well – none of his projects ever did, unless they were huge dams and waterfalls, which he contrived with the greatest ease – and the war was over before he succeeded in distilling sufficient alcohol to make a drink. On VJ-Day, however, the machine excelled itself and produced three pints, which he shared among his fellow prisoners. They all became extremely ill, and the raw spirit acted so fiercely upon the emaciated body of Sir Gerald that he nearly died. Indeed, when at last he arrived at Brensham the porter at the station failed to recognize him; and Joe Trentfield, seeing him go by the Horse and Harrow, asked who the devil was that little wizened fellow like a Chink.

Now, in the gracious house called Gables at the top of the village, the two old friends while away the twilight of their days with Pottering and Port; and Mr Chorlton had the satisfaction of blaming the Government for the occasional attacks of gout which he had previously laid at the door of Messrs Cockburn. Because he was temporarily immobilized by one of these attacks he had asked me to go to tea and tell him the village news; and we sat on the lawn, beside the lily-pond which leaked and the rockery which was the grave of so many rare Alpines, and feasted our eyes on the blue splendour of William Hart's flax field halfway up the hill.

'What a colour!' said Mr Chorlton. 'Is it ideological, do you think? Does it not strike you as somehow rather defiant? Perhaps I associate it with the ribbons in the buttonholes of Temperance reformers who used to provoke me in my youth.'

'They were a different shade,' said Sir Gerald. 'I wore one myself.'

This statement caused us no surprise; for Sir Gerald, in the few years we had known him, had dabbled in Christian Science, Spiritualism, Yoga, the British Israelites and the Oxford Group. He had been a vegetarian for a month, a Blackshirt for a week, and at one time was nearly converted to Islam. Dabbling, as he called it, was the intellectual counterpart of his physical Pottering, and was just as harmless. Indeed it was more so, for the form of Pottering in which he was engaged as we sat on the lawn seemed to involve considerable danger to life and limb. It had occurred to him, while he languished in the Japanese prison camp, that mankind was very much to blame for its wicked waste of safety-razor blades. He was reminded of this deplorable fact every morning, because he greatly desired a shave; and as he fingered his long, hot and itchy beard he used to contemplate with sorrow and even with indignation the huge and prodigal expenditure of blades which went on every minute of the day all over the civilized world. He whiled away many hours trying to estimate the daily wastage; but it was incalculable. He remembered bitterly that there were at least a hundred old blades lying in a box in his bathroom at home, because he had never been able to discover any way of disposing of them other than by burial, and he had been too idle to dig a hole. What would he not have given now for the oldest, rustiest, bluntest of them all? From this sad reflection his thoughts turned to the various possible uses of razor blades, other than for shaving the face. One could make them into pencil sharpeners, of course; but nobody needed a hundred pencil sharpeners. It was surely not beyond the wit of man to devise some other employment for those multitudinous little pieces of tempered steel! Therefore when he was not taking to pieces or putting together his illicit still, Sir Gerald devoted himself to the consideration of this problem; and now on his lawn he was engaged in putting his theories to a practical test. He had obtained several strips of metal with holes in – I think they must have been part of a meccano set – and having joined them together in a length of about three feet he was bolting razor blades along them to make a frightful serrated cutting-edge which, he declared, would ultimately form part of a patent lawn-mower.

I could hardly bear to watch this operation, for he was notoriously clumsy and I was terrified lest he should cut his fingers off. Meanwhile Mr Chorlton, who had recently taken up the study of the social insects, was amusing himself by stirring up with his stick a small ants' nest at the edge of the lawn. As he did so he talked, partly to himself and partly to the world at large, as was his way.

'The biblical Fascists,' he was saying, 'who advised us to go to the ant for an example of good behaviour can hardly have realized what a dangerous example social insects set us. Man, when he looks into an anthill, sees the mirror of himself and exclaims with wonder how "civilized" the little creatures are. Why, they establish food stores and have a system of rationing! They cultivate crops of fungi and keep domestic animals! They are so extremely civilized that they establish slavery and indulge in organized war. Theirs, in fact, is almost exactly the same sort of civilization which recently took us six years to wipe off the face of the earth. It's rather comforting to know that the termites have actually gone a little farther than man along the road to complete regimentation. They are the only inhabitants of this planet who have succeeded in socializing their males.'

He twirled his stick deeper into the nest and leaned forward to watch the busy commotion.

'If one aberrant ant does anything different from the other ants,' he said, 'the unsocial insect is immediately slain. There would be no room for William Hart in an ant community.'

My eyes went back to the flax field on the hill and I wondered whether Mr Chorlton was right, that it would lead to a big row. Old William Hart had been in trouble with the War Agricultural Executive Committee ever since it was formed. He possessed more than his fair share of the obstinacy, the rebelliousness, the wildness and the wayward fancy for which crack-brained Brensham is so well known. Because he objected to being told what to do with his own land he had defied the Committee for more than five years. The trouble had started in 1940, about a field which bore the odd name of Little Twittocks. This field was overgrown with teasels, burdocks and small hawthorn bushes, and the WAEC ordered William to clear and cultivate it. This he refused to do, giving the extraordinary reason that it harboured foxes. The argument went on for eighteen months. The Committee, which consisted of successful farmers, was possibly over-enthusiastic and not very tactful, and having tried persuasion without avail they resorted to threats. When threats also failed they sent a bulldozer, which quickly routed up the hawthorn bushes and pushed them into a pile at the corner of the field. The bulldozer was followed by a tractor, which ploughed Little Twittocks, foxes' earths and all, for the first time in its history. The Committee then sent William a bill for the job, which he refused to pay until he was sued in court. A short armistice followed, and the Committee, having exercised its authority, would have been wise to let well alone. Perhaps, indeed, it wished to do so; but the bureaucratic machine, once set in motion, is beyond the power of ordinary men to stop, like Clotho it spins out the fates of men with ruthless impartiality, and William was caught in the toils of the terrible thread from which there is no escape this side of the grave. Therefore he received in due course a cultivation order imperiously demanding that he should plant Little Twittocks with potatoes under pain of extreme penalties. The obstinate old man took no notice whatsoever, and proceeded to plant it with sunflowers, of all things, the seeds of which he proposed to feed to his chickens. It turned out be a cold and dabbly summer, with little sunshine, and the crop failed; the Committee sent their tractor once again and ploughed it in, which saved William the trouble of doing so himself, and once again he refused to pay the bill until he was taken to court. When planting-time came round he received another order, to plant Little Twittocks with oats. The evidence of his final defiance now blazed on Brensham hillside for all the world to witness.

'What do you imagine,' I asked Mr Chorlton, 'the War Ag. will actually *do* about it?'

He shook his head.

'The war being over,' he said, 'I *hope* they'll just laugh. But although they have the cheerful faces of ordinary decent men whom we all know, Mr Nixon, Mr Whitehead, Mr Surman, Mr Harcombe, and such-like, they are in fact the tentacles of an octopus. The inky body of the beast is situated in Whitehall; and it never laughs. I should be extremely unwilling to provoke that octopus, for fear that it should strangle me; which is what I'm afraid it will do to old William. But, by God, what a colour that field is!' he exclaimed again. 'It's like a piece of the Virgin's snood out of a medieval stained-glass window! If a man wanted to throw down the gauntlet to authority, what a vivid, defiant, challenging gauntlet to choose!'

The Ploughgirl

As a matter of fact I don't think William Hart really meant his field of linseed to be a challenge. I think his real reason for growing the crop was the much more absurd one which Susan the land girl told me when I saw her ploughing the field during the previous autumn and asked her what William was going to plant there.

'You'd never guess,' she said. 'We're going to put in linseed.'

'Why?'

'Well, the old man says he's sick of sprouts and he wants to brighten the place up a bit. "Let's have some fun, Su," he said to me. "Let's go in for a splash of colour on Brensham Hill for a change!"'

I believe that was his genuine reason, because he was always one for fun and colour; one might say that the whole of his wild life had been dedicated to fun and colour, jest and laughter and song. 'What a man!' said Susan, who adored him, as all the land girls, and indeed all women, did; and she started up her tractor again and roared away up the side of the hill.

Now that the affair of Little Twittocks has become a *cause célèbre* I remember very vividly that November afternoon when I watched Susan ploughing it; for some reason or other it seems to stand at the beginning of all these happenings. I remember it because of a moment of strange beauty which lightened the dark afternoon and because of the joy which I found in watching Susan's craftsmanship.

When I started to walk up the hill the landscape was sad and sodden, the clouds were down on the summit, and a high wind was blowing. A few of Brensham's inevitable sprout leaves drifted drearily about the lane or hung on the hedges. The only sounds were the low moan of the wind in the bare elms and the monotonous churr-churr of the tractor as it crawled to and fro in Little Twittocks.

Then suddenly the flying clouds were torn apart, as if they were sped so fast by the wind that the pursuing cohorts could not catch up with them. The long ragged tear revealed a patch of very pale blue sky low down over the horizon, and a moment later there was a blink of watery sunshine. And now the hedges, that had been till that moment pitchy-black and lifeless, all at once took on a tinge of warm purple-brown; a clump of sallow bushes touched by the alchemist sun turned pinkish-gold; and Little Twittocks, which lay immediately in front of me, changed instantly from sepia to dark red, the colour of old red bricks or a Hereford cow. A flock of gulls fluttered over it like the aftermath of a paper-chase blown about by the wind.

The narrow slanting rays of sunshine, theatrical as a spotlight, picked out the red tractor as it crept like a beetle up the slope, picked out too the dark green jersey of the girl riding the tractor, and made a tiny splash of light on her hair. It was a cheerful and somehow uplifting sight, like a core of warmth and colour even at old winter's chilly heart; and I leaned for a moment on the gate to watch the tractor crawling round the headland and the gulls sailing like far-off yachts behind the plough.

Having turned the corner at the top of the field, the tractor began to come down the hedgeside towards me. There was a row of apple trees in the hedge, with low-hanging branches which made Susan duck; but she seemed determined to plough the furrow as close to the hedge as possible and she rode the tractor like a jockey, lying almost flat over the steering-wheel when she passed beneath the trees. One didn't need to be a ploughman to be aware of the skill and care implied by those dead-straight furrows and narrow headlands; and somehow it stirred me to think of the small girl on the heavy tractor discovering something that her mother and all the generations of mothers had never known – the ancient pride of Adam in his well-tilled earth.

Like a jockey: surely it was her green jersey and the bright handkerchief tied on her head which gave me that idea. But as she reached the end of the hedgerow and began to turn the corner within a score of yards of me a curious thing happened; the ploughshare must have caught in a root or fouled one of the suckers growing out from the old apple trees; for the tractor suddenly bucked like a horse, its front wheels lifted a good six inches off the ground, then as Susan pulled back the throttle they bumped down on the earth again and I saw Susan rise in her seat as a rider does when his horse plunges.

She reversed, and lifted the plough clear; then opening the throttle she roared past the gate and I had an impression of tousled blonde hair and a flushed excited face from which the momentary alarm was just fading. She saw me, and grinned as if to say 'That was a near shave!' and indeed if the tractor had come over backwards on top of her she would have been crushed to death by it as many an inept ploughboy, used to his slow-plodding Dobbins, has been before now. She stopped, and we had our brief conversation, and then she went off full tilt up the hill, with a wave of her hand and a toss of her head, and a lump of earth from the mud-caked wheels came spinning through the air and plopped down at my feet.

What a mere trifle, sometimes, can change a man's mood! As I walked back towards the village I was light-hearted for no better reason than that the sun had shone for a moment on a green jersey and that I'd seen a young girl ploughing as straight a furrow as a man. I paused at the bottom of the lane and looked over my shoulder just as the sunlight was beginning to fade, and the tractor no bigger than a ladybird was crawling along the horizon, churr-churr, churr-churr, etching yet another of those long parallel lines which made the hump-backed field look like an old engraving.

But while I watched, the sunshine was extinguished as dramatically as if someone had pressed a switch, and the light went out of the land. The wind seemed to blow harder as it lashed the laggard clouds to close the narrowing gap; and soon they caught up with the leaders, piling grey on grey, hastening the swift evening. I went on down the road; and with the gale at my back I felt as if I had seven-league boots on. That trivial fragment of experience, the bucking tractor, Susan's alarmed, excited face, her sudden grin, still warmed my heart; and romantically I cherished it.

Frolick Virgins

Susan was one of a score or so of land girls who were accommodated in a big rambling house which had long been empty, next door to the Gables. ('The Land Girls in their

Hostel, the Young Men at their Gate!' chanted Mr Chorlton with a sigh.) The young men, however, were strongly discouraged and sometimes driven away, by the mournful and harassed-looking woman who was the land girls' janitor and whose unsuitable name was Mrs Merrythought. She was a disillusioned creature with thin sandy hair and the faint beginnings of a moustache, and her life was made wretched by her unceasing preoccupation with the wolfish ways of Men. 'Ah, *Men*!' she would declare darkly. 'They're after my poor girls all the time' – as if the girls were a flock of juicy sheep and the village lads sat howling round the hostel with lolling tongues and burning eyes. Because of this preoccupation she had caused the high wall round the garden to be topped with broken glass; and she took such elaborate precautions about locking up at night that on several occasions she locked some of the girls out, with consequences on which it would be idle to speculate. Moreover, because she herself knew so little about men (with the exception of certain legends about their unflagging concupiscence) she gave them credit for a much greater degree of agility, and a much more reckless disregard for danger, than in fact they possess; and she was firmly convinced that they could and would climb the sheer walls of the hostel for the purpose of looking in at the bedroom windows or even – dreadful thought! – crawling through them. She had, therefore, had all the spoutings down the side of the house wrapped round with tufts of barbed wire.

Luckily for her charges, Mrs Merrythought was so concerned with the problem of keeping the young men out that she gave less attention to the task of keeping the girls in; it never occurred to her that the sheep, from time to time, went off in full cry after the fleeing wolves. Nevertheless I am reliably informed that this phenomenon sometimes happened.

The first batch of land girls had arrived in 1939; and since then they had intruded more and more into the accepted pattern of village life, so that they became part of Brensham, and we should have missed them sorely if they had been taken away. One or two of them had been with us from the beginning. These were practically Brenshamites by now; and the newcomers, taking their cue from them, quickly fell into our ways. This was all the more surprising because few of them belonged to our part of England, and many of them came from the cities. Susan had been a manicurist, of all things, before she became a plough-girl. Margie was an East End Cockney, Lisbeth came from Lancashire and talked like Gracie Fields, Betsy with the freckled face belonged to Ayrshire, the one whose demented parents had christened her Wistaria had worked in what she called a gown shop in Putney, and the red-headed Ive was from Birmingham. These were the six whom Mr Chorlton called the Frolick Virgins. The quotation was from Herrick:

Frolick Virgins once these were,
Overloving, living here,

and indeed the innumerable, intertwined and continually fluctuating love-affairs of Susan, Margie, Lisbeth, Betsy, Wistaria and Ive were the talk of the village. These affairs provided a source of unfailing entertainment when they were going well, but at moments of crisis they preyed upon our minds and tattered our nerves, for they were always conducted more or less in public, and if Lisbeth had been jilted or Betsy had stolen Ive's young man the whole of Brensham knew about it, sorrowed and sympathized and took sides. What made these dramas all the more wearing for everybody was a perpetual uncertainty about who was in love with whom; as Mr Chorlton pointed out, in order to calculate the permutations and combinations of the Frolick Virgins and about a score of young men one would require a slide-rule. For among the six girls there was only one constant, one whose love did not veer and back like the mutable winds or ebb and flow like the tide. Susan loved George Daniels with the single-minded passion of a Juliet, and George Daniels' devotion to her was as steady and unshifting as the Pole Star; and yet, alas, their affair went ill.

Young Corydon

The trouble was a combination of two of the oldest obstacles which beset the thorny path of lovers: the pride of parents and the lack of money. Susan's father and mother, who had made a little fortune out of the refined and genteel business of ladies' hairdressing and lived in a trim little house with its own garage in some trim little suburb where all the houses are like that, thought themselves a cut above the people who work with their hands and flatly refused to allow their daughter to marry a farmer's boy. George, who was not exactly a Lochinvar, knew only too well the inadequacy of his ninety shillings a week and the discomforts of a labourer's cottage; his gratuity, moreover, was quite insufficient to buy even a minimum of furniture. In these circumstances he could not bring himself to take the obvious course of marrying Susan against her parents' wishes. He had been told that he was not good enough for her, and he was foolish enough to believe it. So although the couple walked out religiously every Sunday afternoon, and went to the village hop every Saturday night where they danced every dance together except the Paul Jones; although they took their lovers' stroll down the twilight lanes in such close conjunction that they reminded one of Siamese twins or competitors in a three-legged race; and although the final hug with which they said goodnight in the shadow of the hostel wall went on so long that they seemed to take root there and to be a natural feature of the landscape – nevertheless a cloud hung over their love, and we in the village, hearing the sad story *ad nauseam* from Margie, Lisbeth, Betsy, Wistaria and Ive, grew almost as impatient as the unhappy couple and became partners in their frustration.

We all loved Susan, and we all liked George, who in his modest and unassuming way had quietly won a Military Medal at Arnhem. His gallantry on that occasion made a curious contrast with his behaviour when he first met Susan. On sick-leave from Normandy after receiving a flesh-wound, he had taken a walk up Brensham Hill on a very hot Sunday and by accident had stumbled upon the Frolick Virgins, all six of them, sunbathing in a woodland clearing, where they must have looked, I imagine, rather like the Dryads themselves. George, who had little fear of the German SS soldiers, nevertheless turned tail and fled from this classical spectacle; and in his headlong flight he knocked off his claret-coloured beret against a branch and, being taken with a kind of nympholepsy, failed to notice the mishap until it was too late, when he dared not go back to retrieve it. Susan returned it to him at the village dance on the following Saturday and, his leave ending, a long correspondence ensued, of which the village knew by hearsay because everybody was informed of it by Margie, Lisbeth, Betsy, Wistaria and Ive.

Letter from a Liberator

Goodness knows how George kept it up; because he did me the honour, soon after the invasion, of writing one longish letter to me, in which the smudged indelible and the frequent crossings-out bore witness to the pain he had in writing it. I imagine he must have sucked his pencil for a long time between the words. 'The country,' he began – he was writing from the *bocage* district before Caen – 'is rather like ours. The people are very good farmers. They drink cider. If they didn't speak Frog they'd be just like us. It makes you think.'

Because I was there too, though at a different stage of the battle, I could just imagine George sitting and sucking his pencil beside that road between the orchards which was so optimistically signposted to Paris. Leafless poplars, although it was July, and greyish-yellow dust covering the poplar trunks and the thick hedges and the hedgerow flowers and George's face, hair and hands; a notice on a gate, 'MINEN!' with a skull and crossbones underneath it, and a field behind the gate sown with poppies, corn and death; a cart-horse, to which the notice had meant nothing, lying shattered just inside the gate . . .

Not much like Brensham; but George saw the similarities and ignored the differences. Like most Englishmen abroad he expected to find everything strange and was astonished when he discovered things which reminded him of home. He was enormously impressed by his discovery of a little pink weed which turned out to be the same troublesome bindweed which crawled in the cornfields at home; he'd expected strange and unfamiliar and foreign flowers. And he felt at home among the apple trees, Pearmains and Pippins, with the fruit just forming. Like William Hart's orchard. That made you think, too.

But a painful incident had happened to him which had made him think more than anything else. He set it down at great length and without much evidence of schooling; so I will paraphrase it. He had called at a farm, it seemed, to ask for some water. It was a smallholding really, not much bigger than Alfie Perk's at Brensham. The soil was clean, the headlands were narrow, not a square yard of earth was wasted; but the land, he thought, could have done with a good dose of phosphates.

He met the farmer close to the cottage. He was tending a big dappled cow whose hind leg had been badly shattered by a bomb splinter. She was a magnificent cow; George became almost lyrical in her praise. At home you'd have to pay sixty pounds for such a cow. He wanted to tell the farmer how much he admired her, and to ask how much milk she gave a day and what she was worth in Normandy. But of course he didn't even know the French for 'cow'. He stood and grinned and looked a fool.

Then the farmer shook his hand and things became easier. They looked at the cow's leg together and the farmer said 'Bomb.' George said 'English?' and the farmer nodded and shrugged his shoulders as if to say 'It's not your fault.' But the leg was very bad, and it was awful to think that we had done that.

The farmer took him into the cottage. Inside it was just like home. The earthenware jug of cider, rough, raw, cool and sharp, was so familiar that it made him miserably homesick. He didn't feel at all strange in the company of the farmer, his wife and the three children, and although he didn't understand a word of French he often knew what they were saying. When the farmer's wife turned to her husband and asked a question he guessed at once that she was asking about the cow; and he knew that the farmer's reply meant 'I shall have to kill her.' He wanted to say 'Have you any other cows?' but of course he couldn't and in any case he knew the answer. They had no more. They were poor people, you could see that, and the cow must have been worth a lot of money, especially in wartime when prices were high.

So to make up for the British airman's bomb he took his assault ration out of his haversack and gave all the boiled sweets, which he'd been saving for the battle because he liked to suck sweets in a battle, to the farmer's three children. Then he gave his slab of chocolate to the farmer's wife and his cigarettes to the farmer. But he knew it was all nothing compared with the cow.

When he had to go the farmer walked with him as far as the gate. He said something which George didn't understand. Then he touched the butt of the rifle, and George knew at once. They went to the barn, where the cow was lowing. She was down on her haunches now. George unslung his rifle and handed it to the farmer. He shouldn't have done that really, a soldier should never part with his rifle, but it seemed important that the farmer should do the thing himself.

It reminded him of his father shooting an old dog he was very fond of.

The farmer gave the rifle back and shrugged his shoulders; they shook hands again and they understood each other perfectly, they didn't need any words.

That was three days ago, wrote George; but it still made him think. He wished he could write a proper letter to explain that Frenchmen weren't Froggies but were just like people at home. But he couldn't explain so he finished up in much the same strain as he had begun:

'They are very good people,' declared George. 'Their cider is peart like ours. When we've got this lot finished we'll go down to the local and I'll tell you all about it. They have fine cows and they are just like us. It makes you think.'

'*The Pastoral Loves of Daphnis and Chloe*'

When George came back from the war Susan invited him to spend a weekend with her parents. He put on his demob suit, which didn't fit at all, and his demob tie which was wonderfully striped like a Neapolitan ice, and he succeeded in looking exactly what he wasn't, the gooping village bumpkin dressed up for a trip to town. We never heard what happened during that weekend; but it was clear enough that everything had gone wrong. When it was over George wrapped the precious demob suit away in tissue paper and put on his old paratroop's jacket again and went to work for William Hart. He lived at home with his parents and was able to save about two pounds a week out of his pay; and it was estimated that at this rate he would have saved two hundred pounds in two years' time, with which in some mysterious way he would Better Himself and find favour in the eyes of Susan's parents. But in practice the sum didn't work out like that; for love makes nonsense of mathematics and George would have been a poor sort of lover if he hadn't been moved from time to time by the glory and splendour of his state to buy some absurd and prodigal present for Susan or to squander his week's savings recklessly on squiring all six of the Frolick Virgins to the Horse and Harrow and buying them gin. So it looked as if it might be ten years, rather than two, before George was able to afford to furnish a cottage let alone to Better Himself. Meanwhile the star-crossed pair continued to discover every imaginable delight in each other's company and to say goodnight to each other in an atmosphere of considerable drama outside the land girls' hostel every evening. Mr Chorlton, who liked to walk in the garden at twilight and wrap himself in his thoughts, observed sadly that it was extremely difficult to concentrate while what appeared to be a combination of Troilus and Cressida, Pyramus and Thisbe, and Romeo and Juliet, breathed eternal farewells just outside the gate.

Anon Mrs Merrythought, with much banging of bolts and clanking of chains, would indicate that she was about to lock up and Susan would scuttle inside. But the lovers' parting was not for long; at seven o'clock next morning they would be reunited; for the land girls were hired out to various farmers in twos and threes and needless to say Susan generally contrived to be among those who worked for Mr Hart. And so together, like characters in some ancient pastoral, the lovers mowed and reaped, ploughed and planted, and even discovered a kind of bliss in sprout-picking when they did it side by side. They were accessories to the crime, if it was one, of growing linseed in Little Twittocks; for Susan had ploughed the field and George had sown the seed. As for old William, he was so crippled with rheumatism that he was only able to hobble as far as the gate and lean over it; but that was probably enough, for it was always said of him that he'd only got to look at something to make it grow.

The Wild Old Man

It is high time that I told you something of the history of this wild and strange old man, whose boisterous mischief, or prankishness as our people aptly described it, was notable even in crack-brained Brensham.

This mischief, in his youth and early middle age, had populated the village with numerous bastards, whom he cheerfully and shamelessly acknowledged; in later life it had manifested itself in the form of uproarious drunkenness and elaborate practical jokes. Impish even when he was sober,

Mr Hart in drink had been liable to ring the church bells at midnight or call out the Fire Brigade to an imaginary fire; he had introduced a squealing pig into a choir practice and a donkey into the deliberations of the Parish Council; and he had defended himself against an angry policeman with the effective though double-edged weapon of a swarm of bees. But though his absurd pranks caused annoyance to their victims, everybody agreed that there was no real harm in him. 'He wouldn't hurt a fly,' people said. The constable, smothered in blue-bag and smarting from a dozen bee-stings, might perhaps have contested this; but they meant that his broad buffooning had its roots in a sort of innocence, his sins were original sins, without any later admixture of vice. Even his occasional drunkenness had a childlike quality which robbed it of offence. He drank to drown no sorrow nor yet, as our dreary little cocktail-sippers do, in order to get rid of the critical faculty which informs them how dreary they really are. He drank simply because he liked the stuff. The more he drank the more he liked it; and when at last it made him drunk his happiness exceeded all bounds. He had no desire to fight or to tell boring stories or to sit in a corner and cry; he only wanted to spread the tidings of his joy among his friends and neighbours and indeed the whole world. It seemed to him that the best way to do so was to make a great deal of noise; so on these evangelic occasions he shouted and sang and roared about the village boisterously like a wind, sometimes even knocking at doors and waking people up in order to communicate his enormous happiness to them. If you were coming out of the Adam and Eve, and William Hart in drink was emerging from the Horse and Harrow, you would hear him singing and hollering and bellowing his happiness although he was a quarter of a mile away.

When he was in this condition he was by no means amenable to the reprobation of angry householders or to the policeman's suggestion that he should go home quietly; for he would then draw himself up to his full height, which was some six and a half feet, and lean back to balance the weight of his enormous belly, which had the circumference of some fifty-five inches, and wag at his persecutors an admonitory finger. 'Thee carsn't touch I! Thee carsn't touch I!' he would tell them severely, and then, if asked the reason for his supposed immunity, he would utter in ringing tones his proud boast, which had no basis in fact as far as any one could tell but which he believed throughout his life with all his heart and soul. 'Thee carsn't touch I – hands off, ladies and gents, hands off! – thee carsn't touch I because I be a descendant of the poet Shakespeare!' With a lordly gesture he would wave away the impudent person who had tried to interfere with him; and as he haughtily strode off he would resume his singing.

Carnivorous Cider

Of course that was nearly half a century ago, in William's youth and early middle age; and the old men who sit in the Horse and Harrow now, remembering things past and shaking their heads over the present, will tell you that there are no songs in the beer today. Never a chorus, they say, in ten pints of it. But this does not mean that Brensham has ceased to sing, for the pale, harmless-looking cider which our farmers make in the autumn is stronger by far than even the pre-1914 beer. It is deceptively still, it trickles out of the cask with scarcely a bubble, and looks almost green in your glass, though it has a golden glint when you hold it up to the light. Its taste, until you get used to it, is so sharp and sour that it seems to dry up the roof of your mouth – 'cut-throat cider', we call it. But wait. Beyond the shock of that first astringency lies a genial and unexpected warmth, a curious after-flavour of the sunshine and the earth and the falling leaves, a taste of September. Foolish, flat and innocent did the stuff look in your glass? Wise and wicked and old it seems now as it runs down your throat; for it's been three or four years maturing in the old brandy-cask and as like as not Joe Trentfield from time to time has dropped a few scraps of meat in it, for he has a strange theory that 'cider feeds on meat'. Whether this is true or not I do not know; but I can well believe that so fierce and tigerish a potion would welcome a beefsteak now and then to keep up its strength. The names we give to our Brensham cider are indicative of that strength: 'tangle-foot' and 'stunnem' and one other which I cannot print here. Yet its potency, unlike that of other drinks, seems to act rather upon the body than the brain; while it steals from your legs their ability to take you home it leaves your mind free to meditate upon the awkwardness of your predicament. Indeed it is told of William Hart that he was once accused of kicking up a row all night outside the Rector's windows and he explained that the cider in his legs had compelled him to spend the night by the roadside while the cider in his head had caused him to sing without intermission till dawn.

Mr Hart, Wainwright

His drinking bouts were not very frequent, or perhaps he would not have been the good craftsman he was. For William Hart, during the first twenty years of his working life, practised the trade of a wheelwright, and he made better wagons than anybody else between Birmingham and Bristol. You see can them still if ever you visit the neighbourhood of Brensham – for they were made to last for ever – and at farm sales the auctioneer still draws attention to them, urging the company to bid an extra five pounds. 'Come, come, gentlemen, this is no ordinary job. None of your gimcrack jerrybuilt contraptions here. This is a William Hart wagon – see the name on it! These wheels will still be going round when you're in the churchyard.' They were mostly big wagons designed for carrying hay; Mr Hart always spoke of them as wains and himself as a wainwright. Nowadays most farmers use a haysweep instead to bring the hay to the rick (or they bale it on the ground, so that they do not need to rick it at all) and the wagons stand disused and neglected in rickyards and homesteads, but they never fall to pieces, and the bright yellow paint on them (three coats of it) doesn't flake off like modern paint – you can spot them from a mile away. General Bouverie, our local Master of Foxhounds, still keeps one in use for the curious purpose of providing transport between the coverts at his pheasant-shoot. A huge dappled horse, groomed and polished till it shines like a varnished rocking-horse, dolled up with ribbons and rosettes and shining brasses, goes between the shafts; and a dozen guests, with their loaders, guns, cartridges and enormous luncheon-hampers, pile in behind. As the day goes on the wagon becomes filled with the corpses of pheasants, tawny as the fallen leaves; and it is indeed a remarkable sight to see the yellow wagon returning from the last drive of the day, with General Bouverie sitting high on the front of it like a Roman Emperor enjoying a Triumph, the trophies hung on long poles placed crosswise across the wagon, the guests knee-deep in feather and fur.

It used to take William Hart the better part of a month to make a wagon. He built each with loving care, choosing and seasoning the timber himself, and taking infinite pains over every joint, hinge and spoke. ('Measure twice and cut once,' he always used to say.) But as soon as it was done, the moment he'd crossed the 't' of the 'W. Hart' which although he could only read and write with difficulty he stencilled so neatly on the side of it – as soon as he'd done that he went down to the pub and got drunk. He would come bursting into the bar, and order drinks all round, with that transcendent air of blessed relaxation and utter abandon which artists know when they have put the finishing touches to a work of creation and, all passion spent, allow the tide of life to bear them where it will. Usually he stayed drunk for about a week, and it was another ten days before he regained complete sobriety. So, with repairs and odd-jobs and a bit of undertaking – it was said that his pride of craftsmanship made him take as much trouble over a coffin for his worst enemy as over a wagon for his best friend – he built about eight of his great haywains in a year. This earned him ample money for his needs.

Goodman Delver

At one time Jaky Jones, he who served the visiting anglers with teas and wasp-grubs, was pupil or apprentice to William Hart in the wheelwright's business. When that trade began to die out Jaky turned his hand, which had learned its skill from William, to another trade which will never die out as long as men are mortal: he became the village undertaker. But because Brensham is a small place and its inhabitants are long-lived, a man could not make a living in it out of coffins alone; so Jaky joined the ranks of those free and independent and extremely useful people whom we call odd-job-men. In addition to making coffins, he digs the graves. He will also thatch your cottage, tidy up your garden, clean your car, or mend your burst pipes after a frost. If there is anything the matter with your drains, you call in Jaky; likewise you send round for him if you want a lock mended or a tree felled or a chicken-house knocked together out of a few old boards. Perhaps the strangest of the duties which he performs for the community is connected with cats. He is an expert gelder; and it is a village joke that all the toms in the village flee when they hear him coming.

He is a peaky-faced, sharp-nosed little man with a curiously nasal voice, who always wears an ancient bowler hat on the back of his head. His speech is larded with pet phrases which he utters with a small sly grin, phrases like 'Matey' and 'How's your father'. Both his manner and his conversational style are somewhat macabre, as befits a member of his profession, and I remember in particular a gruesome piece of dialogue which I heard one night in the Horse and Harrow.

'Twenty-two inches across the shoulders,' said Jaky.

'Only twenty-two?' said Joe Trentfield. 'Well, well. I should have thought 'a' was more than that. A beamy chap.'

Jaky Jones pushed his bowler hat on to the back of his head and consulted a crumpled and dirty piece of paper.

'Six foot one and twenty-two across,' he said. 'They tends to shrink when they gets older.'

There was a pause, and then Jaky uttered one of his favourite *dicta*.

'A green Christmas makes a full churchyard,' he said, with a shrug of his shoulders.

As he spoke, the ghost of a grin played upon his sardonic features; and I was troubled with a curious sense of familiarity, as if he reminded me of someone else or I had heard that voice long ago. He went on:

'Rector wants 'im put at the bottom end by the yew-hedge.

But I says to the Rector, Matey, I says, 'tis too wet, I says; 'tis too near the culvert; afore you gets down three feet you finds the water seeping through the clay. Matey, I says, I wouldn't put a dog in there.'

Again and again, throughout this sombre speech, some gesture or trick in Jaky's manner struck a chord in my memory. It was like a pin-table game when the ball bouncing from pin to pin makes a contact and lights a momentary flicker of electric bulbs. Such a flicker occurred when he said ''Tis too wet.' 'How macabre!' I thought. 'But I suppose he gets accustomed to it . . .' and the word 'custom' went flickering along another memory-track, custom, custom, *custom hath made it in him a property of easiness* – and then the flicker became a flash, illuminating all. I suddenly saw the stage brightly lit and within that glowing oblong framed by the dark proscenium there leaned upon his spade the very spit and image of Jaky Jones. At Ophelia's half-finished graveside stood Hamlet and Horatio; and Jaky with his hat on the back of his head and the ghost of a grin on his clownish face looked up at them. '*And water*,' said the gravedigger, '*is a sore decayer of your whoreson dead body*.'

Gravediggers haven't changed much in the countryside round Stratford in three hundred-odd years.

The Poacher

Like most of the Brensham men, Jaky is a devoted fisherman, but he possesses the curious eccentricity that he prefers to fish without rod, reel, line or hook. Legitimate angling bores him; and on the rare occasions when he takes a rod he must needs add spice to his pastime by using illicit baits, such as salmon roe, which he prepares according to a secret method which he discovered in an old book. This book, which he once showed me as a special favour, contains some horrifying recipes for the making of pastes with such ingredients as 'Cat's Fat and Heron's Oil, and Mummy Finely Powdered', and there is one which runs like this: 'Take the Bone or Scull of a dead man, at the opening of a Grave, and beat the same into a powder, and put of this powder into the Moss wherein you keep your Worms; but others like Grave-earth as well . . .' I asked Jaky whether he had ever tried this experiment, and although he shook his head I think I detected a guilty look in his eyes. The anglers from Birmingham certainly suspect that he uses some kind of dark and mysterious wizardry; for he does a roaring trade every season in 'Jaky Jones' Special Red Worms', which he sells in little canvas bags for half a crown a quarter-pound.

But as I said, a rod and line, even when it has a Special Worm wriggling on the end of it, does not appeal to Jaky and he prefers to go fishing with such unusual implements as a shotgun, a spear, a willow-wand, a length of rabbit-wire, a tin of carbide, a sledge-hammer, or a wicker waste-paper basket which has had the bottom knocked out. With the shotgun he shoots pike as they bask on the surface in high summer. With the spear, which resembles Britannia's trident, he catches eels as they wriggle up the muddy ditches. With the willow-wand and the wire he fashions a noose which he can dangle far out into the stream and slip over the tails of fish lying near the top of the water. The carbide he pours into screw-top bottles, weighted with stones, to which he adds a little moisture before he screws up the top. He then casts the bottles into the river and awaits the explosion, which stuns all the fish within twenty yards. When they come to the surface he paddles round in his boat collecting the spoils like a punt-gunner picking up the bag after a successful shot.

The sledge-hammer and the waste-paper basket are used

in a very ingenious way. He takes them to some part of the river, such as a lock, where an old brick or stone wall runs along the bank. First he splashes about in the water so that the fish take refuge in the holes and crannies under the wall; and then he smites the top of the wall two or three times with the sledge-hammer so that the fish are knocked out by the vibration and float belly-upwards to the surface. If any should escape him, by darting out of the wall into the weeds, he takes his waste-paper basket, wades out to the weed-clump, and drops the basket neatly over the clump so that any fish which were lurking there are imprisoned. Then he rolls up his sleeves and pulls them out one by one.

There is one kind of fishing which particularly delights Jaky, and that is catching elvers with a cheese-cloth net when the little eels run up the river in springtime. He sets out at night with a lamp slung round his neck and returns in the morning with three or four bucketfuls of the small transparent fingerlings, which he hawks round the village at one and six a pound. It is a familiar thing in Brensham, at breakfast-time on April mornings, to hear Jaky's nasal voice vying with the cuckoo as he marches up the village street, with his bowler hat cocked on the back of his head and a couple of buckets slung over his shoulders on a yoke. '*Yelvers! Yelvers! Yelvers all alive-o!*'

The Trophy

In the last war, although he was nearly fifty, Jaky joined up and fought in the Battle of Alamein. He once told me a story about that battle while he sawed the side of a coffin in his workshop, and a draught coming in under the door teased the sawdust into miniature dust-devils which reminded him, he said, of the sands of Egypt. 'I minds as if it were yesterday,' said Jaky, 'boiling a can of strong tea over a petrol fire . . .' A small man wearing an Australian hat had suddenly appeared as if from nowhere and offered him a cigarette. Thinking the man was some sort of war correspondent, for such people were free with their cigarettes, Jaky had conversed with him in his usual free-and-easy manner for several minutes. He had also expressed a forcible opinion about Generals. The man smiled slightly and got into his car. Jaky was about to light the cigarette when he noticed the flag on the car's bonnet; so he saluted as smartly as he could (but in the manner, I expect, of one who touches his hat to the squire) and put the cigarette away, swearing that he'd never smoke it, not if he was dying for a puff, but would take it home as a trophy for his son and his son's sons. This high resolution was sorely tried next morning; for he was wounded in the first assault, and as he jolted down the line in an ambulance the pain came on suddenly and he wanted a smoke more than anything else in the world. He resisted the temptation, however, and there was the cigarette – 'in case you don't believe me, Matey' – in a neat little glass case, suitably inscribed, hanging on the wall over his work-bench. 'How's your father,' observed Jaky, for no reason in particular; and he began to whistle, as he performed his sombre task, that gay and lilting air which was one of the fruits of our desert victory, that piece of unsubstantial booty which we took from Rommel's men, the tune of *Lilli Marlene*.

'*A Foolish Thing Was but a Toy*'

William Hart had a hobby which he practised in his wainwright days and which made all the children love him. It was the reason why one would almost always see a crowd of brats hanging about outside his workshop on their way back from school. He could never pick up a piece of wood without wanting to carve it into some fantastic shape or other – 'What would you like,' he'd say, 'a Helephant or a Cock-yolly Bird?' and swiftly in his strong, blunt-fingered hands, the knife and the chisel would fashion the curling trunk and the great ear-flaps, or the long beak and the extravagant plumes. Being a born carpenter, he loved wood above all other materials, the feel, the smell, the grain of it, the sweet sawdust and the white shavings and the flying chips; if he saw an odd-shaped piece of oak or pitchpine lying about on his bench he couldn't keep his hands off it, he perceived at once the hidden possibilities lying dormant in the wood, the possibility perhaps of a hunch-back dwarf or a giant with a club or a caricature of his next-door neighbour; and almost at a touch, it seemed, he caused the creatures to spring to life. There was hardly a mantelpiece in Brensham which did not bear two or three of these curious sprigs and offshoots of his fancy which he poured out from his workshop as from a cornucopia to all the children who eagerly waited there.

But there were other figures which he carved for his private amusement only; for sometimes he would put too much of his own quintessential mischief into a caricature, and then he would hide it from the children or say that he had spoiled it and make them a cat or a pig instead. Later he would paint and varnish it and add it to the collection in his back-room, where upon a table covered with a dust-sheet was Brensham village in miniature, with its inhabitants all caught in their most characteristic and sometimes unfortunate attitudes – Briggs the blacksmith and demagogue addressing a political meeting, Sammy Hunt the teller of endless tales cutting a long story *bloody* short (which meant that it would go on for hours), Dai Roberts Postman going to chapel in his black Sunday clothes with a poached rabbit sticking out of his pocket, and so on. Some of the little wooden figures were cunningly articulated so that they could be made to perform various gestures – a policeman, for example, an excellent caricature of the constable who had been stung by the bees, took off his helmet with one hand and mopped his bald head with the other; a fat man resembling Joe Trentfield raised a cider-mug to his lips; a companion-piece, which surely represented Mrs Trentfield, possessed a bosom like a pouter pigeon which became agitated and bounced up and down when you turned a handle in her back. And there were more complicated – and much naughtier – contrivances than these. Yet there was no cruelty nor malice in these caricatures, although William took pains to hide them from the victims; rather were they tokens of affection and tenderness, of William Hart's wide and catholic love for life in all its moods and manifestations, curious, comical, strange, infinitely various, life budding and blossoming everywhere about him like a garden of multiform and many coloured flowers.

Old Adam

There was another thing he did supremely well. Long before he became a farmer he demonstrated that he possessed a genius for growing things; for whatever he planted in his garden flourished so vastly that he carried off most of the prizes every year at all the Flower Shows in the district. Other gardeners had reason to be envious of him, for he seemed to take very little trouble over his crops and he scorned to use any of the patent fertilizers and such-like in which his competitors put their trust. 'I turns over the good earth,' he would say. 'I puts in the little seeds, and up they comes!' Up they came indeed like Jack's beanstalk. You could have made out of his sweet-peas one year, people said, a hedge thick enough and tall enough to confine a bull! His tomatoes were as big as cricket-balls; his gooseberries were a match for some people's greengages; his potatoes were apt to weigh two or three pounds apiece. As for his vegetable marrows, there was something gross, something hardly decent, about the way they swelled and pullulated and waxed fat, until they looked like a herd of farrowing sows lying close together among the luxuriant foliage. Sometimes, indeed, even the judges at the Flower Show were appalled by the size of them, and disqualified them on the grounds that no ordinary housewife could handle them and that only a factory could be expected to turn them into jam.

I remember seeing William bearing away one of these gigantic marrows after the show. He carried it cradled in his arms, like a baby, but it was so heavy that he was soon compelled to pause for breath; and as he did so he looked down at his burden and smiled. Somehow it gave me a moment of exquisite pleasure to see him thus, smiling down in a proud fatherly way at the monstrous vegetable wedged against his huge belly and supported by his strong arms.

The ferocious fecundity of William's little garden might have embarrassed or even frightened a lesser man; for there surely dwelt Priapus himself, Dionysus' son and Aphrodite's, he who makes the green things to multiply and the trees to be fruitful and gives fertility to the loins of men. But William, who had never heard of Priapus, was only slightly puzzled by the phenomenon. Sometimes he would shake out a packet of seeds into his hand, and stare at them, and wrinkle his brow. 'They be so very, very small – but look!' and he would point to a prodigious broad bean thirty inches long, or a stick of 'sparrow-grass' twice as thick as a man's thumb, or a carrot which he'd just dug up and which, obviously, had been seeking the Antipodes. 'So very small,' he'd repeat with a wondering smile, 'but I puts 'im into the good earth and up they comes, Hey Presto!' And then, chuckling merrily, he'd retire into the teeming thicket of lilac, clematis, laburnum and honeysuckle which wildly overgrew his garden path.

As if to demonstrate that it was the special favour of Priapus, and not William's skill alone which made his garden flourish, some of his fattest potatoes and longest broad beans were self-seeded strays which came up of their own accord – as he put it 'without an ounce of muck or a drop of sweat spent on 'em'. He called them 'randoms' and on one occasion, to the vast annoyance of all his rivals, he won first prize at the Flower Show with a pound of tomatoes picked from a 'random' plant which he found growing at the bottom of his garden, beside the ditch where the sewage ran into it. I believe that these waifs and strays, these casual come-by-chance by-blows of his garden, pleased William more than all the regimented, orderly, carefully-tended rows. ''Tis like winning something out of old Nature's sweepstake,' he said, and grinned: 'I often thinks maybe I'm a bit of a Random myself.'

William had married young – the story of that marriage shall be told later – and his wife had died when he was still in his twenties; so he continued for many years to live with his old parents in the cottage by the wheelwright's shop and to carry on the business during his father's retirement. When his parents died – this was about forty years ago – William came into a little money; and thinking that he might as well profit by his extraordinary ability to grow things he bought the 150-acre farm on the green skirt of Brensham. He built himself a new yellow wagon – the biggest and the best wagon he had ever made – and at

Michaelmas he piled all his possessions into it, sat his two schoolgirl daughters on top of the pile, and moved up the hill.

He had bought the farm from Lord Orris, our local landowner, as he was then; and he had bought it exceedingly cheap, for two reasons: the Mad Lord, as we called him, was in debt as usual, and therefore needed the money; and, since his madness took the form of wild generosity, he could never bring himself to exact the full value for anything he sold.

The Ruin of Orris

Lord Orris was at that time about halfway to ruin; far speedier than Hogarth's Rake he was progressing towards penury, through his incorrigible habit of giving things away.

Once he had been rich, some say very rich; but he had handed over all his money to indigent nieces, profligate nephews, drunken wasters, scoundrelly spongers, and indeed to everybody who could persuade him – and that was not difficult – that they were in temporary or permanent need of it. To people who remonstrated with him about his indiscriminate charity he would make this sort of reply: 'Well, the poor chap drinks, you see – and he's very foolish about women too. He just can't help it and nowadays, I understand, that sort of thing costs a great deal of money; whereas my own necessities are really very small . . .' Nor was he content to give away only his cash. He bestowed his valuable library piecemeal upon various persons who said they were fond of books ('For honestly I read extremely little, and these old black-letter things are quite useless to an ignoramus like myself'.) He gave presents of furniture to people who said they collected antiques ('The fellow's a bit of a connoisseur and really *appreciates* that Louis Quinze stuff'). He made the Saturday afternoon gunners free of his woodlands ('Take what you can find, my dear chap – I have an absurd prejudice myself against killing things') and the Sunday afternoon anglers free of his trout-pond ('Though I warn you there's little in it beside eels, which I understand are not highly regarded by sportsmen'). And he even handed over bits of his land to tenants who were hard up, pretending to his critics that he actually gained by the transaction because 'The man has paid me no rent for years and now at any rate he'll have to pay the tithe.'

By the time he had got rid of the whole of his patrimony in this fashion he had fallen into an incurable habit of giving, and like a dipsomaniac he was unable to stop; and so with a kind of sublime innocence he went to the moneylenders and borrowed at a high rate of compound interest the largesse which he continued to distribute to all comers. His bank manager tried to point out the folly of this behaviour: 'Really, sir, the equation doesn't work out!' 'Alas, I am the worst mathematician in the world!' smiled the Mad Lord. His friends, seeing him drift towards bankruptcy, renewed their attempts to persuade him to mend his ways; and he answered them with sweet reasonableness and a logic which does not belong to our hard world. 'But, my dear friend, it is not strictly accurate to say that I *gave* the man a hundred pounds. He was very clever with figures – so unlike me! – and he had discovered an infallible system of winning money at roulette; but he'd lost all he had in trying it out at Monte Carlo. All I did was to *lend* him a hundred pounds so that he could return there and win it back again!'

So it went on, until the dilapidated mansion and the untended gardens were a match for their threadbare owner, and the shabby-looking beggars who slouched almost daily along the weedy drive were joined by shabbier-looking duns, and at last there came a time when neither beggars nor duns found it worth their while any longer to make that pilgrimage; for nothing was left but the crumbling stones of Orris Manor and the green acres in which it stood and which alone of the Mad Lord's possessions they could not carry away.

O Fortunatos Nimium

Without a doubt William had the trick of making things grow. Much of the hillside land was thin and chalky, sheep-grazing ground rather than arable; and like all the Mad Lord's estate it had been woefully neglected. Nevertheless within two or three years William was growing such crops of oats and barley and clover as Brensham had never seen. It was true that the weeds came up as well – perhaps the Garden-god is not selective! – and the good and the bad flourished together, the golden corn and the rank tares. William's was not a tidy or orderly farm. Nevertheless he got a huge yield off it, and in a period of scarcity, during and after the First World War, he made, from time to time, a good deal of money. He never kept it long, for that was not his way, and he still had his occasional bouts of wild drinking during which he let the farm go hang and spent every shilling he could lay hands on.

In 1924, being then well over fifty, he courted, in a boisterous and highly indecorous fashion which you shall hear of later, the cook from Brensham Rectory. The Rector's reluctance to marry them (for she was an excellent cook) was offset by his suspicion that there was a child on the way; and sure enough the child was born five months later, and was christened, perhaps inappropriately, with the name of

Prudence. About the same time William's two daughters by his first wife, who had married village lads, were also having babies; so what with the teeming crops and the outrageous weeds in William's fields, and the squalling brats in his house, one got the impression of a vast fecundity.

It was in this year that I had occasion to see William about some business and called at his farm about teatime on an afternoon in late summer. I remember very well the sense of fruitfulness and prodigality; the enormous yellow wagon lumbering along, piled house-high, it seemed, with golden stooks, and a field of uncut corn beside the drive with the straight stalks standing up to my waist, and yet with such a crop of poppies among the stalks that they made a crimson glow beneath the gold, like embers at the heart of a fire. And within the house, in the big kitchen which small farmers always use for living in, I discovered a cheerful bear-garden filled with babies, nappies, laughter, sizzling bacon, the steam from a kettle boiling over, and the intermingled smells of burning fat and scorched toast. There were, I suppose, only three babies, but I had the feeling that there were at least ten, because they all crawled on the floor in company with a number of dogs, cats and kittens, so that it was practically impossible to take a step without treading on something which yelped, mewed, squeaked or hollered. Betty and Joan (the two married daughters) also took up a good deal of room, for they were naturally buxom and there were two more babies on the way. Mrs Hart, the Rector's late cook, was reasonably ample, and William, who had just come in to his tea, towered over all. I remember him picking up Prudence (and as he did so a black cat jumped on his shoulder) and holding her up in his arms so that she could tug at his beard. Just then I accidentally trod on the fingers of another baby, who let out a loud yell. Everybody roared with laughter, one of the dogs began to bark, the water from the boiling kettle hissed furiously on the fire, the cat leaped off William's shoulder into the general mêlée, and the kitchen wore an aspect of confused pandemonium which Mrs Hart, 'hoping I didn't mind', referred to with considerable meiosis as homeliness.

We sat down to tea, and I amused myself by trying to count the number of animals in the room. There was a terrier and a spaniel bitch in pup, and a lot of cats all of which either had, or were obviously about to have, kittens. William loved cats, and two of them perched on his broad shoulders during tea. A fox cub appeared as if from nowhere and began to play with the terrier, and William told me how he'd picked it upin a cold wet furrow last spring (the vixen had been moving her litter away from the floods) and how he'd fed it with milk out of a fountain-pen filler until it was strong enough to fend for itself. When tea was finished he scraped up a handful of crumbs and threw them out of the window; and there suddenly materialized what I can only describe as a *cloud* of birds, sparrows and finches and thrushes and tits – they darkened the room for a second with their fluttering shadows as they showered down from the eaves and spoutings and bushes and boughs where they'd been waiting for the bounty scattered by William's prodigal hand.

'It will have blood, they say; blood will have blood.'

Though he loved birds and beasts and all wild things and liked to have them about him, it was not in William's nature, itself so wild and free, to wish to cage or confine them. The pet fox cub therefore had its freedom to come and go at its will. It showed no particular interest in the poultry, but it often went hunting for rats and moorhens in the osier-bed adjoining the lower boundary of William's farm; and there, one morning towards the end of the cub-bing season, General Bouverie's huntsman saw it sneaking down the brookside and holloaed the hounds on to its line.

They were, without a doubt, the slowest, stupidest and most riotous pack in England; and as most of them were pursuing moorhens, whimpering after water-rats, or simply standing at the edge of the osier-bed and waving their sterns, the fox cub had a fairly good start. It ran in a circle for about two miles, and gave the Hunt their fastest gallop of the season; but the hounds were close behind it when it came lolloping back towards the farmhouse and slipped through the hedge-gap near William's drive gate.

William had heard the hounds, and as he rushed out to rescue his fox cub he had armed himself, rather absurdly, with a shotgun, which in any case was unloaded. He was in time to see the hounds pull down the cub in his orchard – it was their first and last kill in the open during the whole of that season – and he was also in time to intercept General Bouverie and the rest of the field as they came puffing and snorting, a long way behind the hounds, full gallop up to his gate. There he confronted them, looking rather like a prophet of old with his bristling white beard, holding the shotgun at the ready.

General Bouverie, a mild and courteous person when he was not on horseback, always became so excited during a hunt that he went purple in the face, blasted everybody he encountered with weird and terrible oaths, and demanded of them in furious tones, 'Have you seen my fox, damn you?' Peaceful shepherds, market-gardeners ploughing their land, and even passing motorists who were not aware there was a fox for miles, were often cursed up hill and down dale be-cause they were too stupefied by the General's demented appearance to answer this terrifying question. But now, as the General pounded up to the gate and yelled out to William, 'Have you seen my fox, damn you?' he received a reply which he had certainly never had before.

'I have seen *my* fox,' said William sternly, 'and your hounds have just killed it.'

'Your fox?' spluttered General Bouverie, who believed like all Masters of Foxhounds that he had a prescriptive right to all the foxes within the boundaries of his hunting-country, 'What the devil do you mean by *your* fox?' And he uttered his favourite oath, which was the most extraordinary one I have ever heard: 'Fishcakes and haemorrhoids!'

'All the same,' said William, with quiet dignity, 'it was my fox; and this is my land; and if any of you dares to step over the boundary of my land I've got a gun.'

A ridiculous situation arose, in which everybody talked except William. A woman with a drawling voice said, 'The fellow must be drunk,' several times. General Bouverie's huntsman encouraged his hounds from a distance (although they needed no encouragement) to 'tear 'im up, my beauties, tear 'im and worry 'im, worry, worry, worry!' The General himself called upon fishcakes and haemorrhoids repeatedly but with diminishing conviction. And the Secretary of the Hunt, who was a lawyer, endeavoured to reason with William in a very learned way by pointing out that foxes, like other wild beasts, were legally considered to be animals *ferae naturae*, that is to say of a wild nature, in which the law recognized no private property whatsoever.

But William, who was somewhat *ferae naturae* himself, took no notice. Perhaps he didn't even listen, perhaps he was too full of grief for his little fox and of horror at the worrying noises of the hounds. But he continued to stand at the gate holding the gun awkwardly (for he hardly ever used it) and looking rather like a stiff sentry 'On guard' in a bad Victorian oleograph. Anon the huntsman blew his horn, and the hounds began to come back to him in twos and threes, bloody and stinking of fox, carrying tatters of fur in their mouths. General Bouverie called and cursed them alliteratively:

'Hey, Barmaid, Bosphorus, blast the bitch, Bellman, Bountiful! Here, Dimple, Daisy, Dairymaid, Dauntless, damn the dog, Daffodil!' and at last he turned his horse and rode away, followed by the disconsolate company. 'I *did* want to see them break up their fox,' said the drawling lady. 'It's so rarely the poor darlings ever get the chance... What an uncouth, what a *barbaric* old man!'

Ups and Downs

After that William gave notice to General Bouverie that he would never allow the Hunt on his land; and this action of his was to have far-reaching consequences, as you shall see. It had one immediate consequence, which was that the Hunt no longer bought their hay from him, and because the Depression was just beginning he was left with two big ricks of seeds on his hands. Then one of his cows got foot and mouth disease, and the Ministry of Agriculture sent their slaughterers to kill every beast on the farm. They had to fetch the village policeman before they dared to do it, for they had heard tales of how William had threatened the Hunt with a gun. In the end, however, he gave them surprisingly little trouble. When he saw the preparations for the burning, the faggots and hedge-brash piled high in his Home Ground, the fight went out of him suddenly and the policeman, who knew how to handle him, led him broken-hearted into the house.

Because of this loss, and the time it took him to re-stock his farm, the Depression hit him badly. For two or three seasons there was a glut of fruit and nobody to buy it; the price of sprouts didn't pay for the cost of growing them; sometimes it was actually cheaper to plough a crop into the ground than to try to market it. William, like all the other farmers round about Brensham, got into debt with the bank, the seed-merchant, the local tradesmen, and even the village pub; but unlike some of the others he paid them all in full when the new war began to loom up on the horizon and the farmers were suddenly prosperous again.

Neither debt nor disaster could tame him, and even during the worst of the Depression he would often blow into Brensham like the wind, shattering the uncomfortable quietude of those stricken days when it seemed indeed as if we were taking part in the obsequies of a dying countryside, as if a graveside hush lay over the land. Into the Adam and Eve or the Trumpet or the Horse Narrow blew William, boisterous, thunderous, always discovering at the bottom of his trousers-pocket a forgotten half-crown to pay for another round of drinks; then out into the street at closing-time, singing and shouting his defiant happiness to the world at large, banging on the windows and doors of friends, acquaintances and strangers alike, and answering their sleepy protests with that strange proud boast about his apocryphal ancestry – 'Thee carsn't touch I! Thee carsn't touch I! For I be descended from the poet Shakespeare!' and so, with huzza and tolderolloll, away home to the farm on the hill.

One of the most endearing things about William Hart was his complete lack of any shame or remorse afterwards; indeed he seemed to glory in the memory of his bouts and to look back on them with only one regret, that they were over. When the Rector happened to meet him on the morning following a particularly riotous night, and said to him sternly, 'I hear you were very noisy last night, William,' the wild old man threw back his head and roared with laughter. 'Noisy?' he said. 'Why, I was drunk – rascally drunk!' And he fairly smacked his lips over the night's junketings – '*Rascally* drunk, Rector!'

Liberty 'All

William's favourite pub was certainly the Horse and Harrow, because it had a boisterous atmosphere in which he felt at home. Its landlord, Joe Trentfield, who was a retired sergeant-major, and his huge wife who moved with the ponderous dignity of a full-rigged ship sailing into action, were boon-companions for William because like him they possessed an infinite capacity for laughter. Little came amiss to them as a source of fun; and the world as they saw it was a rich plum-pudding stuffed with joke and jest.

Mimi and Meg, being brought up in this genial air, soon added their quota to the general merriment. They were both serving in the bar (illegally, I dare say) before they were fourteen; and in one of my earliest memories of William Hart I can see the two strapping little girls sitting on his knees, while he warmed a pint of beer with a red-hot poker and told them stories. He was a born storyteller and I think the only time he was ever serious was when he was inventing tales for the children. He would then tell the most comic story with that quiet gravity which children love. I remember very well the beginning of one of these tales, which will show you what kind of a storyteller William was.

'Once upon a time there was a village called Merry-come-Sorrow and the folks who lived there were so mean, you'd never believe it, on Guy Fawkes' night they actually let off their fireworks down a deep well so as the folks in the next village shouldn't see 'em for nothing . . .' He had a fund of old country sayings which he worked into the tales like proverbs worked into the design of a sampler – sayings like 'It isn't spring until you can plant your foot on twelve daisies' and 'Mists in March mean frosses in May'; and his vocabulary was crammed with peculiar words such as 'tomtolly' and 'mollock' which seemed to possess large and comprehensive meanings – 'mollock', for example, meant 'the-sound-and-sensation-when-you-slipped-up-in-the-mud-and-fell-into-a-puddle'. I never found out what 'tomtolly' meant; but the children seemed to understand William's kind of shorthand, for they listened in grave silence and never dreamed of interrupting him to ask for explanations.

For those who were hardy enough to put up with the high wind of laughter which was always blowing there, the Horse and Harrow was the perfect pub; and Joe was the perfect landlord, for he stood in direct apostolic succession from Chaucer's Host – 'Eek therto he was right a mery man.' His free-and-easy bar – 'Liberty 'All', he called it – was probably the most important social institution in Brensham.

Now social institutions do not occur by chance or spring up suddenly; they are the product of gradual evolution, they grow up like trees in the landscape of our lives, they root themselves deep into our history and entwine themselves round our hearts. The Horse and Harrow like our oldest oak tree has been several hundred years a-growing; and like that somewhat similar institution, the Church of England, it is the consequence of a whole series of characteristic compromises. Its ancestry is mixed, complex and by no means wholly to its credit. It has evolved gradually out of the wayfarers' inn and the coaching-house, the dirty little gin-palace and the village drinking-den; and today it is not merely, or even primarily, a place for drinking in but forms one of the kingpins of our society.

If the Horse and Harrow were to disappear tomorrow I do not know what we should put in its place nor how we should contrive a substitute to carry out its multitudinous functions. It is our club, meeting-place, recreation-room, social centre and goodness knows what else rolled into one. Our farmers meet to discuss their business there, our young men in the early and late stages of their courtship take their girls there in preference to the pictures, our married men take their wives there after supper in the evenings. All classes come together in its bar, play darts and shove-ha'penny and cribbage together, tell tales and sing and debate and argue about village politics and about the larger politics of the country and the world.

Whatever changes and chances may happen to me, I think I shall cherish for as long as I live the memory of certain evenings in the Horse and Harrow after cricket, when the whole village team with their wives and their daughters and their girls crowded into Joe's little bar, and the wind of Joe's laughter blew about among us, and Mimi or Meg began to strum on the piano. Almost always before long Joe in his sergeant-major's voice would propose the absurd game which always delighted him: 'Now then, Ladies and Gentlemen, what about a round of Sing, Say or Pay?' The principle of the game was that everybody had to sing a song, tell a story, or pay for a round of drinks; and the pleasant absurdity of the game was that we knew beforehand (since most people's repertory was limited) exactly what favourite piece everybody would perform. Thus the familiar songs and the oft-told stories became associated with particular characters, became as it were part of their characters. Sammy Hunt, our cricket captain, who had also been a sea captain in his day, always sang a song called *The Fireship*:

'As I strolled out one evenin' out upon a night's career,
I spied a lofty fireship, and after her did steer;
I hoisted her my sig-a-nals which she very quickly knew,
And when she seed my bunting fly she immediately
hove-to-o-o.'

Alternatively he would tell an interminable story, which never came to an end although he continually promised to cut it *bloody* short, about how he nearly married a geisha girl in Japan or how he quelled a mutiny in the engine-room of his ship. We all knew these stories by heart and sometimes when Sammy paused we used to finish the sentence for him by chanting it in unison. But Sammy was quite unperturbed by this, and would gravely correct us if we got the sentence wrong – 'No, it wasn't the little yeller feller I hit on the nose – I clipped him behind the ear, see, just like this, because you can always put a Chink out by hitting him behind the ear . . . Well, to cut a long story *bloody* short . . .'

Alfie Perks, the Cricket Club Secretary, a tousled little man who looked like a terrier, could scarcely sing at all, and of his only song he could only remember five lines, like this:

'The Red Red Poppies,
The Red Red Poppies,
Down where the Red Poppies Blow.
The Red Red Poppies,
The Red Red Poppies,
Oh—'

He always said 'Oh' at this point, because, he said, that was where he forgot the rest of the song; and soon the 'Oh' became a traditional ending to the song, which we all sang in chorus.

Jaky Jones, needless to say, told a gruesome story about a man who got drunk and fell into an open grave in the churchyard; Mimi sang a tinny little song about Thinking of You When Skies are Blue; Mrs Trentfield laughed so much at her own story that we never understood what it was about; and Joe's song consisted mainly of a lively imitation of a pig grunting. Mr Chorlton, as you might expect, was the most versatile of our singers; he sang with equal enthusiasm, and equal disregard of tune, in English, French, Italian, German or Latin. We used to persuade him to sing *Mihi est propositum In taberna mori* because it had a good rollicking air and because the unfamiliar sound of the words always made Joe Trentfield laugh – to Joe, who as a soldier had seen most of the world, anything Foreign was automatically funny. But oddly enough the performance which the village liked best was Mr Chorlton's recitation of the Frogs' Chorus from the *Batrachoi*: 'Brekekekex, ko-ax, ko-ax!' of which he gave a very spirited rendering indeed. I often used to think that there was surely not another village among all the thirty thousand villages of England where you could hear a recitation from Aristophanes and see a score of market-gardeners and farm-labourers taking up the chorus one by one so that soon they were all making a passable imitation of the noise which the frogs made in the Athenian Marshland two thousand years ago.

William Hart sang a song as prodigal as himself, an old folk-song dating I think from the time of George the Second, about a soldier and a sailor who join together in a prayer:

'And the first thing they prayed for was a pound of good steak,

And if we have one pound may we always have ten . . .
"*God send us a bellyful!*" said the sailor, "*Amen.*"

'And the next thing they prayed for was a pint of good ale,
And if we have one pint may we always have ten . . .
"*God send us a bellyful!*" said the sailor, "*Amen.*"'

And so on for half a dozen verses. But old William's favourite song of all, when he came blustering into the Horse and Harrow like a March wind, was the noisiest, merriest, naughtiest song in the world, with twelve verses each more shocking than the last one and a rollicking chorus in which even Mrs Trentfield, laughing till she cried and shaking like a jelly, shamelessly joined:

'Roll Me Over!
In the clover!
Roll Me Over – lay me down – and do it again! . . .'

'Well, well, we do see Life,' choked Mrs Trentfield, wiping away her tears.

Fermented Happiness

But now at long last the years began to take their toll of William. Just before the war he had his seventieth birthday, and shortly afterwards his only infirmity – an arthritis in the knees – became painfully acute. People prophesied that he'd snuff out like a guttering candle when he could no longer manage to walk to the Horse and Harrow or even hobble as far as the Adam and Eve. But he was tougher than that; and when his legs began to fail him he determined, in a less compromising spirit than Mahomet's, that if he could not get to the drink the drink should come to him. There were obvious physical difficulties, however, in stocking his small farmhouse with sufficient beer for his needs; the brewers' lorry would have had to climb the hill every week at least. Moreover, he had noticed and he deplored the fact, that the beer got thinner as the years went by. He decided that the time had come to renounce his customary drink in favour of one which contained a higher percentage of happiness in a smaller bulk; and it would be convenient, obviously, if this happiness could be manufactured on the premises. So William went in for home-made wine.

He was provident in this matter if in nothing else; for he began to lay down his first vintage, as it were, several years before the arthritis finally immobilized him. He took back from one of our annual Flower Shows, pushing it upon a large wheelbarrow, his biggest-ever vegetable marrow, which had been rejected by the judges and unkindly compared by those Philistines with Epstein's Genesis. He hacked it into convenient pieces, fermented it with sugar, and turned it into wine. He certainly had no lack of the raw material of happiness in his proliferous garden; and that same autumn he fermented a great quantity of damsons, greengages and plums. Thanks to this piece of forethought there was no thirsty gap in his life, no dry desert in his years. One evening he drank his last pint of beer in the Adam and Eve, hobbled painfully home on two sticks, and immediately celebrated his safe arrival by broaching the first cask of plum jerkum. He took to the stuff at once; and cottagers who passed along the lane on their way home from the pub often declared that they had heard him bellowing with joy.

The plum wine was finished in a couple of months, and then he started on the damson; and when that cask was dry he tackled the marrow, the gooseberry, the rhubarb and the blackcurrant in turn. His taste was extremely catholic, and he was always experimenting; for he believed that there was no wholesome vegetable, flower or fruit which couldn't be improved by turning it into wine, and he boasted that his cellar was capable of providing him with a different sort of nightcap for every day of the month if he felt inclined for variety. 'Sometimes,' he said, 'I'm in the mood for Artichoke and sometimes I feels like Dandelion.' He even made wine out of parsley, which caused the villagers to shake their heads, for we have an old superstition about parsley wine, that it's for lazy husbands and shy wives – 'What would old William want with such stuff, at his age?'

He soon became noted all over the district for his wonderful brews which seemed to be much more powerful than anybody else's – perhaps Priapus saw to it that the sugar-content in his home-grown fruit and vegetables was exceptionally high. His friends and neighbours formed the habit of dropping in for a cordial glass or two to drive out the cold on chilly mornings or the damp on wet ones. But these guests reported that his stocks, despite the steady drain upon them, by no means diminished; for Mr Hart continued to be provident, and he was very mindful of a principle which politicians and economists, too, would do well to remember: consumption must not exceed production, the supply must keep pace with the demand. He therefore devised a long-term plan; what industrialists would call a production-schedule; and the cheerful assumption underlying this plan was that he would live to be a hundred and that he would tend to drink more as he grew older.

Pru

Meanwhile his third daughter Prudence had grown up very unlike her buxom, bouncing step-sisters. She was a little pale wisp of a thing, with a wan-looking expression, a codlins-and-cream complexion, and large china-blue eyes. They always looked slightly moist, as if she were about to cry. She was as quiet as a mouse, as prim as a Victorian maid, she spoke when she was spoken to and suffered herself to be mildly bullied by her step-sisters. We thought of her as Cinderella.

At the beginning of the war, to everybody's astonishment, she went off in her quiet mouselike way and joined the ATS; and very pathetic she looked, when she came home for her first leave, in a rough khaki uniform which was much too big for her. She'd never stand up to the life, people said; she had a weak chest; she was coughing badly already; sleeping in those draughty huts would kill her; and so on. But in 1940 Brensham heard that she was stationed at a lonely gun-site somewhere on the east coast. Imagine little Pru actually firing those great guns! Almost everybody in the village started simultaneously to knit her pullovers and balaclava helmets. Some even sent her their sweet rations. 'Our little grumbles seem very silly,' said the Rector's wife, 'when you think of the Hurricane pilots, and the men in the destroyers, and frail girls like Pru sacrificing themselves to keep us safe!' Pru, in fact, became the village heroine.

But alas, not for long. The gun-site was undoubtedly lonely, and if Pru was not homesick I am sure that she looked homesick. She was the kind of girl whom all men want to comfort, care for, and protect, though sometimes of course they go about it in a rather curious way. So early in 1941 she was invalided out of the ATS and returned to

Brensham, where a few months later in her quiet mouselike way, without fuss or bother or complaint, she gave birth to a boy. She called him Jerry; and explained calmly to her scandalized step-sisters that she did so because the Jerries had been over at the time.

Shortly after this the second Mrs Hart died, and Pru was left with the job of keeping house for William, which she did with serene efficiency, cooking almost as well as her mother had done, cheering and comforting him in his loneliness. She was his favourite daughter, because the others, who had found husbands and respectability, were both ashamed of his past and disapproving of his present, and never lost an opportunity to tell him that he'd kill himself with drinking that nasty home-made wine. Pru, on the other hand, let him drink to his heart's content, helped him up the stairs when his knees were stiff or his legs unsteady, and did everything that a dutiful daughter could do to make his old age easy and contented. She was Cordelia to his Lear.

She had, however, one fault; and William was tolerant of it as she was tolerant of his drinking. She seemed to have some kinship with the owls and the bats, the luminous-eyed cats and the soft downy moths, for not bolts nor bars nor chains nor locks could keep Pru in at night. Not even her twelve-month-old baby; but she was a good mother as well as a dutiful daughter, and because it would have been unreasonable to leave the crippled old man in charge of it, she solved the problem by the simple method of taking the baby with her. She wrapped it up in plenty of woollies, tucked it into the pram, and laid a mackintosh sheet on top in case of rain; and off she went. Pru's pram, parked after dark by the side of a road and generally close to a stile, became a familiar sight in the district round Brensham; for she was courting again, and this time it was an American.

She had her second baby in the spring of 1944, by which time the American soldier had been moved to an extremely secret headquarters where, it appeared, no letters could reach him. Whether Pru grieved, in her quiet mouselike way, nobody ever knew. To outward appearances she was utterly unmoved. She brought up the new baby, a fine bouncing girl, with the same thoughtful care which she had lavished on her first one; and she continued to look after William as well, keeping the house spotless and cooking all his favourite dishes for dinner. She also milked the cows, fed the poultry, and at busy seasons helped with the picking of plums and sprouts. It was a wonder how she found time to do so much; and still more of a wonder when the soft dark autumn nights came again and Pru, her day's work finished, resumed her late-walking with two babies in the pram.

This time it was an airman. He came from the extreme north of Scotland, speaking a tongue which only Pru could understand. Perhaps even she could not properly understand it, for he stoutly maintained during the subsequent proceedings that he had repeatedly told her he was a married man and that she had said it didn't matter in the least. Pru celebrated VJ-Day by having her third baby which turned out to be another girl.

She herself, who accepted life as it came, would never, I think, have troubled to sue for a paternity order against the Scot; she was badgered into this course by Mrs Merrythought, who persisted in regarding her as an innocent victim of the wolfishness of men, and by Mrs Halliday, the wife of our newly-elected Member of Parliament, who ran a crèche in the village hall during the plum-picking season and was moved by what she regarded as Pru's pitiable condition to start a sort of crusade on her behalf. 'The girl must have her Rights,' said Mrs Halliday, who believed that she had a vocation to see that everybody received justice in a manifestly unjust world. But the only Rights which Pru got in the end consisted of ten shillings a week and the right to appear in the Magistrates' Court at Elmbury, where her moist eyes and innocent expression so deeply moved the Chairman of the Bench that he described the unfortunate airman as a blackguard and a cad whom he would have had the greatest pleasure in horse-whipping personally if only the Law had allowed it. When the court was over Mrs Halliday, whom we suspected of being a crypto-communist, took Pru to a café where she bought her a cup of coffee and spent twenty minutes or so telling her how much better the Russians look after girls who got into trouble; but Pru's step-sisters, who had accompanied her to court and to the café, said that Pru paid very little attention, and that she kept looking over her shoulder, with those large love-in-the-mist eyes, at a sailor on leave who happened to be sitting at the next table.

Our MP

'Simple folk,' Mr Chorlton once remarked, 'often become Socialists because they are poor and others are rich; more complicated people sometimes do so because they cannot bear to be rich while others are poor.' Our Member of Parliament was one of the latter sort; and we knew quite a lot about him because it had turned out that he was the same M. R. Halliday (Halliday minor) to whom Mr Chorlton had taught the appreciation of Virgil's hexameters about the year 1919. Old schoolmasters delight to indulge in a complicated sort of detective-game when the names of their ex-pupils get into the papers; and Mr Chorlton, who had an enormous acquaintance among gossipy old dons at

Oxford, succeeded in piecing together what was probably a fairly accurate history of Mr Halliday's career.

It seemed that he was one of those people who are driven into scholarship almost against their will; for he suffered from a slight deformity of his foot, which at school and at Oxford had prevented him from playing the usual games. 'I've had half a dozen boys like that,' said Mr Chorlton, 'they slog away at their books with a sort of melancholy fanaticism while all the time they're eating their hearts out to do the absurd things which footballers do after matches – to run riot in the streets and climb lamp-posts and make away with the helmets of policemen. And when they get Double Firsts and become Presidents of the Union and Senior Wranglers and whatnot it's an empty triumph because they'd much rather have had a rugger Blue or rowed in the boat-race!'

Maurice Halliday went down from Oxford with a brilliant reputation, plenty of money, and good prospects in any profession he cared to choose. But he chose to become a Socialist and to bury himself in the office of a Left-wing publisher who clung precariously to the brink of bankruptcy until he finally toppled over the edge in the summer of 1939. Meanwhile Halliday, the unwilling bookworm, had made himself an authority on the social history of England during the Industrial Revolution and had published a fat book on the subject which hardly anybody had read ('except me,' said Mr Chorlton. 'I used to read everything. It's rather good'). He had also married his employer's daughter.

Then the war came, and being debarred by his twisted foot from joining the Forces he spent the next five years in the Ministry of Information: 'just like his student-days,' said Mr Chorlton, 'tied willy-nilly to his desk, with the war like another envied rugger-rag going on outside his study window.'

In 1945 he had won the Elmbury Division for Labour, by eleven votes after two recounts, and he had already begun to make a reputation as a promising backbencher and in particular as an indefatigable asker of Questions about almost every conceivable subject.

'So there you are,' ended Mr Chorlton, 'we know all about him. But old schoolmasters like me are very foolish really to pursue these inquiries. It is only once in a blue moon that we have the pleasure of teaching a boy who is not a dolt or a blockhead or a rugger hearty or a simple cretin; and almost invariably, when we follow his subsequent career, we discover that he either writes immoral novels or unintelligible poetry or preaches a political doctrine which is highly repugnant to us. These are Time's revenges upon my miserable profession!'

Mrs Halliday

We had come across Halliday's wife through her activities in connexion with the crèche and because she had been searching, in vain so far, for a house in the neighbourhood. She was a brisk, businesslike and self-possessed young woman with a new-laundered smell who looked as if she ought to be a gym-mistress but turned out to be a bluestocking; her extremely attractive head was crammed chock-full of all the latest dogma, she had no doubts about anything under the sun, and she obviously prided herself upon her Rational Approach to Life. And indeed she was terribly rational, except about the Russians and the Tories, who provoked her respectively to the most unreasonable transports of love and hate, and about germs, which she viewed with similar sentiments of mistrust and horror to those she entertained for the Conservative Party. When she was in charge of the crèche at the Village Hall she sprayed the room with so many sorts of disinfectant that it smelt like a chemist's shop. I sometimes wondered whether her husband ever grew tired of the antiseptic aura which perpetually clung to her, whether he found himself wishing that for a change she would drench herself in scent – the cheapest, the most cloying, even the most tarty scent. But even if he did I doubt if he brought himself to the point of telling her so. She was not the kind of girl to whom one could say such things.

Her age was about twenty-eight, and she was tall, long-legged, shapely and hygienic-looking, with gentian-blue eyes and reddish-blonde hair cut rather short. Her whole delight, it seemed, lay in organizing other people's lives. She had organized Mr Halliday into Parliament and poor Pru into the police court and now she threatened cheerfully that if only we could find her a house in the village she would 'wake up' our sleepy Women's Institute, revive our moribund Youth Club, redecorate the Village Hall and get an artist friend to paint bright and modernistic friezes round the walls, and reorganize the Amateur Dramatic Society on what she called a more democratic basis. She also promised to get her husband to ask a Question in Parliament about our sewage system, which was somewhat out of date.

'They'll tidy us up,' sighed Mr Chorlton, shaking his head, 'and at my age I've got a horror of being tidied. For God's sake let's bribe the house agents to keep them away!' But it wasn't very long, as you shall see, before we needed the help of Mr Halliday in the matter of William Hart.

The Irreconcilable

The trouble between William and the War Agricultural Executive Committee had begun as long ago as 1940, when the Committee ploughed up Little Twittocks and destroyed the foxes' earths where he loved to watch the vixen playing with her cubs at dusk on summer evenings. It went on, in the form of a long skirmish about weeds and thistles and nettles, for the next three years; and then as I have told you came a period of open warfare about the sunflowers, which William grew on Little Twittocks in flat defiance of a cultivation order to grow potatoes.

It must be admitted that the WAEC had been, on the whole, pretty patient with William. He was extremely wayward and obstinate, and I suppose to some extent he was even what prim reformers call an irreconcilable. At any rate he was either unable or unwilling to fit himself into a world in which there are a great many regulations and multitudes of forms.

His attitude to forms was very peculiar indeed. He could write only with difficulty, he could read simple statements only if they were in large print, and in common with some of His Majesty's Judges he was utterly unable to understand the language which civil servants use when they try to make their orders and regulations clear to the ordinary man. Being a farmer, he naturally received a large number of these forms. They asked him to make a return of all the labourers he employed, 'differentiating between male and female'. They demanded from time to time a census of his horses, cows, sheep, pigs and poultry. They wanted to know whether his hens suffered from fowl-pest or his blackcurrants from Big Bud, and whether the wire-netting he had applied for was to keep Rabbits (Domestic) in or Rabbits (Wild) out. Pestered as he was with these forms, William at last grew cunning and wary of them, and developed a sort of defensive mechanism against bureaucracy which for a season or two served him very well. He had learned by experience that forms bred like guinea-pigs: the answer to any one question, even if a man could comprehend the question and write out the answer, engendered a litter of new questions each more troublesome than the last. Nor was it any use writing in the blank space provided 'You bloody well find out'; he'd tried that, with disastrous consequences. But these forms, he discovered, could nevertheless be gelded like tom-cats by the simple process of writing NIL all over them. A nice short simple word, and you never heard any more from the clerks in their office if you answered NIL to every question on the form. Having made this discovery, William no longer troubled to read the questions or to ask Pru to read them for him; he merely filled in each of the blank spaces with a large, blotchy and spidery NIL. Later he improved on this method. Instead of NIL he wrote SEE OVER (actually he spelt it SEA OVER) and matched it with a second SEA OVER on the other side of the page. He had thought out this manoeuvre very carefully, and for nearly two years it seemed to work like a charm. But Governments, like the Gods, remember everlastingly; and the time arrived when William's sins came home to roost like a flock of homing pigeons and he was assailed, not with forms only, but with hosts of angry letters, reply-paid letters, and even threats of prosecution if he failed to provide a true and correct answer to paragraph 5 sub-section 2 (d) within seven days.

Among this considerable correspondence which Dai Roberts Postman delivered almost daily at William Hart's farm was a document headed DEFENCE REGULATIONS: CULTIVATION OF LANDS ORDER, 1939. We hereby direct you, it said, to carry out in respect of the lands described in the schedule hereto the works of cultivation specified in the said schedule. *Parish*: Brensham. *No on Ordnance Map* 123. *Acres.* 71·34. known as Little Twittocks. *Required Cultivation*: to plough and plant with potatoes in a good and husbandlike manner.

William, I regret to say, took no more notice of it than he took of all the threatening letters. He ploughed the field, it is true; but when the time came for planting he had forgotten all about the cultivation order, and because he was short of food for his hens he took it into his crackpot old head to grow sunflowers. He'd only got enough seed to plant a small part of the field, so he decided to grow maize on the rest. The subsequent wet weather suited neither the maize nor the sunflowers; and the Chairman of the War Agricultural Executive Committee, making an inspection in August, was unable to see them for weeds.

About this time, to make matters worse, the Committee received a complaint about his bad husbandry from William's neighbour; or perhaps I should say 'neighbours', for the land all round his farm was owned by a Syndicate consisting of some financial gentlemen from London. William's 150 acres, forming a little island in the middle of their estate, was probably a great nuisance to them; and it was certainly an obstacle to some mysterious plans which they had for future 'development'. They looked upon it as Ahab from his palace looked upon the vineyard of Naboth the Jezreelite; and they offered William the worth of it in money, but he refused to sell. And so when the light breezes of summer blew the thistledown from Little Twittocks on to their tidy field over the boundary-hedge, they said to themselves that it was an ill wind which blew nobody any good and instructed their solicitors to write a complaint to the War Agricultural Executive Committee. In due course that letter found its way from desk to desk and office to office and took its proper place in the docket about William Hart which wandered to and fro about the Ministry and now grew bulky and gravid as it ponderously approached gestation.

PART TWO

LORDS OF THE MANOR

The City Rusticates – The Allies – 'Exercise Paratroops' – 'Oi?' – 'My mother said—' – The Good Fight – The Reconciliation – The Wind on the Heath, Brother – The Patriarch – Works of Darkness – Three Swashers – 'Booze and the Wenches Take the Lot' – The World's My Oyster – At Tolpuddle Hall – A Purgatory for Planners – The Pig-killing – Crusaders by Proxy – The Boy David – The Baby Show – 'We'll Tame Her'

The City Rusticates

NOW LET us turn for a moment from the case of William Hart to the affairs of the Syndicate, which had been causing a good deal of excitement in Brensham for the last eighteen months and which now suddenly came to a head. First you must hear a piece of old history.

Long ago, when the addle-pated Lord Orris first began to borrow from the moneylenders, he had pledged a portion of his estate to some City financiers who had already bought up a good deal of land on the other side of Brensham Hill. Subsequently he had increased his borrowings and pledged still more of his land; until at last only the dilapidated mansion was left and he raised his ultimate loan on that. Meanwhile the clever financiers watched and waited, and when they thought that the time was ripe they foreclosed on their mortgages and took possession of the property. It wasn't a very valuable property; for the house through years of neglect had become draughty and damp, the wasted land grew just enough coarse grass to support its unparalleled population of rabbits, the muddy Moat had breached its banks and turned the garden into a snipe-marsh, and even the spinneys and copses had been despoiled for firewood by the gypsyish families in tents and caravans whom the Mad Lord had permitted to camp upon his Park. The financiers, however, were not primarily interested in agriculture; it was rumoured that they intended to build holiday-bungalows on the side of the hill, to turn the Manor into a country club and the Moat into a swimming-pool, and to lay out the Park as a golf course. In the years immediately before the war they had bought up two more farms in the district, and they even got their long talons into Brensham village itself, where they snapped up the few cottages and holdings which happened from time to time to come into the market.

At first the various members of the Syndicate used the Manor as a weekend residence for themselves and their guests, while Lord Orris lived on sufferance in the small Lodge at the end of the drive. It was an odd thing about them that although they came and went, with their wives and families, almost every weekend, they failed to establish distinct identities, and we always thought of them collectively as 'The Syndicate' or 'The folks from London'. They all had big cars, and the men all wore black homburg hats, and the womenfolk seemed inseparable from their furs even in summer so that one tended to think of them not as human beings covered with smooth skin but as creatures bearing pelts, like animals. Nor did the village get to know them any better when they established themselves in the

Manor on a permanent basis, as soon as the bombs began to fall in London. Immediately they started to exercise what they called their rights. They evicted the gypsyish folk from the Park, and set keepers to chivvy the labouring men who thought it no theft to take an occasional rabbit out of the teeming abundance. (Only Dai Roberts Postman was undeterred by the keepers; and he who because of his high moral principles had previously poached only on week-days poached now with a kind of religious and revivalist fervour on Sundays as well.) They prosecuted the village children for 'stealing' their apples even though in a season of glut the fruit lay rotting on the ground, and they put up notices that Trespassers would be Prosecuted along every field-path and beside every gate. They drove off Brensham Hill not only the seasonal mushroom-gatherers and blackberry-pickers but also the courting couples and the families out for a Sunday afternoon airing, although it was pointed out to them that our people had wandered foot-free over those grassy slopes for as long as anybody could remember. Because of these things the village passionately hated them, and there was an element of fear in the hatred, for it really looked at one time as if the Syndicate would overwhelm Brensham and impose their shabby get-rich-quick régime upon it, tyrannize and subdue and cheapen and emasculate it, and turn it at last into a tributary province of their far-flung financial empire. As you will see, however, Brensham dealt with the threat in its own way; our turbulent, obstinate, intractable and crack-brained people dealt with it so effectively that within six months of the end of the war the posters went up advertising the whole estate for sale by auction; and the inhabitants of the Manor were reported to be packing up and preparing to take themselves off again to the slick, smooth, West End world which was all they understood and where, as Joe Trentfield suggested in the Horse and Harrow, they doubtless 'felt at home in the same way as snakes feel at home in the jungle'.

The Allies

A Triple Alliance was responsible for this victory: the village, the evicted gypsies, and Lord Orris' daughter Jane.

The weapons employed by the village were mostly very ancient ones, though by no means blunted by time, the weapons of boycott, obstinacy, petty obstructiveness, and assumed stupidity. Hardly anybody, for instance, would work for the Syndicate; they could get no domestic help, no gardeners, and few labourers on their farms. When they obtained servants from elsewhere the village proceeded to undermine the morale of these servants by various subtle and ingenious means, ranging from suggestions that the Manor was haunted, or that everybody who lived there for more than three months died of TB, to more libellous allegations that the members of the Syndicate sacrificed goats to Satan, performed the Black Mass, and practised unnatural vices. (There was a private chapel in the Manor grounds in which generations of Orrises had worshipped God, and one Lord Orris, assisted by Mister Jack Wilkes and some other rapscallions from London, used with great earnestness to worship the Devil.) It had kept its bad name, and the wickedness of the eighteenth-century lord was still legendary in Brensham, which now wished all his known sins on to the Syndicate with the addition of a few invented ones.

Another method of dealing with the imported servants, costly but well worth the expense, was simply to make them drunk; and indeed one ancient butler, who needed little encouragement in that direction, became so drunk that he suffered an attack of the willies during which he set fire to his bedroom. The local Fire Brigade, called to quell the outbreak, took care to play their hoses unnecessarily upon every piece of furniture in the house which looked as if it might possess any value.

'*Exercise Paratroops*'

It was about this time that the Home Guard took a hand in the affair. During one of the recurrent 'flaps', when the risk of invasion seemed very real, Joe Trentfield was instructed to inform the neighbourhood as tactfully as possible that there was a chance of enemy parachutists landing on Brensham Hill. Carrying out these orders, he called at Orris Park, where the drunken butler ushered him into an oak-panelled entrance-hall decorated with stags' heads bought at a taxidermist's and suits of armour picked up at a junk merchant's. Joe was kept waiting a long time in this chilly place, which did not accord with his sense of his own dignity, whether he regarded himself as the not-unimportant landlord of the Horse and Harrow or as a Lieutenant in His Majesty's Home Guard. At last there came down to him (said Joe) 'one of the furry women', whom he might have mistaken for a pack of silver foxes save for her pale peaky face which peered out between the heads and tails. She addressed him as 'My man', which added nothing to Joe's regard for her; so he delivered his message sharply and urgently, going a bit beyond his orders perhaps and 'slightly exaggerating', as he put it, the risk of parachutists landing on the hill. 'We've been told to keep a special look-out,' he said, 'on the Park itself, which being flat would make a likely dropping ground.' He added some hair-raising instructions about what to do if the Germans arrived, and some colourful speculations about what the Germans themselves would do, at which the pale face among the silver foxes went whiter, if possible, than it had been before. At that moment two fat men, and another furry woman, came down the staircase into the hall. Some imp of mischief prompted Joe to say casually:

'And of course you realize that if the Huns do come they'll probably be wearing British uniforms.'

One of the fat men stammered:

'B-but do you mean to say that there will be no way of telling f-friend from f-foe?'

'The Huns,' said Joe grimly, 'are likely to be the more peremptory.' He then took his leave.

On the following Saturday night the Home Guard paraded at eight-thirty and marched up the hill for the purpose of carrying out an anti-invasion exercise. There were two sections, commanded respectively by Sergeant Jeremy Briggs and Sergeant Alfie Perks. The latter were instructed to conceal themselves in a quarry until nightfall, where they whiled away the time by burning corks and blacking their faces. When Joe inspected them at dusk they were practically unrecognizable as men of Brensham. 'It don't matter much about not being able to speak the lingo,' said Joe, 'but it wouldn't do any harm if you was to say *jar vole* and *Hare Gott* now and then and click your heels when you get an order. And remember that though you're Huns there must be no damage to persons or property.' The section then moved off into Orris Park, where they sent up some Very lights (meaning '*parachutists just landed*') and proceeded to play soldiers with great verisimilitude according to the agreed plan, which was as follows.

Sergeant Briggs' section, less Corporal Dai Roberts who was engaged in setting rabbit snares, were to surround the Park as soon as they saw the signal and attempt to contain the parachutists within the pale. When the German parachutists broke out, which was inevitable, they were to occupy the outbuildings of the Manor itself and defend themselves against a further assault by the British. This tactical exercise, which had been invented by Joe himself, was perfectly legitimate and plausible; for it represented what would probably have happened if the Germans had really landed.

In the event certain things happened which had not been planned or anticipated; but it is by no means certain that they too would not have taken place if the 'invasion' had been genuine. The black-avis'd Alfie Perks, having led his section out of the Park and established it in the gardens and outbuildings of the Manor, was assembling a Lewis gun at the edge of the shrubbery when he was suddenly confronted by two furry women and two fat men who seemed to be half-demented with terror and who demanded tremulously: 'Are you German?'

And Alfie, who had entered into the spirit of the game but who never imagined (or so he says) that he would be taken seriously, answered: '*Jar vole.*'

The effect of this utterance was unexpected and shocking. The two men and the two women began, said Alfie afterwards, to quiver and quake and shiver and shake like frog-spawn. 'The silver-foxes' heads was jigging and dancing about on them women's shoulders so's I could almost fancy they was snapping at me.' Meanwhile the owners of the foxes gibbered at Alfie, and then the men joined in, and soon all four were speaking together in a sort of catch or chorus, like a quartet singing madrigals.

They wanted Alfie to know that they had no personal
 feelings against the Germans.
Politics didn't interest them, anyhow.

We'd always been friends, hadn't we?
They were peaceful civilians. It wasn't their war.
If there was anything the soldiers wanted—
They bore no animosity against Herr Hitler or anybody else.

Alfie listened to this extraordinary performance with mounting horror, but he said nothing except occasionally *Jar vole.* Before long, according to his own story (but Alfie is given to exaggeration), they'd offered him 'the whole works, including the best bed'. At this point, however, Sergeant Briggs delivered his assault upon the Manor. There was a rattle of rifle-fire, a thunderflash landed at Alfie's feet, and the shrieking women fled into the house. ('The men got there before 'em,' said Alfie grimly. 'They was helluva swift-footed.') A few moments later some pyromaniac in Briggs' section set alight the shrubbery with a Molotov cocktail, and the Home Guard spent the rest of the night trying to put out the fire. Nothing more was seen of the inhabitants of the Manor until the morning, when Joe called upon them, ostensibly to make his explanations and apologies.

Needless to say, they were extremely angry. They said that they were law-abiding citizens robbed of their sleep and terrified out of their wits by a lot of thugs playing at soldiers. They declared that the fire in the shrubbery had destroyed some valuable rhododendrons recently imported from Kashmir. They claimed compensation for the damage, and they threatened to write letters to *The Times*, their Member of Parliament, the Area Commander, and the Minister for War, who was, they said, a distant relation of their aunt. Joe listened to all this in silence, and when they had finished he answered briefly and to the point. He answered in two syllables: *Jar vole.*

As a matter of fact, they did write their complaint to the Area Commander; and it is said that this busy officer, who already had before him a somewhat mis-spelt but forcibly worded report from his obedient servant Alfie Perks, Sergeant, Home Guard, submitted for immediate attention through the proper Service channels, took exactly sixty seconds to consider the complaint. He then turned to one of his staff officers and said: 'If you had a large half-empty mansion, occupied by some people who we want to keep our eyes on, what would you do about it?'

'I'd billet a company of Poles there,' said the resourceful staff officer.

'Exactly what I was thinking.' Next week the Poles arrived at Orris Manor, and among them was one Count Wladislaus Pniack, who took only ten days to fall in love with Mimi Trentfield, three months to marry her, and the minimum period thereafter to father her twins.

'*Oi?*'

That was an uncomfortable winter for the Syndicate. They did not get on with the Poles, whose Commanding Officer, a polished gentleman in most respects, possessed an idiosyncracy about candles which has also been recorded of the great Dr Johnson: when they failed to burn well he held them upside down and shook them over the best carpet. It was during this winter, too, that our local garage-man took to introducing sugar into the petrol whenever he filled up one of the Syndicate's big cars; he also was a member of the Home Guard, and he made the excuse that he wanted to test the effect of sugar in petrol in case the Germans came. Generally speaking, however, the village refrained from actual sabotage. It was thought better, on the whole, to cause a multitude of small niggling inconveniences than a few large and obvious ones. So Mrs Doan, at the Village Shop and Post Office, took a hand by making innumerable mistakes over the rations, muddling up the weekly bills, and giving wrong telephone numbers, all of which things she did by the light of nature, and Dai Roberts contrived to deliver the Syndicate's most important-looking letters to the wrong addresses or even to drop them down a rabbit-hole when he was setting his snares.

But perhaps the deadliest weapon of all, and certainly the one which Brensham most enjoyed using, was the assumption of sheer, block-headed, gawkish stupidity. The village which had mucked the church spire to make it grow lived up to its reputation and put on its zany's expression for the Syndicate's benefit. And this, after all, is the traditional weapon of our countryfolk against all forms of tyranny; poachers, rick-firers, sheep-stealers often saved their necks by it two hundred years ago. It is so simple an armament that the veriest fool can use it; indeed it is most effective when employed by a fool. It consists of saying 'Oi' when asked a question and then reiterating 'Oi?' with a faint note of interrogation every time the question is repeated. Many of the present inhabitants of Brensham owe their very existence to the fact that their astute ancestors, threatened with deportation to Australia, stood for hours in the dock doltishly saying 'Oi?' to the clever counsel in their august wigs and even to His Majesty's Judges of Assize.

Crack-brained Brensham has a reputation for this kind of thing. Indeed in many of the stories which are told about our oafish simplicity there is also a suggestion of sly mischief; it generally turns out in the end that we are not such fools as we seem. Once upon a time, they say – telling what is surely the oldest story of them all – a gentleman from the City lost his way and found himself in Brensham on a dark and dirty night. He stopped his carriage and leaned out and asked a stupid-looking puddin'-faced chap the way to Gloucester. The chap said he didn't know, so the gentleman asked the way to Elmbury, being aware that it was only a few miles off. Once more the chap shook his head, and the gentleman neighed angrily in his whinnying London voice: 'Don't you know anything, you stupid fellow?' There was a short silence, and then the Brensham man said quietly: 'Mebbe I'm stoopid; but I knows where I be, which is more than thee does, mister.'

The gypsies' tactics against the Syndicate were more direct and less lawful than those employed by the villagers. We didn't altogether approve of them, and we were in any case distrustful of the rough and riotous tribes. Little love was lost between Brensham and the gypsies; but our temporary alliance with them was less extraordinary than the armistice between the gypsies themselves, who belonged to two hostile families called respectively the Fitchers and the Gormleys. These families, like Montagues and Capulets, bore each other an ancient grudge. Fifty years ago one of the Fitchers had murdered a Gormley, cleaving his head with a hatchet during a quarrel over a woman and subsequently casting his body into the river, whence by ill-chance it was carried down to the Severn by a sudden flood and found its way into a salmon-net operated by some relations of the Gormleys above Elmbury Weir. In due course the murderous Fitcher was hanged and ever since then the families had lived in perpetual enmity, for although the cause of the original trouble was half forgotten the implication of insult remained like an ineradicable taint in certain words and phrases – 'hatchet', 'rope', 'gallows-bird' and 'What's in the salmon-nets today?' – which the factions abusively hurled at each other whenever they wanted a fight. Their hatred of the Syndicate, however, proved stronger than their internecine enmity; and they made common cause to take their revenge.

'My mother said—'

If they knew of the Syndicate's intervention in the Case of William Hart, the gypsies had another good reason for joining in the fight; and doubtless they did know, for they seemed to have some sort of bush-telegraph which informed them of everything that went on in the neighbourhood. William was the only man in Brensham for whom these feckless, fickle and secret families possessed any respect or affection; he was the only person, apart from their patriarchal chieftains, who had any authority over them, who could settle their quarrels and quell their fights and even send them packing from the village pubs when they were drunk. Indeed these Heathens, as Joe Trentfield said wonderingly, 'worshipped the ground he trod on', and to find the reason for this phenomenon we have to go back more than fifty years and listen to a strange old tale which has been told a hundred times on winter nights round the fire at the Horse and Harrow.

Imagine William, then, in his hot youth; 'prenticed to his father who was a wainwright before him, but apt to play truant from the workshop whenever his father's back was turned if there was any football or cricket to be had, or if the Fair with its itinerant boxing-booths happened to come to the district. By all accounts he was a young giant who lorded it over the rough football games, and swiped the bowling out of the cricket-ground and into Cuckoo Pen or beyond into the river itself. (They say that he once slammed three balls in succession as far as Sammy Hunt's osier-bed, where they were lost for ever in the tangled undergrowth and the squelchy mud; and that was the end of cricket for the season, although it was only August, for the Club couldn't raise enough money to buy any more.) He could swim as fast under water as most people can on top of it, and he used to terrify his companions by diving off the top of Elmbury Weir; he won prizes at the Regatta for rowing; and he could stick on the back of any half-broken wild farmer's colt until it was tired of trying to unseat him. His favourite sport, however, was boxing. Whenever the Fair came to Elmbury or Brensham you would always find William hanging about round the improvised canvas ring where the showman strode up and down uttering his brazen challenge like the champion in an ancient battle: 'Walk up, ladies and gentlemen, and see who's got the courage to step into the ring with Terrible Twm the Tonypandy Tornado. Ten silver shillings for anybody who beats him on points and a golden sovereign for anybody who knocks him out. Now then, you sportsmen, here's your chance to show the girls what you're made of. Who'll dare to climb over these ropes and face the Man-eating Tiger from Wales?'

Then William with great deliberation would take off in turn his coat, his waistcoat, his shirt and his singlet, fold them into a neat pile and set a friend to keep guard over them, and purposefully stride forward towards the ropes. And the showman, of course, would keep up his swift patter, knowing that words won as many fights as fists. 'Well, well, well, here's an upstanding young chap. They breeds 'em big in these parts. But I fear he's over-young for the Tornado. He likes 'em young, does Terrible Twm. He'll *eat you up*, young feller-me-lad, Fee-fi-fo-fum, I smell the blood of an Englishman . . . Still keen to have a try? You're mammy oughtn't to let you loose, that she oughtn't. Well, don't say I didn't warn you . . .' Then, while William went quietly to his corner and put on the gloves, perhaps the showman would say:

'On my right, ladies and gents, Terrible Twm the Tonypandy Tornado, Champion of the Valleys, now on tour to challenge all comers. On my left – what might be your name, young feller-me-lad?'

'Never you mind,' said William, and grinned: 'I be a descendant of the poet Shakespeare!'

Only the very old men, who were boys when he was a boy, remember seeing William fight and tell tales of it in the Horse and Harrow. Doubtless they exaggerate, as old men will, but they all agree in one thing: he fought, they say, 'like the wind'. Whether there was much art or science in it they are not sure; but they say he rushed out of his corner like a gale and Terrible Twm or Basher Joe or whoever the broken-nosed, cauliflower-eared wretch happened to be went down before that fierce buffeting like a rotten elm tree before the March wind. A score of times, they swear, William *blew down* his opponents at Elmbury Mop, until at last the travelling showmen became wary of him, and would no longer offer their golden guineas as a reward, and their poor peripatetic pugs as a sacrifice, to the young man who uttered the word 'Shakespeare' as if it were a battlecry. No doubt, as I say, the old men embroider these stories with the fanciful embroidery of fifty years; but there must be a great deal of truth in them, because they help to explain William's triumphant encounter with the Fitchers and Gormleys, which happened when he was twenty-five.

By then William had already begun to sow his crop of wild oats, which didn't fade as most people's do but went on sprouting green for thirty years. You may be sure that he was as practised with his lips as with his fists and that the brown slip of a gypsy girl who used to sneak secretly out of the camp in Lord Orris' Park wasn't by any means the first to discover how gentle as well as strong his big hands could be.

She was only seventeen, in that far-off spring when she and William began their secret courtship; but the gypsies are quick to mature, and the old men say that already she walked with the lovely arrogance of the gypsy women, which has the pride of Lucifer and the slyness of a fox mixed up together in it, and like them she would toss her head and like them give the furtive look over the shoulder – but what do the old men remember of such things? You can imagine her striding up the hill to her trysting-place with William among the bracken and the furze and the may-bushes which were smudges of white in the twilight, her brown eyes like a fawn's peering this way and that, half-eager, half-timid, till she found him waiting by the accustomed stile; you can see her running back on swift sure feet in the darkness, pausing breathless at the Park pale because a twig had crackled under his tread, crecping through the gap in the broken fence, whispering hush! to the lurcher dog which stirred beneath the caravan, and the rough terrier which whimpered in its sleep beside the dying fire.

The Good Fight

I don't know how long it was before the gypsies got to hear of the affair. Not many weeks, I suppose; for though the girl knew how to be secret there was never anything clandestine about William. Sooner or later, surely, he would drink publicly a toast to his Pheemy in the Adam and Eve or the Horse and Harrow, or shout her name for all to hear in a song which he made up as he rolled home half-drunk with love and beer. Nor was Brensham hilltop, even at night, so secret a place as lovers were wont to imagine.

There were other couples besides William and Pheemy, and farmers looking to their lambs, and mischievous boys benighted after bird-nesting, to say nothing of Peeping Tom and Paul Pry. There were poachers too (though it was long before Dai Roberts' day) and these poachers no doubt kept their eyes and ears open for their enemies the keepers and so would not fail to notice the parted bracken which stirred and swayed even though there was no wind. The Fitchers and Gormleys themselves set snares on the hill for rabbits and hares and sought out the snuffling hedgehogs there which they loved to bake in clay upon their smouldering camp-fires. Foolish Pheemy, if she thought that waist-high bracken and sheltering may-bush and love-performing night could keep her secret for long! As for William he cared no more than Antony cared whether the whole world saw him at the side of his Cleopatra.

But, of course, as soon as the Fitchers and Gormleys knew there was bound to be trouble. Perhaps this is the only integrity which they have left – that they keep themselves to themselves and have no truck with the village people. Generations ago they renounced, for what reason I know not, the major portion of their gypsy heritage: they ceased to be wanderers on the face of the earth and made a colony on Brensham Hill, rooting themselves in the neighbourhood. By doing so they sacrificed the ancient freemasonry of road and common, and cut themselves off from the other gypsies and tinkers, who now seem to despise them and who give Brensham a wide berth when they pass it in the course of their seasonal migrations. No true travelling gypsy will camp near the Fitchers and Gormleys if he can help it. In spite of this, or perhaps because of it, the Fitchers and Gormleys cling all the more fiercely to the tradition of gypsy isolationism; because it is the last relic of their gypsydom. They drink in our pubs when they are thirsty, they beg at our back doors when they are hungry, they steal our chickens and dogs and hedge-stakes, they pick our peas or plums for hire, and their women come wheedling at our gates with baskets of clothes-pegs every spring; but these tenuous contacts are the only communication they have with us, they give us no friendship and get none from us, and now I come to think of it I have never once seen a handshake between our people and theirs. I have sometimes thought that we actually hate each other – they hate us because of our possessions and our security and we hate them because their need of neither makes a mockery of all we believe. Certainly our housewives fear them, for they cunningly mix with their cajoling a kind of intimidation which keeps just on the safe side of the law. Surely the women must have been briefed before they set out by some wickedly-wise old grandmother gypsy who has taken infinite pains to study the silly laws of the gorgios! For if a gypsy says 'Buy my clothes-pegs, lady, or you'll have bad luck,' she is uttering threats and telling fortunes and goodness knows what else which may land her in a police court. But if she merely looks slyly at the housewife who happens to be wearing a green blouse and says 'Green is a very unlucky colour, lady,' she is simply voicing a common superstition and if the housewife finds it necessary to cross her palm with silver to counteract the bad luck, well, that's not the gypsy's fault!

The back door, then – or the foot unobtrusively placed just inside the back door, to prevent it being shut in their faces – was as near as the gypsies got towards intruding into our lives. Their numerous encampments, scattered all round Brensham Hill, formed a microcosmos within our larger world; but there was no common citizenship, and it would have surprised the village less that one of our lads should have brought home a Zulu or an Eskimo as his wife than that he should marry a Gormley girl. To the gypsies, whose isolation from us was somehow bound up with the last vestiges of their self-respect, such a match must have been still more unthinkable. Therefore the whole Gormley clan, including the girl's parents, looked upon her courtship with William as an act of treachery and proceeded to deal with her as a traitor. Rumours began to fly about the village, that she was being beaten and starved, or locked up in solitary confinement within one of the caravans; that they had cut off her hair as a mark of shame; or that they proposed to cast her out of their tribe penniless into the world. Whether there was any truth in these stories I cannot tell; but before long William got to hear of them – perhaps he had waited night after night at the trysting-stile in vain – and at once he girded up his loins for battle.

The old men who tell this tale say that he strode into the Horse and Harrow one September dusk and that he was 'rascally drunk', having already spent two or three hours at the Adam and Eve and the Trumpet. At the Horse and Harrow he drank no less than six pints of beer; but instead of making him more drunk this fabulous draught seemed to sober him, and he became all at once very quiet and thoughtful, and refused to play darts or to join in the usual Saturday evening singing. At last he handed his gold turnip-watch to the landlord, asking him to look after it until the morning; and without another word he walked out into the dark night.

He reached the Gormley's camp in Orris Park at about half past eleven, when the last of their fires were flickering out and the majority of the inhabitants of the tents and caravans were settling down to sleep. The camp contained about thirty men and boys, to say nothing of the women, who are famous viragos. Note that it was a Saturday night, when most of the men had probably been drinking in the various local pubs; and the Gormleys after a bout are as quick to strike as a nest of adders suddenly wakened from their slumber in the sun. Furthermore it was pitch-dark, and William did not know his way among the tent-pegs and caravans; and he was alone.

You can imagine the howling set up by the score of mongrel dogs as he strode into the camp; the whinnying of the horses; the grunts and growls and oaths and snores of the awakening Gormleys. They may have thought that the midnight visitor was a policeman come to make unwelcome inquiries about a lost dog or somebody's hens which had unaccountably vanished; at any rate they were in no hurry to show themselves, and were content at first to challenge the intruder with sleepy shouts of 'Who's there?' And then William smote them like a gale.

He had provided himself with a sheath-knife, long and lovingly sharpened on the whetstone. First he slashed the headropes of all the horses and with a great holler drove them full-gallop through the encampment. Their hoofs sent the sparks flying from the still-smouldering fires, and by that little light, and the flicker of a few twigs rekindled, William went among the tents cutting the guy-ropes. The Gormleys are notoriously slovenly in their camping arrangements – they lost their woodcraft long ago when they ceased to be nomads – and I dare say most of the guy-ropes were rotten and many of the tent-poles depended on a couple of ropes instead of half a dozen. William had laid half the tents flat before the Gormleys realized what was happening, and he had also in his fine fury pushed over a ramshackle caravan, which by chance had a paraffin stove inside it, so that it immediately caught fire. The blaze, which added to the Gormley's confusion, helped William to see his enemies as they gathered about him. He threw away the knife, for it had done its business, and he did not fight with knives; and with his bare fists he went into the fray.

The Gormleys, you must remember, had been taken entirely by surprise. William's sudden onslaught had caught them when they were sleepy and fuddled, and at least half of them were trapped beneath the fallen tents, where they writhed and struggled helplessly. The galloping, neighing horses, the yelping dogs, and the flame and smoke from the burning caravan completed their bewilderment. There were probably not more than a dozen men on their feet when the real fight started; there was only one on his feet when it ended.

William fought, as the old men put it, 'like the wind'. Now he was a tornado, a typhoon, a hurricane blowing through their camp, knocking over the tents like ninepins and toppling the men as a woodcutter fells trees. It must have seemed to the Gormleys that there was not one but a hundred Williams, shouting upon the name of Shakespeare and challenging them in a voice of thunder: 'You carsn't touch I! You carsn't touch I!'

So he smote them, as Joshua smote the Seven Kings by the Waters of Merom: 'he houghed their horses and burnt their chariots with fire . . . and smote all the souls that were therein.' And then, so the tale goes, in the midst of the confusion he seized a small boy who fled before him, and holding him by the scruff of the neck whispered with what blood-curdling threats I know not: '*The yellow caravan, show me the yellow caravan, quick.*' That much at least he knew, for Pheemy had told him; her parents lived in a yellow caravan with scarlet shafts and wheels. The boy, terrified for his life, showed William the way while the bewildered Gormleys shrieked and howled and wriggled beneath the canvas and started fighting each other because they did not know who had laid the tents about them.

William smashed down the door of the yellow caravan and found Pheemy confined there, cowering in a corner. He picked her up and slung her over his right shoulder, to leave his left hand free in case he had to fight his way out. But his bruised and bloody fist was needed no more that night. The Gormleys, still uncertain who or what had assaulted them, were crawling out of their tents, trying to catch their frightened horses, and pouring buckets of water on the burning caravan; a few continued to fight among themselves. Nobody challenged William as he made his way out of the firelight into the black night beyond. He carried Pheemy home, and knocked up his astonished parents, and declared to them as he stood bloody and triumphant in the doorway: This is my bride.

He married Pheemy three weeks later, and the village policeman, reinforced by a sergeant from Elmbury, kept guard outside the church in case the Gormleys should come down from the hill to take their revenge; but they kept sullenly to their camp, and did not show their faces in the village for more than a month. When at last they did so the Fitchers, their deadliest enemies, mocked them in the streets with new catchwords and catcalls: 'Biters bit! Biters bit! What about the wife-stealers no-ow!' So a new fight began, and raged up and down the crooked street of Brensham, and an old harridan of the Fitchers was so badly mauled with a hatpin that she had to go to the doctor and have three stitches put in her nose.

The Reconciliation

Of Pheemy after her marriage the tellers of tales have little to say. She rarely came down to the village, and did not often venture farther than the garden gate, being frightened, perhaps, lest she should encounter any of her own clan. William's parents were kind, and William cherished her – he even gave up for a time his Saturday night visits to the pub, and people smiled knowingly: 'The young rascal's settling down at last.'

Nevertheless there was a vague feeling in the village that all was not well with the match, and the old men still shake their heads about it in a puzzled way. ''Tain't natural to marry a gypsy, any more than it is to cage a wild bird. They don't thrive within bricks and mortar, they pine under a roof.' Whether Pheemy was happy we shall never know. The few people who remember her speak of her as 'over-quiet' and 'timid-like' and say that she'd start and turn her head at the least sound – 'like a small brown squirrel she were, always darting her looks this way and that'. Perhaps in time she would have got used to the gorgio walls and the gorgio ways, but she had little time, poor child, to get used to anything. Three years after her wedding, when she was scarcely twenty-one, she died in childbirth. She had already borne William two daughters, but she took the third baby with her upon that last journey. William, they say, 'was crumpled up sudden-like as if he'd took a mortal sickness': for a season the young giant seemed to shrivel and shrink. Then one day he threw back his shoulders again and broke out 'wilder than ever before'. He was back upon the familiar merry-go-round of fights and football and pubs and wenches; but love sets its mark upon a man, and if he has known it he is never quite the same afterwards. The mark which was left on William's character took the form of a most unexpected tenderness towards all wild and timid things. It was as if he saw Pheemy in every wounded bird or hunted fox or frightened hare; or in the children for whom he invented stories and made toys. Among men and women he laughed and sang and hollered and went his wild noisy ways; but in the company of a child or an animal he became at once both gentle and grave.

Meanwhile something very queer and inexplicable had occurred which ended for ever the bitter quarrel between William and the Gormleys. On the evening of the day when Pheemy died William went for the second time alone to the camp in Orris Park. Since the Gormleys had solemnly sworn to murder him if he showed his face near the camp this action was either fantastically foolhardy or fantastically brave; but I doubt if he thought of the danger at all, for he had a last duty to perform for his dead Pheemy and an angel with a flaming sword could not have stopped him. In broad daylight he walked into the camp and he held his hands behind him, for there must be no fighting on this day: he would not hit back even if they struck him. The dogs set up their customary howling, but neither man nor woman nor child spoke or stirred. The tent-flaps were drawn, and the doors of the caravan were shut; but half a hundred faces peered out at William through the tent-flaps and the caravan windows. In the terrible silence William walked through the camp, and all the eyes followed him. At last he stood before the door of the yellow caravan and knocked upon it. There was no answer, and he stood there with bowed head, listening to the silence; then he knocked again, and still there was no answer, and so for the third time he clenched his fist and thundered upon the door so loudly that all the dogs howled together at the imperious sound. As that dreadful chorus died away, the door was opened to William. He went inside, and delivered Pheemy's message, whatever it was; then with a hundred eyes upon him still, he walked slowly back through the camp and down the hill towards Brensham.

Nobody knows what passes in the Gormleys' minds; nobody can say for sure whether their respect for William, which grew later into something much more than respect, was due to the thrashing he gave them when he stole

Pheemy away or to his action in going back to their camp with Pheemy's last message to her parents. However it was, he alone of all the people in Brensham had somehow found the way into their hearts; and very slowly as the years went by there sprang up a relationship between William and the gypsies which is difficult to explain or define except by saying that they looked up to him as children to a beloved father, or as tribesmen to a trusted prophet, or as a nation to some elder statesman who has reached the calm waters which lie beyond the storms and hurly-burly of politics. All this, of course, happened very gradually, for there is no short cut into the confidence of the gypsies, who do not even trust each other. At first it was noticed that the women carrying their baskets of clothes-pegs would curtsy when they met William in the street; yet they never went to his door begging and whining as they did at all the other back doors in Brensham. Then, one sunny season, all the fruit ripened at once and there was a sudden shortage of plum-pickers. It was soon after William went into his farm; he was said to be in bad straits financially, but he had a splendid crop of Victorias and the price of plums was high. It would fall, however, as the market became glutted and possibly in a week or two the plums wouldn't be worth picking. Do not ask me how the Gormleys knew all this, for they were away picking in the Evesham Vale on the other side of the hill; but suddenly without warning they left the orchards where they were at work (they did not even wait for their wages, which was unheard of) and tramped twenty miles back to Brensham, where they presented themselves bright and early on the following morning at William's farm. They picked his plums in three days, and earned him two hundred pounds, which may have saved him from bankruptcy; then without waiting for thanks they tramped off on the road towards Evesham.

After that, at pea-picking and plum-picking, you would always see the gypsies working in William's fields and orchards. The bright dresses of the women, and the red and yellow neckerchiefs of the men, made even the drab fields of peas blossom like a garden. On William's farm (and nowhere else) the Fitchers and the Gormleys worked side by side in amity; they worked harder for him than for anybody; and they paid him the ultimate and rather touching tribute of respect – *they did not steal!*

Gypsies love a patriarch, and as William's splendid beard became grizzled and then slowly went white his authority over them grew greater. The Fitchers as well as the Gormleys began to come to his house with their troubles, and even to lay their disputes before him as it were for Solomon's judgement. I have seen the women with their baskets and their babies (slung from their shoulders in a shawl in the ancient, primitive, comfortable way!) going down the path to his farmhouse to ask his advice or settle a quarrel; and I have seen them actually step inside the back door into the kitchen, which was a wonderful thing, for except when perforce they go shopping the gypsies never have a roof over their heads from year's end to year's end. William, in his middle age, took to visiting their camp from time to time and knew them all by their Christian names, even differentiating between their grubby babies. Sometimes he would sup with them, taking an honoured place beside the camp-fire and sharing the meal which came out of the big bubbling pot like a witch's cauldron. Two or three times I went with him and took part in that feast; for it happens that I too possess some small privilege among the gypsies, not through any merit of my own, but because my grandfather used to doctor them long ago. Now doctors are very important to the gypsies, for though in almost all other respects they are self-supporting within their own community, providing their own tradesmen and having no need of parsons or lawyers, they are still dependent upon the outside world when the surgeon's knife or the physician's diagnosis becomes imperative. They possess, it is true, their wisewomen who treat the ordinary ills and infirmities with herbs, salves, purges and charms; but when the long wasting sickness comes, or the pain gripes deep in chest or belly, or the baby comes feet first – then mortal terror seizes the gypsies and a sense of their own helplessness drives them post-haste into the town to knock timidly upon the doctor's door. My grandfather was not only a good doctor, but a good man; and knowing their poverty he always treated them for nothing. He was also in some respects a rather eccentric man; he once took on a prize-fighter with his bare fists and downed him within five rounds, a feat which was bound to appeal to the Fitchers and Gormleys. Moreover he took more pleasure in the company of gypsies, tramps, poachers and various kinds of scallywags than he did in that of his respectable patients; and when he was sick of the drawing-room conversation and the bedside manner and the spoilt pampered brats and the rich women with their *maladies imaginaires* he often sought relief in the gypsies' camp, where he would tether his horse and sit down to a hearty supper. The gypsies have long memories, and, although my grandfather died more than fifty years ago, because I bear his name they make me welcome.

The Wind on the Heath, Brother

It is a curious experience to sit with the gypsies round their pot in the twilight and to take your chance with them regarding what comes out of the pot on the end of your fork. For the cauldron is literally a lucky dip, and makes no allowance for finicky choosings. You plunge in your fork and whatever may happen to be speared upon it falls to your portion; you can make no guess beforehand what it is likely to be, for the brown bubbling stew gives away no secrets. But when you have impaled your piece and dragged it forth on to your plate (if the Gormleys are so formal as to provide you with one) then experience plus an elementary knowledge of anatomy will generally solve the riddle. A rabbit's shoulder-blade, a pheasant's leg (especially if there are a few feathers still attached to the drumstick), or a chicken's wishbone provide simple clues, and I once fished up a whole partridge on the end of my fork and felt as if I had drawn out Leviathan with an hook. Sometimes, however, the diagnosis is less easy, for the stew may contain such assorted ingredients as hedgehogs, hares, moorhens, grey squirrels, lapwings, fieldfares (which are excellent) and many small birds, with all kinds of herbs and vegetables, mushrooms, truffles, and the late autumn fungi which we call blue legs. The gypsies are not averse to curing the hams of a badger when they can lay hold of one, and it is difficult to distinguish the meat from good lean bacon; and every year in the winter they take their toll of the cygnets on the river, catching them for preference just before the brown plumage becomes flecked with white. So you see there is plenty of variety in the gypsies' diet, and when you sup with them it is best on the whole to put aside all uncomfortable speculations – in fact to 'open your mouth and shut your eyes and eat what the good Lord sends you'. Otherwise you are apt to remember your Macbeth and the Weird Sisters' recipe, and to read into the morphology of even the most delicious morsel a suggestion of fenny snake or newt's eye, lizard's leg and birth-strangled babe's finger. That way nausea lies.

The last occasion when I went with William Hart to dine

with the gypsies was in 1938, about the time of Munich; and I remember thinking how remote their lives were from ours, for they were quite oblivious of the coming catastrophe. The successive wars and crises of civilization scarcely touch them at all; for it is a task beyond the wit of bureaucrats to conscript them into our armies or direct them into our factories. They pay no income tax and belong to no trade union; and since for the most part they live on the countryside, when the gorgios are rationed the gypsies continue to feed as well as before. Life has always been hard for them, and now that our own high standard of living is dwindling fast, and the cold winds of the world are blowing one by one our precious amenities away, they might laugh at our discomfiture and our grumbling – if they ever troubled themselves enough about our affairs to be amused by them.

The joke is certainly against us, and it is a good joke. We have built up an extremely elaborate and inter-dependent form of society while the gypsies have sat peacefully by their primitive camp-fires. But those camp-fires will still be burning if our great blast-furnaces should go out through lack of coal, and the oil-lamps in the caravans will still give light if the failure of the power-stations should plunge all our cities into darkness. These queer secret people whom for so long we have pitied, despised and deplored, are nevertheless completely unaffected by the ills and catastrophes which our complex civilization has brought upon itself; and I don't mind betting that their hens will be scratching about under their caravans when our last dollar has bought the last packet of dried eggs from America!

The Patriarch

On that misty autumn evening ten years ago William was already beginning to hobble with the arthritis which was soon to cripple him; I doubt whether he ever managed to visit the Gormleys' camp again. Perhaps they guessed that it was the last time, for they guessed so many things; and they waited upon him with special courtesies and even with a kind of awe, as if he were a prophet soon to be translated who had come among his people to take his farewell. When the meal was over there fell a long silence, and then one of the children piped up in a timid voice:

'Father Hart! Father Hart!' – for thus they addressed him, almost as if he were a priest – 'Father Hart, tell us a tale!'

'What tale do you want tonight?' said William, by which I learned that he was in the habit of telling them tales.

Another child said timidly:

'Tell us, please, how you came to our camp at midnight and cut the tents down!'

'Tell us, tell us!' cried all the other children. There is magic here, I thought: a legend is being born. Five centuries hence the gypsies will tell the fabulous tale round their fires. William then will be a giant twelve cubits tall.

'Tell us how you pushed over the caravan and burned it with fire!'

'Listen, then, my children,' said William. 'In those days I was more powerful than I am today. I simply *leaned upon* the caravan and it toppled over . . . '

I shut my eyes and listened in a sort of ecstasy, for it is not often that a man may be present at the very fountain-head of a fable where the crystal-clear source bubbles out of the ancient rock. Thus it begins, I thought: this is the eternal spring of stories which never fails, whence flowed the tale of Angoulaffre who leaned against the Tower of Pisa and made it crooked; of Roland who slew him; of Samson; of Ajax and Achilles; of Polyphemus and of Odysseus who laid him low; perhaps – who knows? – of Odin and great Jove.

'And who came against you, Father Hart, when you had pushed over the caravan?'

'Some dozen only. But leading them was *your* grandfather, little one, who was then in his prime, and he'd plucked a tent-pole out of the wreckage which he whirled round his head as if it were no bigger than a walking-stick . . .'

'But you knocked him down, Father Hart?'

'One blow; and then came three men together . . .'

So it went on until at last William had reached the door of the yellow caravan and was smashing it down. But there the story ended; for though I saw a young girl with a brown elf's face, eager and beautiful in the flickering firelight, part her lips to ask a question, and I guessed what the question was going to be, an old woman at that moment stretched out her hand and laid it on the girl's arm so that the words were never spoken: 'Tell us about Pheemy – was she beautiful?' Even the Gormleys had their reticence; and as for William, he never spoke her name.

Works of Darkness

So now you will understand that the gypsies had a double cause to hate the Syndicate, whose members had turned them out of the Park where they'd camped for three or four generations and had also wronged old William. William's quarrel was their quarrel, his wrong was theirs; and love of him added zest to their hatred when they set to work against the Syndicate in their age-old mysterious way.

None of us really knew how they performed their dark mischief. Nobody actually saw them breaking down the Park palings to enlarge the Prize Bull, which terrified the neighbourhood for five days and ultimately had to be shot because it was a danger to the children. Nobody caught them stealing the little weaner pigs which disappeared mysteriously from the styes. Nobody could guess at what secret hour they opened the fowlhouse doors, making a present of their inhabitants to the keen-nosed hill-foxes with which perhaps they had a gypsyish fellowship. Nobody was quite sure what killed the five cows and the two horses which were found dead one morning in a field, for though the vet said they had been poisoned with yew the nearest yew tree stood in the churchyard two miles away.

No: there was not a tittle of evidence against the Fitchers and Gormleys; but it was significant that for two years they were unusually quiet and well behaved, they drank together in the pubs and refrained from brawling even when they were full of beer, and so powerful was the loving-kindness between them that they actually intermarried for the first time since the ancestral Fitcher had plunged his fatal hatchet into the Gormley skull. This unheard-of event happened at Easter, when an extremely timid-looking Gormley girl, wearing the expression of one who is about to be thrown to a pack of wolves, was led to the altar by a young Fitcher who kept glancing nervously over his shoulder as if for his part he already heard the wolf-pack yelping at his heels. After the wedding the relations of the bride and the bridegroom, dressed in their best clothes but probably armed to the teeth, adjourned together to the Trumpet, where the respective heads of the families ordered drinks all round. When the drinks arrived the swarthy-looking chieftain of the Gormleys dramatically clasped the hand of the patriarch Fitcher and made a short speech. The phrase with which he ended could scarcely have been more ill-chosen. 'Let us bury the hatchet,' he said. At once a dozen Fitchers leapt to their feet and there were dangerous mutterings of 'Rope!' 'Gallows!' and even 'Salmon-nets!' The hands of the women were already flying to their hair-pins, which they employed with deadly effect in every brawl; but the stern glances of the two patriarchs quelled them just in time, and at last the whole company raised their glasses to the young couple and wished them health and happiness with murderous looks.

The third member of the Triple Alliance played an obscure but possibly decisive part in the campaign. Jane Orris, who now lived in London, was married to a young man who had a financial interest in certain newspapers. It was not very difficult to persuade these newspapers to show a polite and kindly concern about the Syndicate's successive misfortunes. They were extremely careful, of course, to print nothing scurrilous or in bad taste; they merely asked, in sizeable headlines, IS THERE A CURSE ON ORRIS MANOR? and then made quite sure that henceforth everything that happened there would be News. They duly reported, circumspectly, accurately, and indeed most sympathetically, the fire, the escape and pursuit of the Prize Bull, the disappearance of the pigs and poultry, the unexplained deaths of the cattle and horses; but as a matter of fact it was a rival newspaper, spurred on by the competitive spirit, which published a somewhat imaginative interview with a hysterical maidservant who declared that she had seen the Devil, accompanied by a spectral goat, wreathed in blue flames at the entrance to the half-ruined chapel. On only one occasion did the papers owned by Jane's husband overstep the boundaries of plain fact: they quoted 'village gossip' as their authority for stating that even in cold weather the milk at Orris Manor curdled within an hour, and speculated playfully whether this was the work of Robin Goodfellow. The wretched inhabitants of the Manor indignantly denied the story and the newspapers humbly apologized, giving undue prominence to the denial.

Shortly after that the posters appeared announcing the forthcoming sale. The obstinacy of the villagers and the malice of the gypsies had made life unsupportable at Orris Manor; but worst of all, I suspect, was the sense of being watched – with however friendly and solicitous a stare – by a number of Argus-eyed newspapers. Nobody could have put up with that for very long; and the Syndicate, whose financial dealings were obscure and complicated, may have had more reason than most people for fearing the limelight.

Three Swashers

I forgot to mention, among the Syndicate's persecutors, the three scoundrelly old soldiers whom I call Pistol, Bardolph and Nym. Nor do I know precisely by what mischief they added to the discomfiture of our foes. I can only tell you that they were frequently to be seen Hanging About, as the policeman darkly put it, in the vicinity of the Manor; and when one hears of these three Hanging About one is instantly reminded of vultures, which do the same thing for the same reason.

They do not belong to Brensham, where most people regard them as an everlasting plague, but come from Elmbury where they are the petty lords of an alley-underworld. Since childhood they have lived by their wits, begging, borrowing, scrounging, pilfering, Hanging About and Hanging On; but those wits, though sharpened by continual adversity, have utterly failed to keep them out of trouble and they are familiar with the inside of many prisons, especially Gloucester jail, which they regard as their second home. From time to time, at the low ebb of their fortunes, they have enlisted under false names in the Army; and although they have invariably deserted or been dismissed before long, nevertheless it cannot be denied that their short periods of service have coincided with some notable battles. They therefore wear many medal-ribbons, though these are so dirty and faded as to be unrecognizable, and in the pub they often recall the long weariness on Mons, the heaving quagmire of the Somme, the tormenting flies of the Dardanelles, and the griping dysentery of Salonika with such verisimilitude that it is at least possible they were there. They also speak, but with less confidence, of Mafeking and Ladysmith and of the North-west Frontier of India; and thus they obtain many free drinks from strangers, who are sometimes profoundly moved by their chance encounter with three battered, tattered, down-at-heel Heroes in a bar.

In the Magistrate's Court at Elmbury they have been convicted severally and together, goodness knows how often, of the trivial inglorious crimes of their kind: Begging, Petty Larceny, Trespassing in Pursuit of Coneys, Stealing Mushrooms, Doing Wilful Damage, Insulting Behaviour, Assaulting the Police, Wandering without Visible Means, Drunk and Disorderly, Drunk and Incapable, Sleeping Out. Often enough they have found little profit in it: Bardolph once stole a bicycle, rode it twenty miles on two flat tyres, sold it for half a crown, and went to prison for a week; thus emulating the achievement of his illustrious namesake who stole a lute-case, bore it twelve leagues, and sold it for three-halfpence. And I dare say it is true of Nym, though he has five convictions for assault, that ' 'a never broke any man's head but his own, and that was against a post when he was drunk'.

Theirs, in fact, are small, sordid and rather ineffectual sins, which make a dreary catalogue when the Inspector reads them out in court. Worthless good-for-nothings, you would say; and you would be surprised therefore to see the shadow of a smile upon the Chairman's face as he passed the usual sentence. The truth of the matter is that they are not entirely graceless; they possess a scaramouch humour, and even a sort of mountebank dignity, which we are bound to acknowledge even while we deplore them. Pistol, as he slopes along with his curious stride (as if he were perpetually stalking somebody or something) wears his mouldy old hat with the jay's feather in it at a jaunty angle of devil-may-care. Bardolph's unlovely features, when he grins, are illuminated by that sheer basic unalloyed mischief which I have only seen elsewhere on the faces of the gargoyles on Elmbury Abbey; and Nym sometimes succeeds in making the stern Magistrate laugh when he pleads with mock gravity: 'Don't send me down for long, your Worship, or I shan't be able to vote for you at the Council election!' Even when they are drunk their waggish self-possession does not entirely desert them; I have seen Pistol, as he was borne away to the police-station, conduct himself with such a lordly air that one might almost imagine he had arrested the constable.

I once encountered all three swashers walking, as bold as brass and in broad daylight, upon my small rough shoot halfway between Elmbury and Brensham. They had already, I was well aware, ferreted out most of the rabbits during a series of Sunday morning forays, and now they were obviously in search of other game, for they had a sly sneaking lurcher-dog at heel and Pistol carried an old hammer-gun with a long single barrel covered in red rust. I had surprised them by crawling down a hedge, and I came upon them suddenly face to face, so that they had no chance of sloping away.

I was very angry indeed. 'I've caught you at last,' I began. 'This has gone on long enough. You know, I suppose, that I *pay* for this bit of shooting?'

Bardolph grinned his gargoyle's grin. Nym shrugged his shoulders. ('That's the humour of it,' I could almost hear him say!) And Pistol politely tugged at the brim of his hat and observed coolly:

'We knowed it was yourn, sir; that's why we come; we knowed thee wouldn't say nothing.'

And after that, what could I say?

'*Booze and the Wenches Take the Lot*'

A very respectable Councillor of Elmbury, who owned half the back-alleys in the town, once took me to task for, as he put it, romanticizing Pistol, Bardolph and Nym. 'You writin' fellers are all alike,' he said 'Sentimental. You don't want to waste your sympathy on that sort, nor your ink neither. Folks don't want to read about that sort. You can take it from me, they're just plain rotten. I know what I'm talking about. Plain scum.'

He certainly ought to have known what he was talking about; for he was the landlord of the particular stinking rabbit-warren called Double Alley in which Pistol, Bardolph and Nym as children had run about stark-naked, as most of the slum brats did in those days. There they learned the light-fingered tricks before they were ten; pinching a few pence, I dare say, out of a drunken father's pocket as he snored. There they learned to drink before they were fifteen, and the rest of what they needed to know they were taught by the shrieking sluts in the common lodging-house which was half a brothel. Mr Councillor owned that too, and exacted for it a weekly rental of three shillings and sixpence. He didn't collect the money himself, however. There were too many unpleasant smells and too many germs in Double Alley for his liking. The ragamuffins might have picked his pockets, or the drunken old women might have emptied the contents of their chamber-pots upon his respectable grey hairs. So he hired a cheap bully to collect his rents for him, on the strict commission basis of a shilling in the pound.

Thirty or forty years ago he sent young Pistol to prison for stealing bull's-eyes from a sweetshop. ('Honest tradesmen must be protected.') Bardolph and Nym incurred his displeasure soon afterwards and completed their education in Gloucester jail. Oh yes, he certainly knew what he was talking about! 'Just plain scum,' he said again. 'It's the way they were bred, see. You can't do anything for people like that. Society has got to defend itself against them.'

He paused, and then with an odd sort of resentment he went on:

'And what have they got out of it? I ask you? Thirty years of drinking, stealing, poaching, setting 'emselves against the world – and look at 'em now? What have they got out of it?'

Then I realized suddenly that to this respectable man the crimes of Pistol, Bardolph and Nym seemed all the more shameful because of their pointlessness and futility. If they had made any profit out of the business he wouldn't have thought so badly of them. Their continued poverty was an added crime, and perhaps the worst of the lot. That they would pick his pockets of half a crown was bad enough; but that they set no value on the half-crown and would spend it within half an hour on sluts or cider – that was the real anarchy. For, you see, the truth about Pistol, Bardolph and Nym is that they not only lack the respect for *other people's* property, they lack respect for any property at all.

And while I listened wonderingly to the fat prosperous

Councillor I recollected the gay and bittersweet and mocking words which Maître François Villon, nearly five hundred years ago, had addressed to some cut-throat, crib-cracking, sneak-thieving boon-companions of his who were the Pistols, Bardolphs and Nyms of the back-alleys against the Seine: his *Ballade de Bonne Doctrine a ceulx de Mauvaise Vie.* What have you got out of it, he asks with a wry grin, out of your pinching, filching, rifling, sharping, dice-cogging, thimble-rigging and what not? In three verses and an envoi he asked the same question – *Où en va l'acquest, que cuidez?* Where has the swag gone to? – and always he gives the same shoulder-shrugging answer, the same devil-may-care sardonic answer which respectable Mayors and Magistrates through all the centuries have never been able to understand: *Tout aux tavernes et aux filles!*

The World's Mine Oyster

But I am writing too much about things past; and I shall do less than justice to Pistol, Bardolph and Nym if I fail to record the change that has come over their fortunes during the last two or three years. Gone are the days when they thought it worthwhile to get their feet wet in my squelchy marshes for the sake of a pot-shot at a hare; gone are the hard times when Pistol would stalk me down Elmbury High Street and wheedle out of the corner of his mouth, 'Give us 'alf a crown, Master John; I've just come out of the jug.' Today the dock at Elmbury police court and the cells at Gloucester jail know them no more; and surely the Magistrates and the warders would scarcely recognize them now, for the scarecrow jackets and the tatterdemalion trousers and the shapeless boots are discarded in favour of clean blue suits (Nym's had a pin-stripe in it, and Pistol's is padded at the shoulders) and shining new shoes (Bardolph's are bright orange, and pointed at the toes). In their declining years – for none of them is less than sixty – they bask in prosperity as in an autumn sun. The door they have so clumsily fumbled to unlock is opened to them, the secret they have sought so long is revealed, the faith they have held on to through so many vicissitudes is justified in the end. For they have always believed (and they have paid dearly for their belief) that if only a man could find it there must be a way of making a lot of money without doing any work. At last they have found it. They have discovered the Black Market.

By themselves, perhaps, they would never have hit upon it; for they had got into a rut of useless and unprofitable wrong-doing, they were conservatives and traditionalists in crime, they were set in their foolish old-fashioned ways, always poaching on the same farms, sleeping out on the same hayricks, stealing bicycles simply because bicycles were easy to steal. Pistol, however, had a son called 'Enery who had followed in his father's footsteps by joining the Army and deserting from it – just after Dunkirk, lest he should be put in such mortal peril again. Because it would have been unsafe to return to Elmbury, where everybody knew him, 'Enery took refuge in the pleasant haven of Soho and went into some sort of partnership with a friendly French-Canadian, who had deserted as soon as he arrived in England, being so harrowed by reading about Dunkirk that he took it to be a warning from heaven to have no more truck with the Army. When the war was over 'Enery came home, accompanied by his friend Pierre, and together they set up in business under the style of Hauliers, though what they hauled in their ramshackle lorry was nobody's affair. They always seemed to have plenty of money, and they spent it freely in the pubs; and before long they allowed Pistol, Bardolph and Nym to share in their prosperity, either out of sheer kindness of heart (which is unlikely) or because they found their local knowledge useful. The business, whatever it was, flourished exceedingly. Soon 'Enery bought an old car in addition to the lorry, and it was amusing to see Pistol, Bardolph and Nym sitting up very straight and formally in it – perhaps a little self-consciously too, for their previous experience of motor travel was connected with the black maria which had taken them so often to Gloucester. At night 'Enery and Pierre would often go off to dances in their car. They dressed up in tight-fitting dinner jackets, they wore side-whiskers, their hair was smarmed down with grease, and they talked with imitation American accents, and in their hip-pockets they carried flasks of gin; and they had a great success with many of the local girls, for they had certainly learned a thing or two in Soho.

What Messrs Pistol, Bardolph, Nym, 'Enery and Pierre, Hauliers and General Dealers, actually dealt in I do not know. If you had asked them they would have told you 'old iron'. But if you had then said you were not interested in old iron, but could do with a pound of butter, a dozen eggs, a few petrol coupons, a bottle of whisky, a salmon, or even half a pig, I am pretty sure that one or other of them would have whispered 'How much?' in a suspicious sort of way, and if your offer was acceptable they would have said 'Let's 'andle,' and you would have received your brown paper parcel in exchange.

'Let's 'andle' was the phrase which was always on their lips. It was the motto and watchword of their business, the seal of every bargain. 'Pay cash down at our price, let's 'andle, and we'll see you get the goods.' On such terms how could they fail to prosper in 1947, when as Mr Chorlton never tired of pointing out, England provided a classic illustration of the truth of a saying by Tacitus: *Corruptissima republica plurimae leges?* Nor did they fail.

No doubt it is all very reprehensible; but whenever I see Pistol, Bardolph and Nym nowadays, see them strutting like peacocks who used to sneak like jackals, see them pulling out a wad of notes who used to display the lining of their pockets in search of sixpence, I am led into a series of most uncomfortable reflections concerning ethics, morals, social justice, and the theory of rewards and punishments in general. For example, when Pistol, Bardolph and Nym went about with empty bellies and half a shirt to their backs committing a lot of silly little crimes which did more harm to themselves than to anybody else – 'sleeping out' for example, or getting drunk on the cheap cider which we call tanglefoot or stunnem – we sent them to prison on the average about twice a year. Now that they no longer have any need to beg or to wander without visible means they go free. However, I don't suppose that these considerations trouble the minds of Pistol, Bardolph and Nym, who are accustomed by now to accepting the rough justice of the world. They would probably say, if they thought about it at all, that they have received their deserts; for the long lean and scrounging years are recompensed at last by the autumnal glow and glory of their present fortune.

Their brief dealings with the Syndicate must, I think, have helped to augment this fortune. At one time all three of them found employment at the Manor. Pistol is said to have called himself a Steward, whatever that may mean; Bardolph 'worked in the garden' – though 'worked' was obviously a euphemism; and Nym's duties must have taken him amongst the poultry, for he conducted a flourishing black market in young cockerels and eggs. 'Enery, I think, acted merely as liaison with the outer world; and Pierre contented himself with seducing the last, the very last, housemaid.

The fact that any of them were employed in any capacity

was a measure of the desperate straits in which the inhabitants of the Manor found themselves; and when we heard about it in the village we knew that it was the beginning of the end.

Shortly afterwards the Syndicate left and the whole estate was sold by auction. The farms and small holdings mostly went to their tenants, who had done well in the war, and these fetched a good price. The Manor was offered as a separate lot, and the newspapers on the very morning of the sale took the opportunity of asking once again whether there was a curse on it; so Mr Halliday, who didn't believe in curses, was able to buy it cheap.

At Tolpuddle Hall

It was some weeks before the Hallidays moved into the Manor, and meanwhile Mr Chorlton happened to notice the advertisements of a Grand Rally of the Elmbury Labour Party at which our MP was giving an address. 'I think we ought to go and listen to the Lord of the Manor,' he suggested one day. 'After all he spent a good deal of his young life listening to *me* talking. Let's collar him afterwards and take him out for a drink; if he does drink, which I doubt.' He turned to Sir Gerald. 'You'll come along as well? Two old Drones, they'll call us. But I was a man-eating Fabian when I was at Oxford. Now I suppose I'm the last Gladstonian Liberal, a museum piece like a stuffed great auk.'

So on the following Saturday the three of us drove into Elmbury and duly took our seats in the back row at the Tolpuddle Memorial Hall. This remarkable building stood in one of the narrow side-streets of the old town, and made a striking contrast with the half-timbered houses which adjoined it. Glazed red bricks, in the public-lavatory style, made up its façade, and yellowish stones of various shapes were set among the bricks to form a mosaic of the most revolting pattern. Within, the place was austere and cob-webby, and one got the impression that it was haunted by the spirits of innumerable Temperance Reformers who in the past had preached there. A couple of hundred hard-arsed chairs faced a unusually high platform upon which even a shuffling foot rang hollowly and which was so bare and sombre that whoever climbed on to it felt rather as if they were mounting the scaffold.

In these dreadful surroundings we sat and waited the arrival of Mr Halliday, who was late. His Agent, who had a nervous habit of biting his nails, strode anxiously to and fro between the door and the platform with his fingers in his mouth. The Branch Secretary, an earnest little woman with horn-rimmed glasses and an unpowdered nose, followed at his heels complaining every few moments: 'Oh, *dear*, I can't *think* what's happened to the dear Member!' The pianist on the platform fussed nervously with her tattered scores and played a couple of ten-year-old tunes, of no ideological significance, with excruciating ineptitude. The Honorary Treasurer got up and proposed his conventional plan to wipe out the usual deficit by means of a jumble sale. And the senile and inaudible County Councillor in the chair seized the opportunity provided by Mr Halliday's lateness to talk for fifteen minutes instead of three.

At last Mr Halliday arrived and mounted the platform with as much enthusiasm as if he were indeed going to his execution. He explained that he had had a puncture and, forestalling his Chairman, who was rising to make a second speech, he plunged straightway into his address.

I took to him at once. He was a rather serious and desperately sincere politician of forty, with slightly rounded shoulders, greying hair, a keen, thoughtful face, and some anxious wrinkles on his forehead. Yet I suspected that his seriousness was not so much native in him as something which through force of circumstances he had gradually acquired; it was like a monk's habit, which is no part of him and yet if he wears it long enough he grows grave to match it. He certainly had a sense of fun, which showed itself once or twice in his replies to a heckler, but it was suppressed and well-disciplined and kept under; whenever it peeped out he metaphorically spanked it and sent it back whence it came from. For the most part his address was cool, factual and unrhetorical. He didn't abuse his opponents and so he got little applause.

Then came the time for questions. Sitting all round us in the back rows were the people who go to every meeting for the sole purpose of airing their own views. One by one they jumped to their feet, the cranks and the honest-doubters and the earnest-inquirers and the exhibitionists, to ask about the Member's attitude to vivisection or to Russia, to gambling, blood sports, divorce, equal pay for women, proportional representation and goodness knows what else; and among them was a man with a red face in which the veins made a pattern like that of a railway system on a map, and a pimple on the end of his nose with hair sprouting out of it, and a rainbow-striped Old School Tie of unfamiliar pattern. This man was obviously Mr Halliday's sworn and dedicated persecutor. He clutched numberless pieces of crumpled paper in his hands, and referred to these documents every time he asked a question. He had evidently gone to great pains to learn the more intimate details of Mr Halliday's career and barbed with that knowledge his questions sped like poisoned arrows straight to his victim's heart. When, for instance, the school age was under discussion, he rose with a bland smile.

'Will the Member please inform the audience where *he* was educated?'

'Winchester and Balliol.'

'*Ah*,' said the red-faced man darkly. '*Ah*.' And with that he sat down, turning right and left to glance significantly at his neighbours.

But a moment later he was on his feet again. He had armed himself with quotations from speeches which Halliday had made in the past, phrases torn from their context, sentences obviously twisted out of their original meaning, and he demanded to know whether that was a true report of what the Member had said. 'No lengthy explanations please. Yes or no.' And then with a small regretful sigh, a long-drawn '*Ah*', a slight commiserating inclination of the head, the red-faced man subsided.

But the arrow with the deadliest poison he kept for the last. The subject under discussion was conscription. The red-faced man got up very slowly, like one who takes leisurely aim, being certain of a kill, and asked deliberately in his oleaginous voice

'*Will the Member be good enough to let us into the secret of what* he *was doing between the years* 1939 *and* 1945*?*'

The arrow struck. Halliday jerked his head, and for a moment I wondered : is he going to tell them about his twisted foot or isn't he? There followed what seemed a long, a painful silence, during which I reflected that of all the professions in the world I should least like to indulge in politics. Then the answer came, short and factual:

'I was in the Ministry of Information.'

'*Ah*.' The persecutor's tone was more smooth and suggestive than ever. That is all we need to know, it seemed to say; thank you very much, that explains everything. Triumphantly he nodded and smiled to his neighbours and turned round in his seat to grin at the people behind him. '*Ah*,' he repeated. '*Ah.*' And he sat back with folded arms and a beastly satisfaction in his smile while Mr Halliday answered the next question, speaking perhaps a shade too loudly and a shade too fast.

'A credit to his prep-school,' Mr Chorlton whispered to me. 'For that, I think, was literally his Achilles heel.'

The meeting ended ten minutes later. Mr Chorlton intercepted Halliday as he came down off the platform and having no doubt made an apt and suitable quotation in Latin – I am sure he was unable to resist that temptation – he brought him round to the door where Sir Gerald and I were waiting. 'We're going to slip round to the Swan,' said Mr Chorlton in a conspiratorial whisper. In the Swan bar we sat in a corner and drank pints of beer, which Halliday obviously enjoyed. 'You can't imagine,' he smiled, 'how long it is since I had a free moment to sit in a pub and drink a pint. Months and months. During the session I seem to be in a tearing hurry all day and half the night. And when I come down here my Agent takes charge of me. He disapproves of my going into pubs. He says it upsets the Nonconformist conscience and loses votes.'

'Pubs for Politicians,' laughed Mr Chorlton. 'There's a policy for you.'

'We make such a lot of laws,' said Halliday seriously, 'that we get bewildered and bemused by them. We desperately need to sit down and think. And a pub's a good place for that.' And indeed, as I glanced at him across the table, I thought that was probably what he needed more than anything else: the chance to sit down and think. He was the tiredest-looking man I'd seen since the war. His eyes reminded me of the eyes of men coming out of battle. Soon he looked at his watch and got up to go. 'I've got another meeting at 8.30,' he said, 'ten miles away.' He hurried off, and Mr Chorlton said quietly: 'The squirrel in his cage, endlessly turning a little treadmill. I wonder if he realizes yet? But where the devil,' he added, 'has Gerald got to?' He'd given us the slip, just outside the Memorial Hall, muttering that he'd left something behind. I got up to order another drink, and at that moment he came into the bar. He was looking somewhat shamefaced, and he had a small piece of paper in his hand which he hurriedly tucked away in his pocket.

'Come here,' said Mr Chorlton, 'and tell us what you've been up to.'

'Nothing,' said Sir Gerald. 'Er – nothing. At least—'

'You Seventh Day Adventist, you Good Templar, you Buddhist, Moslem, Spiritualist, Oxford Grouper,' roared Mr Chorlton. 'I know you, you anabaptist, polytheist, gymnosophist, fire-worshipper, you hanger-on of sects and societies. Make a clean breast of it and show us that piece of paper. For unless I'm very much mistaken you have just joined the Labour Party.'

'Well,' said Sir Gerald, 'he *did* talk a lot of sense, didn't he? And you know I always believe in trying everything. But it was that horrible red-faced man who did it really. I thought: goodness me, if that sort of person is a Tory – well, after all—'

'Did you not,' accused Mr Chorlton, 'only three weeks ago send off your annual subscription to the Elmbury branch of the Conservative Association? Are you not also a regular subscriber to the Liberal Party funds?'

'It is one of my few principles,' said Sir Gerald firmly, 'to keep an open mind.'

On the way back to Brensham Mr Chorlton talked about Halliday.

'You know,' he said, 'I could make a diagnosis of that young man's trouble. He's never had much fun in his life. He is suffering, in the modern jargon, from serious fun-deficiency. I believe Brensham might cure him. I should like to watch his reaction, anyhow, on one of the occasions when the village takes its hair down and goes a bit crazy. I wish he could meet old William Hart when he's full of home-made wine and roaring his happiness to high heaven in his great voice like the Bull of Bashan. I wish he could see the Frolick Virgins, with all their young men, giggling and cuddling on their Saturday evening out. I'd like to take him into the Horse and Harrow, say, when Joe Trentfield's telling his naughtiest stories, and Mimi and Meg are strumming on the piano, and everybody's singing all our wildest songs, on Christmas Eve!'

A Purgatory for Planners

The Hallidays came to live at Brensham a fortnight later, and while their furniture was being moved to the Manor they spent a night at the Horse and Harrow. For Mrs Halliday at any rate this was a most unhappy introduction to Brensham ways. She was obviously a girl who above all things abominated disorder. She had an almost physical abhorrence of the haphazard, the unorganized, and the unplanned. But in order to enjoy a night at the Horse and Harrow one has to be appreciative, or at any rate tolerant, of the most uncompromising individualism. The plumbing, indeed, has so much individuality that it might be described as anarchic.

Even the journey up to her bedroom must have seemed a nightmare to Vicky Halliday. I have taken a good many visitors to stay at the Horse and Harrow, and have carried their suitcases upstairs for them, so I am familiar with the experience. You are led first into the kitchen, which is small and generally full of children belonging to Mimi and Meg.

Mrs Trentfield mountainously rises up from an armchair and Mimi and Meg, often with babies at their breasts, appear like foothills beside her. 'I'll have to lead the way,' says Mrs Trentfield, 'because the staircase is a bit awkward.' It is indeed. It goes up in a corkscrew spiral, in pitch darkness even by day, and the suitcase jams against the banisters. At every bend a low beam juts out, upon which you bump your head. At the sound of the bump Mrs Trentfield chuckles, and when she does so the whole staircase creaks. 'Sorry,' she says, 'but visitors *always* bump their heads and I *always* has to laugh.' At the top of the staircase there is a narrow crooked corrider with an uneven floor; here you invariably trip up; and at the end of it you climb another convolute staircase, and reach the Guests' Bedroom. 'Here we are at last!' says Mrs Trentfield, as triumphantly as if she were a pilot who has brought his vessel safely to anchor through the treacherous shoals. The room, which is a fairly large one, is almost completely filled by the largest bed you have ever seen. 'Take care you don't get lost in it,' says Mrs Trentfield cheerfully. 'It's feathers. Now I must explain about the bathroom. I hope you won't mind; but the fact is the bathroom was built on separately, by a local jobbing builder, and to get to it you have to go down the way we came up, and through the living-rooms, and through the bar, and up the other side. It's a nuisance, but it can't be helped, and of course if you like you can always arrange to have your bath during closing-time . . .' As like as not, while she stands beaming there, a most extraordinary noise, which seems to come from the ceiling, startles you out of your wits. It is a sort of deep gurgling chuckle, interspersed with choking gasps, and ending with what sounds like a loud belch. 'That's just the plumbing,' explains Mrs Trentfield, kindly, 'and it only means that somebody's pulled the lavatory plug downstairs. The water tank makes that noise when it's filling up again. Joe – my husband – he calls it *Minnehaha Laughing Water*. Lord, he's a merry man!' she adds. 'Twenty years we've bin here and twenty times a day he's heard it, but I should begin to wonder what was up with him if it didn't make him laugh!'

Poor Vicky Halliday! I called at the Horse and Harrow in the evening, and took her into the bar for a drink. (Her husband, in his usual tearing hurry, had driven off to a meeting at the other end of his constituency.) In protest, I think, against the untidiness of her surroundings she had over-tidied her hair and reduced it to that state of symmetry and order in which she would like to see the disorderly world and especially the disorderly village of Brensham. She looked rather like a model for Hitler's ideal of Aryan womanhood. There was, however, a large and angry-looking bump on her forehead.

While I ordered the drinks she stared with disapproval at the remarkable assortment of curios, curiosities and unseemly odds-and-ends which decorated the walls of the bar. Her cool and unamused glance wandered from the old top-hat which surmounted the moth-eaten stag's head to the stuffed parrot and to the fox's mask upon which in the late hours of VE-Day Joe had ceremonially hung up his Home Guard cap. She had no sense of the comic or the absurd, and she found nothing funny in Joe's extraordinary collection of malformed and contortionist vegetables which occupied the mantelpiece – potatoes with legs and arms, a parsnip like a mermaid, a pear like a wizened old man, a marrow with a caricature of Winston Churchill engraved upon it, a hob-goblin tomato putting out its tongue. When she had taken a long look at all these she turned to me and made her considered comment.

'A bit prep-school, isn't it?' she said.

I forbore to ask her if she liked her room, because I felt

quite sure that she had an antipathy to double beds, especcally enormous ones, and that she regarded feather mattresses as an affront to good hygiene. So we talked uncomfortably about the weather and the Village Hall which she proposed to redecorate and the Women's Institute which she proposed to wake up. Then Mimi's husband, Count Pniack, came into the bar, and I introduced him to her. He sprang to attention and loudly clicked his heels. 'The P is silent,' he barked; and clicking his heels once more, and bowing stiffy from the hips, he went out to the kitchen.

'He was here during the war,' I explained, 'and married the landlord's daughter.'

'Oh, I see. One of those *reactionary* Poles,' said Mrs Halliday.

A moment later Mrs Trentfield came through the kitchen door, a surge of flesh accompanied by the smell of frying fat and boiling pudding.

'Supper's ready, my dear! There's chit'lings, and suet roll, and, if you've got a corner to fill, bread and cheese and pickled gherkins and home-made piccalilli!'

There was something anarchic even about the hospitality at the Horse and Harrow.

The Pig-killing

Next weekend the Hallidays had another unfortunate experience. Mr Chorlton had offered to 'show them round the village', but it turned out to be a drizzly grey day, November had shut down, the countryside was brown and sodden, and most of the population of Brensham, looking their most oafish, were engaged in picking sprouts. The squealing of a pig, shrill and tremulous upon the still air, accompanied the sightseers wherever they went.

Normally Mr Chorlton would not have noticed this bucolic sound; but whenever it became exceptionally loud Mrs Halliday gave him a look of inquiry and at last when the squeals reached a crescendo she observed to her husband:

'Maurice, I believe they're doing something awful to that wretched animal.'

Now Mr Chorlton was aware that Jeremy Briggs the blacksmith was preparing to kill his pig (which was called Mr Molotov because of its exceptional obstinacy) for he had noticed the preparations in the smithy yard as he passed by: the well-scrubbed bench, the pile of straw, the earthenware jug of cider on the bench, and the neighbours hanging about because a pig-killing was always a bit of a ceremony in Brensham. Guessing that the Hallidays would disapprove of public butchering, he didn't tell them this, but took them into the church to see the memorial brasses. Not even the thick walls of the church, however, were impervious to the pig's squeals, which sounded even more blood-curdling as they echoed in the vaulted roof; so Mr Chorlton conducted the Hallidays down to the river, and walked them about half a mile along the footpath, despite some warning twinges of gout in his big toe. But wherever they went the intermittent squeals followed them.

Dusk fell at last, and Mr Chorlton, already limping badly, turned for home; but the smithy lay between the river and his house, and unless he led his charges across the muddy sproutfields there was no way round it. He therefore took them back by way of the village street and by a most unhappy chance the squealing ceased abruptly and significantly just as they approached the smithy. There was a short grunt, such as an old gentleman might make as he settled down for an afternoon snooze at his club, then silence. And here let it be said that the execution, without doubt, was performed swiftly and mercifully by Dick Tovey the butcher, who takes as much pride as a bullfighter in making a clean kill. The squealing which had provided such a lengthy prologue to the drama had been, like most prologues, completely irrelevant; it was no more than the pig's protest against the invasion of his rest and quietude. The Hallidays, however, were not aware of this.

Nor were they familiar with the traditional epilogue to a pig-killing, which involves among other things the burning-off of the bristles; so that when they arrived at the gate of the smithy and saw the flames leaping high from the pile of straw, out of which the animal's blackened face peered grotesquely like that of a half-charred heretic, they got the impression that the pig having been only partially butchered was now being roasted alive. And indeed to their unaccustomed eyes the sight must have been a fearful and horrific one. There was blood upon the ground and upon the beefy hands of Dick Tovey, who looked like a murderer in the firelight as he busied himself with his deadly knives. The flames danced above the straw-pile and two of Jeremy Briggs' grandchildren, excited as children always are by a bonfire, were dancing too. They joined hands and jigged round the pig's funeral pyre, singing and laughing, like little savages.

'Children!' breathed Vicky Halliday. 'Maurice, it's disgraceful!'

Meanwhile Mrs Briggs energetically scrubbed a wooden trough, somebody else filled a can with boiling water from the furnace, and Jeremy set up a spring-balance over the door of the smithy to weigh the pig; for all the neighbours, as usual, had taken tickets in a sweepstake about it. Vicky watched all these formalities with growing horror, understanding nothing, but thinking, no doubt, in terms of cannibal feasts and druidical sacrifices. To make matters worse Dick Tovey came to the gate to have a word with Mr Chorlton, and his appearance was enough to daunt any stranger, let alone one so fastidious as Vicky. He was a hefty, gap-toothed fellow with red hair, always smiling like *le bourreau souriant*, who wore a pigskin apron smeared with grease and blood. In his belt, scabbarded like a soldier's bayonet, he carried a long knife; at his hip hung a larger scabbard or pouch which contained an assortment of more frightful cutlery still – bone-handled, murderous-looking blades which rattled together when he moved, terrible gouges, and a thing like a marline-spike. He must have seemed to Vicky the personification of all the livers and lights, kidneys and tripes, which throughout her life had gruesomely affronted her; and she shied away from him as if she were a timid horse that smelt blood.

'Well, we've killed old Molotov,' observed Dick cheerfully. 'Seventeen score if he's a pound.'

'Molotov?' said Halliday.

'Jeremy Briggs,' said Dick, 'always gives his pigs names after chaps he don't like. He grows too fond of 'em else. At one time it was Ramsey Mac; and then it was Old Chamberlain. In the war it was Hitler and Goebbels and Musso, of course; but generally it's politicians.'

When Dick went away Vicky said to Mr Chorlton, in as matter of fact a tone as she could manage (she always believed in Facing Facts): 'Tell me, why do they kill it here? I thought animals were always taken to an abattoir nowadays.'

'In Brensham,' said Mr Chorlton, 'the executioner goes to his victim.'

'Why?'

'Well, if you'd ever tried to shift a pig when it didn't want to be shifted, you'd understand that Dick Tovey on his bicycle is much more mobile.'

They went back to Mr Chorlton's house to tea. Vicky, who couldn't eat anything, remarked later:

'Maurice, I'm still thinking about those children. The harm done by this sort of thing might last for the whole of their lives. It could produce a really serious pyschological trauma. You must take steps to get it stopped. You must put down a Question . . .'

And sure enough a few weeks later, as Mr Chorlton happened to glance through the Parliamentary Report in *The Times*, his eyes lit on a very elaborate Question indeed, a Question which seemed to rise in many tiers like an old-fashioned wedding-cake:

Mr Halliday (*Elmbury, Lab*): 'What regulations govern the slaughter of pigs on private premises in rural districts; whether these regulations have regard to considerations both of hygiene and humanity; whether it is not highly undesirable that such slaughter should take place in circumstances which give it the character of a public spectacle; and whether the presence of children and adolescents at these unedifying events is not to be deplored?'

Crusader by Proxy

Mr Chorlton had an interesting theory that Halliday's wife was the *fons et origo* of most of the Questions with which he pestered his disapproving Front Bench. He pointed out that she possessed a quality which was fortunately uncommon in women and which was very rare indeed in girls as good-looking as Vicky: she was filled, brimful and overflowing, with reforming zeal. She was obviously one of those people, he said, who could not bear to see the wicked flourishing like the green bay tree and who never knew when to let well alone. Her path through life was beset with injustice and inequality; folly and stupidity luxuriated about it like rank weeds; hidden scandals lurked like the poisonous nightshade; dragons and monsters of monopoly, power and privilege uttered their brazen challenge out of the dark capitalist jungle; and Hydra-headed Conservatives lay hidden everywhere in the undergrowth. Like the Knights of the Round Table ('who were also a pretty tiresome lot,' observed Mr Chorlton dryly) she saw a simplified world in black-and-white, a woodcut-world without half-tones, and it never occured to her that dragons might have kind hearts or that some maidens might actually relish the attentions of an ogre; and with boundless energy she strove perpetually to remedy the injustice, to tidy up the disorder, to cast down the wicked, and to expose the scandal to the light of day.

Just like William Cobbett, said Mr Chorlton: abhorring hornets, and having no hornets in her own garden, she goes off and stirs up the hornets' nests of her neighbours. 'I wouldn't mind betting,' he speculated, 'that she pleads with her husband for Questions in the House in much the same way as other girls badger their men for new hats or fur coats. He'd probably much rather give her a hat; but more likely she wants a Parliamentary Question about the egrets' feathers in somebody else's. He'd gladly, I expect, buy her a fur coat; but no, she demands an inquiry into the fur coats with which band-leaders are alleged to bribe members of the BBC. And the poor fellow can't refuse her. As other men might pacify their wives with lollipops, he poses these Questions to please her. And I'm sure he'd bring her the Prime Minister's head upon a salver if she asked for it.'

Curiously enough, although his activities had not made Mr Halliday popular, they had a by no means adverse effect upon his career. The political gossip-writers were already suggesting that he might be offered the next available Under-Secretaryship, to keep him quiet.

The Boy David

Mr Chorlton's theory received fresh confirmation a few weeks later. We had heard that Pru's eldest child, Jerry, following in the family's anarchic tradition, had put a shot from his catapult through the Hallidays' drawing-room window – having missed the mistle-thrush which he was stalking in the Manor grounds. Shortly afterwards we read in the Parliamentary report:

Mr Halliday (*Elmbury, Lab*) asked the President of the Board of Trade how much rubber, in the form of elastic, was allocated for the purpose of the manufacture of catapults; and whether in view of the Wild Birds' Protection Act this wasteful employment of valuable raw material could be justified.'

This roused Mr Chorlton to such a pitch of indignation that he immediately sat down and wrote to *The Times* on behalf, he said, of 'a section of the community which has no Society or Trades Union to defend their ancient liberties'. He stated his belief that a small boy without a catapult in his pocket (and a fluffy, half-sucked bull's eye stuck to the elastic of the catapult) was an unnatural child who was unlikely to make a good citzien. And he ended:

'At least I am thankful that I was a boy before the foolish paternalism of Government began to take cognisance of such trivia; and perhaps it is fortunate that there were no well-meaning MPs in the days when another small boy "chose him five smooth stones out of the brook . . . and his sling was in his hand; and he drew near to the Philistine"'.

The Baby Show

It was not to be expected that Vicky would be able for long to resist the temptation of trying to reform poor Pru, especially as Pru's favourite lane for love-making happened to be the one which led from the village to the Manor. Driving back from Elmbury on a foggy night in January, Vicky collided with a pram which was parked at the side of the lane; and the two small babies in the pram traced a neat parabola through the air and fetched up squalling on the grass verge. They were unhurt, though frightened; Pru, who came over the stile a moment later followed by a shadowy young man, was very frightened indeed; but probably the most frightened person of all was Vicky and her fright very naturally showed itself in righteous indignation. She threatened Pru with the police, and the National Society for the Prevention of Cruelty to Children, and even with a Home, at the very thought of which Pru burst into tears. She would probably have carried out these threats but for an incident which happened a few days later.

The Village Hall had been redecorated and the Women's Institute woken up; and to celebrate the decorations and demonstrate the awakening a Baby Show had been arranged at which Vicky had been asked to judge the exhibits and Lord Orris to give away the prizes. Therefore, on Thursday afternoon, about a score of babies (for Brensham was a very philoprogenitive village) sat about in the hall staring without comprehension at the frieze of formalized tractors which Vicky's artist friend had painted round the wall, while their mothers, who understood what it meant even less than the babies, comforted each other with the assurance that the dust and the cigarette smoke would doubtless fade the daubs before long. In due course Vicky arrived, and also

Lord Orris, who was wearing his only suit which did not hang about him like the rags on a scarecrow. This outfit, miraculously saved from the pawnshops and the money-lenders, consisted of light-grey trousers, almost as tight-fitting as the mess-trousers of a cavalryman, and a cutaway tail-coat, originally black but now bearing faint traces of green mould due to the pervasive damp of Orris Manor. Lord Orris also wore spats, patent leather boots, and a grey bowler hat; and he looked exactly like a 'Spy' cartoon. He was in good heart, however, and got on very well with the babies, who delighted to pull his long drooping grey moustache. Vicky was less at home in his company; for I think she had been brought up on the idea that the aristocracy were all Wicked and Rich, and was having difficulty in adjusting her sense of values to the discovery that a real Lord could be both gentle and poor. Moreover, it probably embarrassed her to find out that she had more or less bought the Lord with the Manor; for he still lived in the Lodge, and if you felt as Vicky did about the evils of privilege it must have been extremely uncomfortable to have a representative of the Privileged Classes living upon your charity.

When the time came for judging, Vicky announced that there must be no suspicion of favouritism and everything must be done in a Democratic way. She would therefore have the babies brought to her, one by one, by the district nurse; then she wouldn't know whom they belonged to. She examined them all with the greatest care, and indeed she did possess some qualifications as a judge for she had originally trained as a nurse and had worked in a hospital during the war. She took a long time to make her decision, and at last she announced that the result was a tie. There were two babies, two little girls, which were obviously healthier, better nourished, and better cared for than all the others; and that was saying a good deal. She suggested that the mothers of these two girls should divide the prize.

There was rather a long pause before Pru, who was the mother of both, padded up to the platform with her soft cat's tread, pushed from behind by the other mothers because she was so shy, and with a demure little curtsy and a look of misty-eyed wonder received her prize from Lord Orris. She was no doubt terrified of Vicky, because of that terrible threat about a 'Home'; but she needn't have worried any more. It would have been very difficult to maintain that the best mother in Brensham was in need of care and protection herself.

Altogether it was a bad afternoon for Vicky. After the judging, the smaller babies were confined in a play-pen while their mothers had tea. Before long the most horrible noises, shrieks and gurglings, gasps and what sounded like death-rattles, began to rise from this pen, in which the unruly children of the Fitchers and Gormleys reproduced in miniature (like a battle demonstrated on a sand-table) their parents' larger strife. At first Vicky watched this dismaying spectacle with the too-deliberate unconcern of the conscientiously broad-minded; having no children of her own she probably believed that if one prevented them from doing what they desired they suffered from inhibitions in later life. However, when a Fitcher boy began to savage the ear of a Gormley girl, and it seemed that the latter might be permanently disfigured, she could stand it no longer and gallantly entered the arena in order to part them. In doing so she got herself bitten on the hand, and since it was to be supposed that the bite of a Fitcher or Gormley would be peculiarly poisonous there was a hurried search for the iodine-bottle, which could not be found. Poor Vicky, whose terror of germs was well known, thereupon lost her self-possession altogether and began to look as if she were going to cry. She was comforted in a very chivalrous and old-fashioned way by Lord Orris, who courteously gave her his arm and took her outside for 'a breath of fresh air'. He was probably the only person who wasn't surprised by Vicky's unexpected behaviour; for he had had nothing whatever to do with women since early Edwardian times, when they were apt to cry or swoon at the least provocation. He was therefore completely master of the situation and dealt with it beautifully.

Since it was generally supposed that he was starving, the committee of the Women's Institute had arranged to present him with a cake; and they had taken great pains, and sacrificed some of their rations, to make a very large and rich plum cake for him, which was said to be his favourite sort. He was delighted; and when the Baby Show was over he carried away a big cardboard hat-box containing this precious gift. Alas, he did not keep it for long. On his slow way up the lane he was overtaken by Pru, wheeling her two babies in the pram. He immediately became convinced that they had more need of the cake than he had; and he was seen by two members of the Women's Institute to bestow it upon them with a little stiff and gracious bow, familiar no doubt in Edwardian drawing-rooms but very rarely seen on Brensham Hill.

'*We'll Tame Her*'

For quite a long time the village always spoke of the Hallidays as 'them foreigners'. It did not mean to imply, of course, that they were un-English, but merely that they were not natives or old inhabitants of Brensham. People who lived in Elmbury, only four miles away, were 'foreigners'; and newcomers to the neighbourhood, even if they were householders, remained 'foreigners' until Brensham got used to them.

However, after the incident at the Baby Show, the village people began to take a kindlier view of Vicky, because they had seen her shaken out of her self-possession, which had previously frightened them. 'She nearly cried,' they said. 'She's human after all.' Even when Vicky began to reorganize the Amateur Dramatic Society on a more democratic basis (which meant that the leading parts were no longer given to people whose feelings might be hurt otherwise), and to revive the Youth Club and to form a Folk-lore Society and a Debating Circle, these innovations were patiently endured, for it was well known that Ladies of the Manor were addicted to troublesome Good Works and that humble folk must tolerate them in the same way that they put up with the interminable Welfare Work of clergymen's wives. 'We'll tame her,' they grinned, meaning that they'd break her in to Brensham ways just as they broke in each successive village policeman, parson and parson's wife. In this way this was a compliment to Vicky, because there had never been any question of attempting to tame the Syndicate. 'We'll give 'em the sack,' Brensham had said.

We noticed too, as the weeks went by, an interesting change in Mr Chorlton's attitude to the Hallidays. He had professed the greatest alarm when they had come to live at the Manor. 'God help us, they'll tidy us up!' But now he gradually began to accept them, as we all did, as part of the Brensham scene; and though he still spoke of Vicky as 'that female Cobbett' with pretended dismay, it was significant that he also called her a female Cobbett to her face, teasing her and pulling her leg in just the same way as he had pulled the legs of generations of schoolboys in the past. On one occasion he took her to a Meet of General Bouverie's hounds, when they met outside the Horse and Harrow, and with the utmost gravity put forward his suggestion that the Communist Party should adopt pink coats and top-hats as their official uniform.

'Hunting-pink,' he said, 'is not pink in the sense of being pale or wishy-washy; it is scarlet, a good revolutionary colour, the colour of blood. Now it may be true that the only sort of hunting practised by the Communists is heresy-hunting, but I do suggest that instead of deploring this uniform as the insignia of the Idle Rich the Party should buy a lot of pink coats and wear them as the battledress of revolution.'

'But I'm not a Communist,' protested Vicky.

'I know, my dear, but I want you to pass on my suggestion to your friends; for I assure you there is a great deal to be said for it. In the first place pink coats look gay and gallant, and the colour is that of the Red Flag and therefore stained with no ideological impurities. In the second, since taxation has practically ruined the Idle Rich, there are plenty of pink coats going cheap and coupon-free. Thirdly, I understand that the Party is not entirely heedless of the trends of fashion which originate in Moscow, and it must be aware that Russian Communists often appear in public in bright and dazzling uniforms bemedalled even more wonderfully than the late Marshal Goering's; in short they have discovered what kings and archbishops discovered long ago: that it's fun to dress up.

'In England there's a temporary reaction against military uniforms; we've grown tired of them. But the quaint and cheerful habit of these hunting-men has no military significance. It's a wholly bucolic uniform which English people regard with humorous affection. If the Communists really want to win their way into our hearts they can scarcely do better than appear next May Day in top-hats, scarlet coats, buckskin breeches, and polished top-boots with spurs.'

General Bouverie tittuped past, tootling some truants from his pack which were whimpering after a cat in the churchyard. Mr Chorlton went on:

'And here's another point. The wearing of this uniform in public would finish whatever is left of the Squirearchy more quickly than a bloody revolution. Imagine the scene at the emergency meeting of the MFH Association. Picture the chaos in the Counties and the confusion in the Shires. Contemplate the situation in Leicestershire, with the committees of the Pytchley and Quorn in continuous session trying to devise a new uniform and to buy in the black market enough coupons to obtain the material! Finally, just think of General Bouverie's anxiety lest he should be mistaken for a Communist. Surely he'll hasten to fit himself out in a suit as threadbare, shabby and unobtrusive as the one in which Karl Marx once walked the streets of Bloomsbury; and then, Comrade, your revolution is achieved!'

When the Hunt moved off I took my car and we followed them a little way up the hill; but the fox which they started almost at once ran into a quarry, where it found refuge in a sort of foxes' catacombs among the rock. The General insisted on trying to dig it out, and sent for mattocks and crowbars. 'My old father always used to say,' he declared, 'my old father who's been in his grave these twenty years, "My boy," he said, "it doesn't matter what you chase so long as you kill it; whatever else you do, see to it that *your hounds taste blood.*" ' None of us wanted to wait for this unpleasant climax, so we took Vicky (who was obviously boiling up for a Question about Blood Sports) back to the Horse and Harrow for a drink. The bar was very full, for it is the custom of Brensham men, at the stroke of noon, to plant their spades and forks firmly in the dark earth, to tie up their horses to the nearest tree or to park their tractors at the end of the furrow, and to make their way to the nearest pub for a pint of beer or cider. There was Alfie Perks, who'd been spraying his fruit trees and whose face was brick-red from the acrid rain of the spraying-mixture; old Sammy Hunt with his bald head like a wrinkled walnut and the smell of tar about him, for he'd been caulking one of his rowing-boats; George Daniels still wearing his old camouflaged jacket with the blue parachute on his sleeve; Briggs the blacksmith in his leather apron; the porter from the railway station and the gangers and platelayers from the line. Vicky became more and more bewildered as we introduced her to each of these people in turn; she was still a stranger to the sort of village microcosmos in which everybody is known by their Christian names. Then Jaky Jones the odd-job-man arrived, and 'Enery and Pierre drew up in their lorry upon some dark business or other (the lorry was loaded with a crate of hens, a hogshead barrel, a roll of wire-netting, and something very mysterious in a bloody sack), Mimi and Meg came bouncing in from the back-room, and Mimi's Pole clicking his heels whenever he could find an excuse, and Mrs Trentfield, who'd left her kitchen, she said, for the purpose of seeing a bit of life. Joe and the girls were kept busy fetching and carrying drinks, and the company fell to darts playing, talking, stamping mud-caked boots on the stone floor, or eating the midday 'bait', which consisted of inch-deep slabs of bread with cold fat bacon, upon which a raw onion was precariously balanced. Vicky, better informed about calories and carbohydrates than about the needs of hungry men, watched the rapid disappearance of these morsels wonderingly through the corner of her eye.

'A penny for your thoughts,' said Mr Chorlton.

'I was thinking about Happy Families,' she said.

'Happy Families?'

'A horrible game we used to play with cards. Do you remember the terrifying *self-sufficiency* of those families when you gathered a whole set together in your hand? I was thinking that Brensham is rather like that. Everybody belongs, everybody has a function and forms part of a pattern. Every single person who has come into this bar this morning immediately fell into place like a piece of a jig-saw-puzzle. "This is Mr Perks who grows fruit and is the father of Meg's husband and Meg is Joe's daughter, the sister of the one who had twins." '

'And don't you approve of it being like that?'

'I don't know.' She glanced about her, at Sammy Hunt and Mimi and Meg and the blacksmith and the railway porter, the odd-job-man and the rest, the Happy Families all complete, and she turned back to Mr Chorlton with a little frown. 'I think it rather scares me. If we were here for a year or two, I believe, you'd absorb us.'

'We always eat our missionaries,' smiled Mr Chorlton.

'Without meaning to, without even troubling your heads about us, you'd fit us somehow into the jigsaw-puzzle, you'd make us part of your little world. Am I right?'

'You're a very intelligent young woman,' said Mr Chorlton. 'That is exactly what Brensham is likely to do.'

PART THREE

THE CASE OF WILLIAM HART

The Scarlet Spider's Web – Poacher, Poet, Postman – 'Both man and bird and beast' – The Last Hope – The Umpire – The Long Man – Plus ça change – Microcosmos – The Siege – The Stirrup-cup.

The Scarlet Spider's Web

THE Hallidays had been at the Manor for nearly a year when William Hart's field of linseed appeared like a banner of rebellion hung out on Brensham Hill.

Meanwhile that bulging docket – '*The Case of W. Hart*' – had continued upon its inexorable way. A kind of spider's web of red tape had spun itself round William's affairs. And now suddenly the threads drew tighter.

In weighing up the rights and wrongs of this matter it is important to remember that the War Agricultural Executive Committee was at no time tyrannical in its dealings with William. It was a quorum of respectable and successful farmers, and after all one of the ancient principles of English justice is the principle that a man should be judged by his peers. Being human, the successful farmers may have been a trifle puffed up by their own importance; but according to their lights they treated William fairly, and even in the matter of the sunflowers, as we have seen, they refrained from exercising to the full their rather terrifying authority. They had the wasted crop ploughed in, and then the Chairman, as he put it, 'gave the old fool a wigging' and that would have been the end of the whole affair if William had not next year planted the field with linseed. His offence in disobeying the cultivation order was made greater by the fact that the crop was unfortunately full of weeds. Even so, I think the Committee would have hesitated to exact the extreme penalty of the law but for three unfortunate complications. In the first place, General Bouverie happened to be Vice-Chairman of the Committee. In the second, some permanent official of the Ministry of Agriculture and Fisheries, having read *The Case of W. Hart* with amazement, had taken it into his head to call for a report on William's state of mind. And in the third, the letter of complaint written by the Syndicate's solicitors some twelve months ago had made its tortoise progress, slow but sure, through what are called the usual channels to this same official's desk. (The evil that men do lives after them!) The official wanted to know what steps the WAEC had taken to deal with the complaint.

The General sat on the Committee by virtue of the fact that he farmed a thousand acres to his own considerable profit although perhaps he was more concerned with the pheasants in his coverts than the stock in his fields. He was neither an unjust nor a vindictive man, but he honestly believed that anybody who was not enthusiastically in favour of fox-hunting couldn't be quite right in the head; moreover it was indisputable that William had threatened him with a gun – and he didn't know that the gun had been empty. To make matters worse he had had a subsequent encounter with William who, being drunk at the time, boasted truculently of his descent from Shakespeare. It was therefore as clear as daylight to General Bouverie that the old man was suffering from delusions, and he put this point of view very forcibly to the Committee. The Committee incorporated his statement in its report; and some say that a clerk, copying this document, accidentally left out part of a sentence, so that it read: 'He thinks he is Shakespeare.' This was particularly damaging; because an Englishman can understand the foible of a man who believes himself to be Nelson or Napoleon or the King, but immediately assumes that the lunacy is dangerous in the case of a man who thinks himself a poet.

By the time the fat beribboned bundle of documents about W. Hart had returned from the Ministry to the WAEC it was high summer, and as a token of William's continued disobedience the linseed blazed blue on the side of the hill. The Committee lost no time in taking up this final challenge (as it must have seemed) to their august authority. They delegated three of their members to inspect William's farm; these three men reported that the linseed crop was not worth harvesting; and a week later Dai Roberts Postman delivered another registered letter at William's door. It contained no complicated forms this time, and no empty threats. The Committee proposed to take over the farm on Michaelmas Day. It was regretted that it would be necessary to requisition the farmhouse as well. Any appeal against this decision must be lodged in writing within twenty-eight days.

Poacher, Poet, Postman

William's notice of appeal was duly written out for him by Pru. She was, he said, a wonderful scholard, by which he meant that she could at any rate read and write. But about the middle of August, when the appeal was due to be heard, the old man was suddenly taken ill. The Committee, knowing nothing of this, waited for him all the morning and finally rejected the appeal in his absence. All the same they were not ungenerous to William; being property-owners themselves, they hated the whole principle of dispossession, and were anxious to put off the repugnant act until the last possible moment. They decided to suspend the take-over of the farm for ten weeks after Michaelmas, in order to give William time to find somewhere to live.

Hearing he was ill, I walked up to his farm one Saturday afternoon to pay him a visit. On the way I met Dai Roberts coming down the hill on his rattling bicycle; long before he came into sight round the corner I knew it was Dai, because he was singing, and although our village lads are as vociferous as larks and thrushes, their favourite airs are merry and bucolic and generally sung out of tune. There is only one man in Brensham who sings beautifully and sadly and who chooses to sing hymns when he is not in church; and sure enough the rat-tat-tat of a loose mudguard accompanied the singing, and Dai appeared round the corner with his postbag flying over his shoulders and a fine fat hare tied across the handlebars of his bicycle.

This spare, wiry, sallow little man came to us long ago out of the dark valleys across the border, settled down in the village, and married a Brensham girl. He had previously, I think, been crossed in love, which was probably why he left home; for I was telling him once how I had hooked and lost a salmon (twenty pounds if it was an ounce and I played it for twenty minutes on a little trout-rod), and Dai nodded his head in respectful sympathy. At last he said, with perfect understanding:

'I once loved a girl and she married another. But it is not so bad as losing a fish.'

A fisherman – whether he fished legitimately with a rod

or illegitimately with dynamite, carbide, salmon roe, gaff or pitchfork – was to Dai as a brother. But he and I had something else in common. He had once won a prize for a poem at an Eisteddfod, he had worn the bays upon his brow, and because I wrote books he regarded me as brother-craftsman though of an inferior degree: his subjects were Sacred, whereas mine were Profane. Now he skidded to a stop and told me proudly that he had completed the composition of a long poem during the course of his round. I didn't gather exactly what it was about, except that William Hart and the WAEC came into it, and also the Syndicate, whom Dai had fiercely hated because they had him prosecuted and fined ten shillings for poaching on their land.

'Biblical it iss and yet modern too,' said Dai, 'for in it the Syndicate iss the sons of Belial, do you see, bearing false witness against their neighbour.'

I asked him how William was, and Dai shook his head.

'Very strange and quiet and suddenly old he iss become. Broken his heart they have and maybe he iss not long for this world. He does not laugh nor sing, and his foot drags after him as he walks. It iss a great shame they have put upon his grey hairs.'

Then Dai remounted his bicycle and prepared to launch himself down the steep hill. Perhaps I had raised my eyebrows at the hare strapped to his handlebars, for he generally hides such things in his postbag, which is why our letters and parcels are so often smeared with blood. He shouted an explanation over his shoulder as he rattled away:

'Constable Banks has boils upon his bot-tom. Afflicted like Job the poor man iss.'

I walked on up the hill and turned into William's drive. On my left the linseed field, scarcely faded since its first blossoming, lay like a thick pile carpet of rarest blue.

'Both man and bird and beast'

I found old William in the garden, and because he was sitting down I did not at first notice the change in him. As usual, he was surrounded by children and animals. Pru's eldest, Jerry, now seven years old, was shooting at a tin-can with his catapult. The two babies were sleeping in their pram under the big mulberry tree on the lawn, and I noticed that Pru, most provident of mothers, had covered the pram with a piece of strawberry-netting lest the birds should peck them. As always the garden was full of birds and the mulberry tree was alive with the cheerful chirruping of flocks of blackbirds and thrushes glutting themselves with the wine-coloured berries. Two young goats playfully butted each other on the lawn, there were three or four cats stretched out in the sun, and William was petting a tame magpie, while Pru sat beside him dutifully darning socks.

The garden looked out on to William's Home Ground, where the men were harvesting what must have been the heaviest yield of barley Brensham Hill had ever seen. I suppose I had half-expected to find an atmosphere of high tragedy lying over William's farm, so it was a relief to hear the laughter of the men and girls in the barley field and to see the yellow wagon trundling past the garden gate with George Daniels driving it and Susan, with a pitchfork in her hands, perched up beside him on the yellow sheaves. George was shirtless, and burned deep mahogany by the sun; Susan's arms and neck exactly matched the red-gold of the barley. The pair waved cheerfully as they went by, and I thought I had seldom seen a pleasanter sight than those two young lovers among the corn. The whole scene reminded me sharply of a passage from the Georgics which I had learned at school and only half-remembered now – something about 'In the sheaf of Ceres' stalk the season richly abounds, and loads the furrows with increase, and overflows the barns . . . the cows hang down their udders fraught with milk, and fat kids on the smiling lawn with levelled horns against each other strive.'

I sat down and talked to William about the weather and village affairs, while the magpie hopped about on his head. Pru sat primly over her darning with downcast eyes like those of a virtuous young lady in a Victorian magazine, a picture of innocence and modesty, speaking only when she was spoken to and favouring me for a second or two with that singular misty look which had caused such havoc among the armed forces of the Crown.

When I got up to go William insisted on hobbling with me as far as the gate; and it was then that I realized for the first time that he had become suddenly old. As Dai had said, he dragged his left foot after him as he walked, and his arm hung awkwardly too, as if he had little use in it. I thought that he had probably had a partial stroke. He leaned heavily on the gate, and said slowly:

'They be going to turn I out, so they say.'

'I've heard about it,' I told him.

'Look,' he said, and made a queer comprehensive gesture with his stiff arm, an awkward and painful gesture which somehow included the Home Ground with its sheaves of barley, the weathered old farmhouse, the garden bright with hollyhocks and flaming peonies, the children, the cats and the goats on the lawn, the merry flocks in the mulberry tree, and away to the right Little Twittocks shining like a blue lagoon. 'Look,' said William. 'They'll turn I out of all this, they say. Can they do such a thing to a man, nowadays?'

'They have big powers,' I said; and it suddenly seemed to me fantastic and unbelievable that we should do such things in England. I thought, 'Perhaps they'll change their minds at the last moment; after all they're good and decent men, Mr Harcombe, Mr Surman, Mr Whitehead, Mr Nixon . . .' But I hadn't much hope really, because I knew what happened even to good and decent men when they became caught up in the huge impersonal machine.

William said suddenly: 'But I wun't go willing,' and for a moment I saw a lightning-flash of his old self, fierce and free. 'I wun't go. They'll have to fetch I,' he said.

Then the fierce flash faded, he shook his grand old head slowly two or three times and fell silent. The magpie hopped about on his shoulder and he put up his hand to scratch its head. 'Hey, Cheeky,' he said, 'what do you want, eh? There, there, Cheeky' – and I realized that he had already forgotten the threat which hung over him, the grief and anger had faded out of his mind, where all thoughts, hopes and fears were now as fleeting as pictures in the fire which old men see as they slump over the hearth with half-closed eyes. And yet, shorn as he was of all his boisterous vigour, I saw more clearly than ever before his essential gentleness. Often his noisy mischief had obscured it; but now that the laughter was silent and the singing done, the turbulent wildness purged out of him, I understood why the children had always loved him and the finches had flocked about him and the wild things had been without fear of his shadow. He reminded me suddenly of the Ancient Mariner – perhaps it was his long white beard! – 'He prayeth best who loveth best All things both great and small.' I left him playing with the pied bird on his shoulder, tickling the side of its head and talking to it, playing with it like a child.

The Last Hope

I was tormented by the thought that William would soon be turned out of his happy and fruitful little farm, and that perhaps he'd end up in the workhouse because he had nowhere else to go. The only hope seemed to be that the Committee might hold its hand if we represented that William was ill and obviously hadn't much longer to live, or if we pointed out that despite his unorthodox ways he had probably grown as much useful food per acre as anybody else in Brensham. I discussed this with Mr Chorlton one evening when I found him drinking port with Sir Gerald, and he proposed that we should take the first opportunity of putting William's case before Halliday. Mr Chorlton claimed that he knew a good deal about bureaucracy, because he had been a temporary civil servant during the first war. 'Even the most savage dog fears its own master,' he said. 'Even the most hide-bound bureaucrat is scared stiff of his own Minister; and all Ministers live in mortal terror of Question Time. We must therefore persuade our tame MP to ask a Question. There shouldn't be much difficulty about that. The job will be to get hold of him. He's always buzzing about like a chimera bominating in a vacuum.'

And indeed, although in theory he lived at the Manor, we saw very little of our MP. During Parliamentary sessions he was in London from Monday till Friday night. He sometimes appeared in the village on Saturdays and Sundays, but he was always in a hurry, always rushing off to address meetings in his own constituency or somebody else's. Even during the recess there seemed to be no respite for him. He spoke for other candidates at by-elections; he sat on numerous committees; and when he was at home he was generally busy answering the bundles of letters which Dai Roberts reluctantly carried up the steep hill to the Manor: 'Forty-seven letters by the morning post! And all for one man! It iss not reasonable. And who knows but a telegram there will be waiting when I get back to Mrs Doan's Post Office!' Dai sadly looked back upon the good old days when the Mad Lord had lived at the Manor and his sole correspondence consisted of bills in halfpenny envelopes which Dai delivered only once a week 'for the sake of his lordship's peace of mind'.

'*Bombinans in vacuo*,' Mr Chorlton went on, 'and unless we can soon persuade him to sit down and think now and then over a pint of beer he'll end up as they all end up, with hardened arteries and shrunken souls like shrivelled nuts rattling about inside the shell. Empty husks through which the wind of what they call Public Opinion blows with a thin sad piping. I've seen some old politicians in my day!'

Mr Chorlton sipped his port.

'We've got ten weeks,' he said, 'before William is actually dispossessed. We must get to work on Halliday before the House assembles again, and he must then ask a question which will make the hide-bound bureaucrats sit up. Isn't it odd, by the way, that we've almost got into the Greek habit of attaching particular epithets to particular nouns? The Press writes of hide-bound bureaucrats just as Homer wrote of the rosy-fingered dawn and the wine-dark sea! Have another glass of Government Port?' He made his ancient and familiar joke. 'It's any port in a storm.'

'You'd think it ambrosia,' said Sir Gerald, 'if you'd tasted my mango-spirit in Burma.'

'*Nihil altum, nihil magnificum*,' boomed Mr Chorlton, '*ac divinum suscipere possunt* . . .' launching himself into a quotation from Cicero to the effect that those who devote their thoughts to low and abject things cannot attempt anything exalted, noble or divine.

The Umpire

As it happened the opportunity of talking to Halliday about William Hart came unexpectedly a fortnight later. To everybody's astonishment he consented to umpire in our annual cricket-match against Woody Bourton.

The team was short of an umpire because Joe Trentfield, who had done the thankless job for years, suddenly declared that he was sick to death of being Vilified by friend and foe alike, and nothing we could say would persuade him to change his mind. 'They Vilifies me,' he repeated, as he shook his head; and he reminded us of the painful dispute after the last match with Woody Bourton, when our opponents asserted that he had lost them the match while our own side maintained that they had only won in spite of him. 'I was absolutely Vilified,' said Joe, and we could see that he was adamant; so the committee began to look round for a successor.

It was Alfie Perks who suggested that Halliday should be invited. The reasons he gave were sound but unusual: in the first place, he said, nobody who was familiar with the bitterness engendered by this particular match would take on the job, and in the second, not even the loathly captain of Woody Bourton would dare to dispute the decision of a Member of Parliament. So on Sunday a deputation was sent to the Manor, where they were hospitably entertained with glasses of sherry, a drink to which they were unaccustomed. When they came to the point Halliday confessed to them that he would have been delighted to accept the invitation if only he had known the rules; but he had never played cricket in his life. Alfie, who had drunk three glasses of sherry, assured him airily that his lack of cricketing experience would make no difference at all; the Laws of

Cricket, he said, were set forth in Wisden, and were much less complicated than the Laws of England, which Mr Halliday doubtless carried about in his head. 'Mug 'em up, sir!' said Alfie, full of sherry and enthusiasm. 'A chap like you could mug 'em up easy in a few hours! And when you've mugged 'em up, all you've got to do is to remember you're the boss and not be frit of nobody. That was the trouble with Pegleg, who used to be our umpire years ago: he was always frit. One day Lord Orris' father brought W. G. Grace to play in a match on our ground, and the very first ball the old man steps in front of his wicket and the ball hits him fair and square on the pads. "How's that?" yells the bowler. "How's that?" hollers the wicket-keeper. And everybody else shouts "How's that?" as loud as they can. Up goes Pegleg's finger, though it was shaking like a leaf, and "Out" says he. But Mr Grace's beard bristles, and he gives Pegleg a terrible look, and then in a voice of thunder which you could have heard on top of Brensham Hill he just says: "What?" That "What?" was too much for Pegleg. "Beg pardon, sir, not out," says he, trembling like an aspen. And W. G. stayed there to make a hundred. But for a chap like you, sir,' finished Alfie, 'if you ain't frit of Mr Churchill in the House of Commons, you won't be frit of nobody I'm sure.'

Next day Alfie provided himself with a copy of Wisden and took it to the Manor. 'I think I can 'tice him,' he said with a grin, explaining that in his belief laws and rules and regulations would always prove irresistible to political chaps if dangled before them like carrots in front of a donkey. This is what he proceeded to do. He opened Wisden at Rule 22 and, remarking casually, 'There's a fair puzzle here,' began to read:

'*Note (f): The striker is out if the ball is hugged to the body of the catcher even though he has not touched it with his hands.*

Should the ball lodge in the fieldsman's clothing, or in the top of the wicket-keeper's pads, this will amount to its being hugged to the body of the catcher.

'Funny thing, that,' said Alfie with an expression of wide-eyed innocence, 'for if a ball sticks in a wicket-keeper's pads, how can you say he's hugging it?'

'I think,' said Halliday, 'that it is one of those cases where a common phrase is given a wide interpretation to cover a large number of possible eventualities. But it's an interesting clause, certainly.'

Alfie continued to dangle his carrot.

'Rule 44 Note c,' he said. 'It always makes me laugh. *The umpire is not a boundary*. Just that.'

'*What?*' said Halliday. 'Let me have a look at the book.'

'Would you like to borrow it for a few days?' said Alfie.

'That's very kind of you. Let me see. *The umpire is not a boundary*. Very odd. But I suppose if you scored four runs every time you hit me – I mean the umpire – it would be a very strong temptation, wouldn't it?'

Alfie, who had not failed to notice that 'me', returned in triumph to the Horse and Harrow. 'I 'ticed him,' he said. 'Now the next thing is to get him trained.' A few days later we took Halliday down to the nets to give him, as Alfie put it, a bit of a try-out. He came through this test with flying colours. Indeed he seemed to know the lbw rule better than we did ourselves. It was a good deal simpler than Company Law, he said, and the man who had drafted it knew how to express himself in plain English.

'It just shows,' remarked Alfie on the way home, 'how easily these MP fellows can mug things up when they set their minds to it.'

The match was fixed for the following Saturday, and we had the umpire's white coat specially washed and ironed for the occasion. Halliday, who evidently took his duties very seriously, brought the copy of Wisden with him, and read the Laws of Cricket in the pavilion to refresh his memory. This somewhat dismayed us, for it seemed to suggest that he did not, after all, know them by heart; but he told us that even the Solicitor-General would sometimes refer to his authorities during a Parliamentary debate. We suggested, however, that he should not display the book more often than he could help before our opponents. Woody Bourton (Bloody Bourton, as we called them) were a suspicious lot, we explained; and Halliday with a most unaccustomed twinkle in his eye tucked Wisden away in his pocket.

'The fellow who drafted those laws,' he remarked, 'seems to have thought of every possibility. Even the most alarming possibilities. For instance, *The ball does not become "dead" on merely hitting the umpire unless it lodges in his pocket or clothing.* There's a good deal to be said for substituting the MCC for a Committee of the House of Commons.'

When Woody Bourton's Secretary came up to me in the pavilion and asked 'Who's your new umpire?' adding rudely, 'It was time you got a new one,' I took pleasure in saying as casually as I could:

'Oh, he's our Member of Parliament.'

'What's his name?' said the Secretary.

'Maurice Halliday.'

I could see at once that he was impressed. 'Good Lord,' he said. 'He's the chap who's always asking Questions. A well-informed fellow, I should think; though I don't agree with him politically.' I felt that the match was half won already. When Halliday put on his spotless white coat I watched the Woody Bourton fieldsmen nudging each other; and when he walked out with measured tread towards the wickets they were so awe-stricken that they even forgot to show off by throwing each other difficult catches as they followed their captain into the field.

But it was not until the innings started that we realized how thoroughly subdued they were. We had won the toss, and we batted first. Now as a rule the Woody Bourton bowlers, the wicket-keeper, the captain and indeed the whole eleven appeal in raucous voices at the least provocation, and often with no provocation at all. '*Howzat?*' they shout, in the hoarse tone of vultures clamouring about their doomed prey. 'HOW-ZAT?' they screech, whether the ball hits us on the legs or the arms or in the belly or in the box. There was none of that this afternoon; and the silence was so unfamiliar that some of our batsmen remarked that it was like a Test match and confessed to feeling thoroughly nervous themselves.

Halliday received only one appeal during the whole innings. The Woody Bourton slow bowler, whose antics when he appeals are generally those of a dancing dervish, asked very humbly and respectfully: 'How was that, sir?' in so quiet a tone that Halliday failed to hear him. He therefore ignored the appeal altogether, and the bowler quailed before his impassive silence. I think the incident had a serious moral effect not only upon the Woody Bourton players but upon their own umpire; in the next over, when I walked in front of the wicket and received the ball fair and square upon my pads, I could hardly believe my ears when he said 'Not out.'

We scored a hundred and twenty all out, and then we had tea. Vicky helped Mrs Trentfield, Mimi and Meg to cut the sandwiches and pour out. 'The girl's getting quite human,' Mr Chorlton whispered to me. He'd been sitting with her all the afternoon on the bench underneath the shade of the willow trees, and gently teasing her, no doubt, about her politics. A year before it would have seemed almost unbelievable that these two opposite characters should find any pleasure at all in each other's company; but although they still argued frequently and sometimes savagely there had grown up between them a sort of comradeship, almost an affection, so that strangers meeting them together often assumed that they were father and daughter. Nobody who was wise and less tolerant than Mr Chorlton, I think, would have got past the brisk, assured, humourless personality and discovered the real Vicky underneath. Perhaps the fact that he had spent most of his life with boys had something to do with it; for boys too, because they lack humour and self-confidence, wrap themselves in personalities which are not their own. At any rate he was the only person in the village who was not at least a bit frightened of Vicky, and he was certainly the only one who dared to tease her. I once heard him greet her in the village street with 'Well, you booksy girl, what's in the *New Statesman* today?' and to my astonishment she actually laughed. It occurred to me to wonder whether Halliday himself had ever tried the effect of pulling her leg.

After tea the Woody Bourton captain came out, looking grim and purposeful, to open the innings. He was, as it happened, the Conservative agent for a neighbouring constituency, and he was also extremely argumentative; it would be very interesting, I thought, if Halliday had to give him out. The first ball pitched well on his off, he swung at it foolishly, and there was a loud click. Our wicket-keeper appealed, holding the ball triumphantly above his head, and Halliday raised his finger. For a fraction of a second the Woody Bourton captain hesitated, as if he were about to remark, as he always did on such occasions, that the ball had hit his pads or his boot or his arm or that his bat had not been within a mile of it. But there was something extremely authoritative about that raised finger; even the most determined hecklers had been silenced by it; and when he had taken a second look at it the Woody Bourton captain slunk away to the pavilion with the air of a criminal who has been sent down for seven years and knows he deserves it.

In the next over, however, Halliday refused two appeals for lbw and this pleased us, because it demonstrated the impartiality of our new umpire, of whom we were already feeling extremely proud. We were confident that we could skittle out Woody Bourton for much less than a hundred and twenty, and perhaps we began to take things too easily, for the batsmen scratched and scraped their way into the forties before we got another wicket. Then we dropped a couple of catches, and aided by extras and overthrows our enemies poked and pottered along in what we considered a typically Woody Bourtonish way until the score stood at ninety for seven. The tail-enders began hitting, and before we knew where we were the match had drifted into a state of crisis: there was a hundred and ten on the score-board, eight wickets were down, and two hefty batsmen, the one a butcher and the other a drayman at the brewery, were scoring precious singles by means of mis-hits between their legs. The vociferous supporters whom Woody Bourton had brought with them clapped and cheered and cat-called, there was an atmosphere of authentic suspense between the overs, and the situation was obviously working up to one of those passionate finishes which seemed to be inseparable from the games (if indeed they were games) which we played against Woody Bourton. To add to the mounting tension, there was a huge sable thundercloud bearing down from the north-west, the light was bad, there was a crackle of lightning and a rumble of thunder, and I felt a cold rain-drop splash on my nose.

It was against this Twilight-of-the-Gods background that the remarkable last scene of the match was played.

The score being then a hundred and fifteen for eight, Alfie Perks bowled to the butcher a slow ball which pitched short and seemed to hang in the air for a moment after it bounced. The butcher began to make a terrific swipe at it, changed his mind at the last moment, and cocked it up in the air. Sir Gerald, who was undoubtedly our worst, but was also our most enthusiastic fieldsman, happened to be standing forward of point. He ran into the middle of the pitch and stood with his hands cupped ready to catch the falling ball. The doomed butcher, in a mighty voice, suddenly called his partner for a run.

Now the butcher and the drayman, between them, must have weighed about thirty-five stone. I swear the very ground shook as they pounded down the pitch. The butcher charged with his head down, like an infuriated bull, snorting like a grampus; the drayman carried his bat like a lance before him as if he were Don Quixote charging a windmill. Sir Gerald saw them coming, or more probably heard them coming, for he was still looking up at the ball in the air. He was never a very self-assertive person, and I think it was politeness as much as fear that made him move as if to get out of the way. But as he did so a great shout went up from Sammy Hunt, our captain, who still employed the majestic terminology of the sea upon the cricket-field in moments of crisis. 'Belay, you blithering fool!' yelled Sammy. 'Hold your course and shiver their timbers! *Catch it!*' For a moment Sir Gerald hesitated; and then, like one who sacrifices himself to Juggernaut, he plunged once more into the middle of the pitch.

But there was not one Juggernaut, there were two; and Sir Gerald, just as he got his hands to the ball, was sandwiched between them. There was a sickening thud and the three men went down in a heap together; but even as he fell Sir Gerald kept his head, and there came from his lips a last despairing cry which seemed to be literally squashed out of him, a kind of squeak such as toy teddy-bears make when you squeeze their tummies, a small faint squeak indeed but nevertheless recognizable as 'How's that?'

'Out,' said Halliday, without a moment's hesitation.

The batsmen ruefully picked themselves up and stood staring at Halliday. Sir Gerald crawled upon the pitch picking up bits of his broken glasses.

'Out,' said Halliday again.

'Why?' demanded the drayman truculently, still waving his bat like a lance.

'For obstructing the field,' Halliday said; and to everybody's amazement proceeded to quote *verbatim* from the Laws of Cricket: '*Rule* 26. *The batsman shall be out if under the pretence of running, or otherwise, he wilfully prevents the ball from being caught.*'

'All right,' said the drayman, utterly confounded by this. 'If it says that then I suppose somebody's out. But the question is, which?'

There was a long pause, and it was apparent to some of us, though not, I think, to the dazed and puzzled batsmen, that Halliday didn't know the answer to this problem. His reading of Wisden had been pretty thorough, but he could not remember any of the Laws of Cricket which covered so unlikely a situation; for the impact had occurred exactly in the middle of the pitch and both the batsmen, running from opposite directions, had collided with Sir Gerald simultaneously. If the butcher was to blame, pounding along like a mad bull, so was the drayman, charging like a lancer. It was impossible to say that one was more culpable than the other.

'*Which* of us is out?' demanded the drayman again.

'Both,' said Halliday firmly.

And strangely enough they went. They went quite meekly, though they muttered and murmured together and shook their heads in a puzzled way; and so the match was over and Brensham had won by five runs. As if to finish off the drama with a good spectacular curtain there was a vivid flash of lightning and a clap of thunder and as we all raced for the pavilion the rain came sousing down.

It was very surprising, and it says a good deal for Halliday's air of authority, that not a single member of the Woody Bourton team openly criticized his peculiar verdict, and indeed the only adverse comment came from our own side – from Dai Roberts Postman who kept the score for us so neatly that it looked like a sonnet and who now complained, 'Out of all reason it iss, and untidy will it make the score-sheet look, for two men to be out together.' He made a neat little squiggle to record his disapproval, and we still possess the score-book with the remarkable entry in it, which looks like this:

<table>
<tr><td>Davidson, I.</td><td rowspan="2">} Obs. Field {</td><td>11</td></tr>
<tr><td>Rowley, R.</td><td>3</td></tr>
</table>

However, as Sammy Hunt said, if Woody Bourton were satisfied, we were more than satisfied. Sir Gerald, especially, despite his bruises and the loss of his glasses, felt like a conquering hero. Alfie remarked that the whole thing restored his faith in the House of Commons.

When we had changed, and Woody Bourton, still puzzled, grumbling, but morally a defeated side, had climbed into their bus and driven away, Mr Chorlton lit his pipe and observed to Halliday between long puffs.

'That was a very remarkable decision, if I may say so. Solomon himself could hardly have made a fairer one. But I wonder if you happen to know what the rule really is?'

Halliday shook his head.

'Nor did Woody Bourton, apparently,' said Mr Chorlton.

'Unless I'm much mistaken there's a note (*a*) in small type under Rule 26: *It should be noted that it is the striker who is out if this law in infringed.*'

'Good Lord! Then they weren't both out?'

'Of course not. Two men can't be out at once.'

'I'm frightfully sorry,' said Halliday. 'I learned the rules by heart, but I must have missed the note. What a rotten umpire.'

'Not at all. A jolly good umpire: you won the match. Let's go along to the Horse and Harrow,' said Mr Chorlton, 'and celebrate it.'

The Long Man

We drove to the pub in my car: Halliday, Vicky, Mr Chorlton, Sir Gerald and myself. On the way Mr Chorlton broached the subject of William Hart and Halliday listened attentively, asked sensible questions, and jotted down brief details of the case in a diary which seemed to be more full of engagements than any diary I had ever seen before. 'Obviously,' he said, 'it would be monstrous to turn the old man out in the circumstances. Our job is to make bureaucracy humane. It isn't easy, within a few years, to turn glorified clerks into benevolent despots. But aristocracy wasn't always humane, was it? What about the dispossessed crofters in the Scottish deer-forests?'

'True enough,' said Mr Chorlton, 'but there were sanctions against aristocracy. If a landowner was wicked enough you broke his windows and burned his ricks—'

'If you dared,' interrupted Halliday swiftly. 'And then you were deported to Australia. But I agree with you to some extent. Public opinion did count for something. The man in his office in Whitehall is insulated against public opinion. Much too often he doesn't feel which way the wind is blowing.' He paused and said almost wistfully: 'There's no wind there,' as if he often longed for a breath of the wind and a sight of the sky. The storm, which hadn't yet spent itself, seemed to please and even excite him, for he looked gayer than I had ever seen him before and when there was a particularly loud crack of thunder he glanced at me and grinned: 'The weather is something you miss, in London.'

We got to the Horse and Harrow before opening-time, but Joe, like most people in Brensham, never locks his door, so we went into the empty bar. I hammered on the counter for Joe, while Vicky once again examined the absurd vegetables on the mantelpiece, which never failed to irritate her. 'Like a harvest festival dedicated to the Devil,' she said.

'Hallo!' exclaimed Halliday suddenly. 'What on earth's this?' The object stood in the shadows at the back of the bar, among the tins of snuff and the pipe-cleaners and the sets of darts; for even Joe, with his easy-going view of what constituted a good joke, had not seen fit to display it to the public gaze. But Halliday happened to notice it and now he leaned over the bar to take a closer look, for at first, I suppose, he thought that some trick of the light had deceived him. This, however, was not the case. William Hart, in one of his most mischievous moods, had been minded to give Joe a present. Liking the sound of Joe's laughter, and knowing well the sort of thing which would make him laugh loudest, he had carved for him a somewhat fanciful and greatly exaggerated version of the Long Man of Elmbury.

The Long Man, I must explain, was the creation of a furniture and curio dealer called Mr Parfitt, who kept a shop in Elmbury. After a holiday at Cerne Abbas, he had been inspired to invent the legend of a monstrous figure which, he said, had once existed on Brensham Hill but had been ploughed up long ago at the instance of a puritanical parson. For years he had made a profitable business out of carving models of this Long Man and selling them to gullible visitors; and in the end the legend had found its way into the learned books of the folk-lorists and the archaeologists, so that Mr Parfitt in his humble way had actually made history. The naughty little figure had greatly appealed to William Hart, who had carved his own lively version of it whenever he laid hands on a piece of wood which had the sort of shape which suggested it.

'Good God,' said Halliday. 'Look at this!' He stretched across the bar, picked it up, and set it on the counter in front of him.

There was a brief silence, while the thunder rumbled and the rain lashed the windows and the Hallidays stood and stared without speaking at the outrageous little statuette. The Long Man, in an attitude halfway between menace and frolic, and with an expression halfway between a grin and a leer, uncompromisingly stared back at them.

'At Cerne Abbas in Dorset,' said Mr Chorlton, 'there is one rather like it carved on the side of a hill . . .'

Sir Gerald, who without his glasses was very nearly blind, leaned down myopically to examine the figure, then suddenly straightened himself and said: 'Dear! Dear!'

Vicky, meanwhile, regarded the figure with studied unconcern. She was extremely well educated and believed that nothing could embarrass or shock her; I am sure she must have read the whole of *The Golden Bough* before she was nineteen. She put the Long Man in his place with a cool stare. It must be admitted, however, that for a moment she had looked slightly startled; and now she gave a kind of snort, expressing her disapproval of the monstrosity. 'Put it away, Maurice,' she said. 'It's disagreeable, and if I may say so, rather silly.'

Halliday, however, seemed to be in no hurry to put it

away. With his hands in his pockets and a rare smile on his face he stood and contemplated it. William Hart had thrown all his boisterous mischief into the carving of the figure; and because he had dedicated it, as it were, to Joe Trentfield, he had contrived to mix a little of Joe's rough humour with his own. In truth it was his masterpiece. There was fun and frolic and laughter and lust in it, and even the lust was a sort of comprehensive lust of life. The sideways-glancing secret eyes beneath the heavy lids reminded me of a picture which had often come into my mind when I was reading the Classics at school: behind the printed text and the solemn notes, behind the dull glossary, behind Liddell and Scott, there had often appeared a cool green glade dappled with sunlight, with a crystal stream reed-girt running through it; and the reeds swaying in the wind were furtively pulled apart by brown hairy hands, and between them when they were parted peered out the secret eyes of the ancient, the Goat-Footed One. Like that were the eyes of William Hart's wooden idol; but no, not quite like that. For they were a man's eyes nevertheless, dreams as well as desires in them. As they followed the light-treading nymph they would discover the lilt of a piece of music in her movements and make the soft curves of her breasts into a sonnet. The wide, loose, slanting mouth, the long lips parted, might equally utter a jest or a love-song, or dare to shout a challenge to the high gods themselves.

Halliday, I think, saw much the same things as I saw in the little statue. He was a person, as Mr Chorlton said, who had suffered all his days from a serious lack of fun. All the more boisterous manifestations of life had passed him by. The furrows on his forehead grew deeper, his hair became tinged with grey, his eyes had wrinkles round the corners from reading late into the night; and when he had spoken of London he had said with a queer wistfulness: 'There's no wind there.' Well, here was a high fierce wind of mirth and mischief, fun and frenzy, man's divinity and man's devilry! Strangely stirred by it, he continued to stare at the manikin which William Hart, bellowing with joy, had carved one uproarious midnight when he was full of wine.

'Fertility rites,' said Vicky, and added rather impatiently: 'Do put it away.' Halliday picked it up and stood it again in the dark shadows where it belonged. As he did so the wind got up, grew loud for a moment in the chimney, and rattled the windows with a new flurry of rain. One could almost fancy one heard in it the ancient laughter and the huge halloo.

Soon Alfie Perks and Sammy Hunt and the rest of the cricketers came into the bar, and we all sat together along the benches by the window and drank pints of beer. I don't know how it happened that the talk got round to the subject of William Hart; I think Mr Chorlton must have engineered it. At any rate, we found ourselves talking about his young days, and his skill in carpentry, and Jaky Jones who'd been his pupil told us how he used to make the yellow wagons and about his favourite motto which no carpenter, said Jaky, should ever forget: Measure Twice and Cut Once.

'Aye, he allus took pains,' said Joe, 'whether he was making a wagon or a coffin or a toy for the kids or something like *this*' – and he indicated the Long Man standing in the shadows among the snuff-tins.

Halliday became interested at once.

'Why, is William Hart the man who carved that figure? We noticed it when we first came into the bar.'

Joe nodded.

'You spotted it, did you?' he laughed. 'As a matter of fact I usually hides it behind the snuff. It might fright the wenches else. I hope the lady warn't frit?'

Vicky said nothing, but looked rather insulted at the

suggestion that she might have been frightened by anything so silly, and Joe went on:

'''Tis supposed to be a sort of charm; though I don't believe in heathen idols myself. Gets you children, they say; but I keeps it because it makes me laugh.'

'You seem to have plenty of grandchildren,' said Halliday, who had no doubt seen and heard a good deal of Mimi's and Meg's numerous babies when he spent the night at the Horse and Harrow.

'Eight,' boasted Joe. 'That's to say, three at the police-station – my eldest girl married the bobby – and five in this house; and two more coming. It's always neck and neck between Mimi and Meg. Mimi had a good start when she took up with the Count, but then Meg married a local lad, Alfie Perks' boy, and first go off she had twins. But in the long run I'd back the Pole.'

'Old William,' said Jaky Jones, 'he didn't need no charms. He'd scarce so much as look at a maid and it was how's your father.'

'He had a lot of children?' smiled Halliday.

'Bless you, yes,' said Joe, 'and most of 'em out of wedlock. And mark you, most of *those* are proud of it. That's a funny thing,' he added reflectively, 'they're most of 'em proud and open about it, aren't they, Jaky?'

'William's a proud man himself,' Jaky nodded.

'Very proud and boastful of his ancestry he is,' agreed Joe.

We explained to the Hallidays about old William's absurd belief that he was descended from Shakespeare: a belief that went strangely with his own inability to read or write. 'Well, he's got the right name, anyhow,' laughed Halliday. He seemed very interested in William, and Mr Chorlton winked at me. 'What's he like,' Halliday asked, 'this strange old fellow who's brightened up the view from my windows with his field of flax?'

'Well . . .' Joe looked puzzled. 'It's difficult to put into words, but the thing I always think about him is that he's full of life. Not in any ordinary sense of the words, either. He's like a new barrel of beer which you can't draw off in half-pints because it froths so; and you feel he'd bust if you corked him. I've never known anybody so full of life in all my time, have you, Jaky? 'Course, I'm talking about his younger days now; we haven't seen him down in the village since he got so lame.'

'Like weeds he was,' said Jaky, rather obscurely; but Joe understood. 'That's it!' he said eagerly. 'Like weeds. I've got a rough and unruly piece of ground which I ploughs and hoes and disc-harrows and cultivates but it's so full of life that the weeds always come up in it fierce and free. It's got a sort of demon in it. Last spring I thought I'd lay down a patch of concrete to make a stand for the horse and dray; because in wet weather it's so mucky that they're like to get stuck. But would you believe it, a little dock, no bigger'n my finger or an asparagus-top, poked up and forced its way through the concrete and cracked it, and then more docks and thistles and nettles, till all the concrete was busted and now it looks like crazy pavement with weeds growing in all the cracks! In the same way, if you can understand me, life was fierce and forceful in William Hart in the days of his youth. There was a demon in him; and yet you couldn't say he was wicked any more than weeds are wicked. They *has* to sprout and riot; and so did he.'

'But how, exactly, did he sprout and riot?' asked Halliday.

Everyone laughed.

'Wenches and drinking and singing and fun,' said Joe. 'And yet there wasn't an ounce of harm in him, was there, Jaky? The maids he wronged always forgave him; and even when he was drunk he was as gentle as a lamb.'

Jaky nodded; and Alfie Perks put in:

'A child could handle him. And yet you wouldn't have thought it, to hear him bellowing about the village after the pubs shut. You'd have thought Beelzebub was inside him; and yet 'twas simply that he was full to overflowing with Life.'

'Funny you saying that,' said Jaky, 'because somehow I just can't fancy William ever being dead. Most people,' he went on, with a sardonic grin, 'when I sees 'em in the street or in the pub I knows they'll come to it in the end.' (To this favour they must come! I thought.) 'But William, somehow, I can never see myself burying him, I can't picture him in the churchyard. Though, Lord knows, he's been familiar enough with the churchyard in his time; and I often used to tell him that he'd know the way there.'

Joe hastened to explain:

'At one time he was courting the cook at the Rectory. He'd slip in through the lych-gate after dark, and cook'd slip out through the Rector's back door, and they'd be up to their games among the owls and the yew trees. Then one day they fell down a hole that Jaky here had dug, and the cook sprained her ankle. There was a fine old to-do about it, and the Rector had it stopped; but by then, of course, 'twas too late.'

'How's your father again,' said Jaky succinctly.

'That'd be, what, twenty-five years ago,' Joe reflected, 'when William was over fifty?'

'Twenty-five years it must be,' agreed Sammy Hunt. 'Young Pru is twenty-four.'

I smiled at Halliday and he whispered: 'I'm enjoying this. I'm beginning to get a picture of your wild old man.' It was a confused and fantastic and rather one-sided picture, but I could see that it delighted Halliday in the same way as the carved figure had delighted him, and probably the Long

Man had somehow got mixed up with William in his mind. Now Jaky Jones told him the story of William's first marriage to the gypsy girl and Sammy Hunt described William's wondrous store of home-made wine, and Joe brought out from the back of the bar a faded photograph of William at the flower show, standing beside his biggest vegetable marrow (rather like the pictures we used to see in the war of airmen standing beside their two-thousand-pound bombs!) Yes; considering they used very few words I think Joe and Jaky and Sammy and Alfie painted a pretty accurate and vivid portrait of William in the space of about half an hour. *Full of life*, like a new barrel of beer, and *fierce and forceful as the weeds*: irrepressible life working in him like the ferment in his own plum wine, bursting out like the trees in spring or the dock cracking the concrete; something demoniac about him, yet withal he was as gentle as a lamb; bellowing about the place like the Bull of Bashan; singing and shouting (the long slanting mouth half-open like that little idol's, the ancient laughter and the huge halloo!); and then, at the age of fifty, sprouting and rioting among the tombstones with the Rector's cook – and the offspring of that union was called Prudence!

My people don't use many words, I thought, but they know how to tell a tale.

'What a man he must have been!' whispered Halliday; and at some story of Sammy Hunt's, about how the parsnip wine had affected the Rector when he called to admonish William and drank two glases of it under the impression that it was a teetotal drink, Halliday suddenly threw back his head and laughed. He filled his lungs with laughter as a man who has been too long in cities breathes deep the un-accustomed country air. We looked at him in surprise, for we had never seen him laugh like that before; and Vicky, who had probably formed her own, and very different, picture of William Hart (a case of arrested development with a low Intelligence Quotient!) stared at him with a sort of bewildered disapproval. But at least she had drunk two pints of beer in a public bar, which I was pretty certain she wouldn't have dreamed of doing six months ago. We were taming her!

Plus ça change

Yes, said Mr Chorlton later in the evening, when we'd said goodnight to the Hallidays and were walking home together up the crooked village street: Brensham was taming them both. The very thing was happening to them which Vicky had far-sightedly foreseen, on that morning when we took her into the Horse and Harrow after the Meet: they were fitting into the jigsaw-puzzle of our little community, they were becoming part of the structure and pattern, they *belonged.*

'And yet,' he said, 'perhaps it's not so strange or unexpected after all. I don't wholly agree with their politics, probably because I'm too old or because having read too much of Pericles and the politics of Athens, I tend to see the whole of politics as a historical merry-go-round, repeating itself in an endless and rather boring cycle. And yet I believe that those two are just as valid an expression of the English Spirit as William Hart; and the English Spirit doesn't greatly change. Halliday's dream is not very different from the young dream of Disraeli, in *Sybil*, when he imagined the aristocracy setting the people free from their middle-class masters; it's only the conception of aristocracy which has altered. And as for Vicky, as I said before, she's pure Cobbett, the English Radical who never changes except in name, and who is truly Radical in the sense of having deep roots. Perhaps Vicky hasn't got very obvious roots yet; but you wait. She's growing them!'

Microcosmos

There followed a long lull in the affairs of William Hart. The field of flax faded at last, became a smudge of faint indigo on the side of the hill, and in due course an unsuccessful attempt to harvest it was made by George and Susan. The WAEC, contrary to everybody's expectations, took no steps to plough it in. Michaelmas brought its mists and its mushrooms, Susan driving her red tractor turned up the brown earth in Little Twittocks once more, the Frolick Virgins started sprout-picking again and demonstrated the truth of the saying 'Cold hands, warm hearts', by all falling passionately in love afresh with each other's young men. Soon after Parliament reassembled Mr Chorlton had a note from Halliday, saying, that he'd tackled the Minister, who promised to inquire into William's case; so we ceased to trouble our heads about it, feeling confident that all would be well.

At the end of September the usual horde of Birmingham fishermen descended upon Brensham in twelve charabancs for their annual Fishing Competition, which was won with a catch of five small eels about as thick as bootlaces; but the fishermen drank our three pubs dry and Joe chalked a sad sardonic little notice upon his front door, which he still kept hospitably ajar:

NO BEER, NO CIDER, NO SPIRITS, NO CIGS, BUT PLENTY OF STRONG POP.

About the same time a curious misfortune happened to Sammy Hunt, whose tiny estate by the river consisted of a cottage, a paddock, a landing-stage where he hired out boats, and a small osier-bed. All this messuage, as the lawyers say, was situated within the bend of the river, where it wound round the base of the hill; in summer, with its yellow flags, water-lilies, purple loosestrife, pink flowering-rushes and overhanging willows, it was one of the pleasantest places where a man might fish or laze or paddle a boat and dream. But some tidy-minded official of the Catchment Board decided that the river would be much nicer if it ran straight; for then the winter floods would drain away more quickly. The Conservancy therefore sent two mechanical dredgers to chop off Sammy's osier-bed and straighten the bend. They had offered him, of course, the usual compensation: much more, probably, than the osier-bed was worth. But Sammy protested in vain that the money was useless to him, he wanted to keep the place as it was '*because it was his*' and because in any case he liked crooked rivers. The tidy-minded official saw no point in this argument, and day by day like caterpillars chewing at the edge of a leaf the dredgers whittled away at the osier-bed, nibbled chunks off the bank, and dragged up the very entrails of the river to make a black and slimy mud-bank at the bottom of Sammy's land. 'It's vandalous, vandalous,' cried Sammy in despair, 'and what's more they're beginning to undermine my garden.' And now sure enough, as the first flood-water came down the river, the bank collapsed and half of Sammy's garden, including his carefully tended three-year-old asparagus-bed, slithered gently into the muddy stream. Moreover a deep crevasse appeared within a few yards of his back door; and the officials who now descended upon him in swarms with offers of still more compensation shook their heads gravely and wondered whether the foundations of the cottage itself might be damaged. 'It just shows,' said poor Sammy, 'what comes of interfering with Nature. What are you going to do about it, anyhow?'

'*You've* got nothing to worry about,' said the officials kindly. 'You'll get compensation on a very generous scale indeed. You'll be able to buy another place if you like.'

'But don't you understand,' Sammy protested desperately, 'it's *mine*; I bought it to retire to; I don't want another place.'

The officials gravely shook their heads. 'If the house were to collapse,' they said, 'we could take no responsibility for any injury . . .' But Sammy, who had twice in his life stood on his bridge while a ship went down beneath him, was not the sort of man to abandon a sinking house. 'Here I am,' he said, 'and here I stays, and if so be as I wakes up one morning and finds myself swimming I'll see you all in hell.'

About the same time Mrs Doan of the Village Shop was also having trouble with officialdom. Some sharp-nosed functionary of the Customs and Excise, who happened to be in the village on holiday, whiffed a strong smell of peppermint, and following the scent like a hound on the trail he came at last to Mrs Doan's wash-house, where she was busy distilling her autumn store against the colds and coughs of November. So he demanded to see her licence, hinting darkly that for all he knew she might use the still for making whisky or gin. Mrs Doan, a lifelong teetotaller to whom the very word gin was anathema, protested her innocence in vain; and a few weeks later she had a letter threatening her with all sorts of persecutions, pains and penalties unless she 'desisted forthwith' from what was described as 'an open contravention of the law'.

October came in with some still days, as translucent and pearly-grey as a pigeon's feathers, the evenings shut in, and Pru heard again the ancient and irresistible call. Quiet as a mouse, soft-padding as a cat, kin to the fluffy-feathered owls and the downy moths of autumn, she crept out into the dusky lanes where the love-performing night drew its close curtain over her. Late wayfarers hearing a faint bleating from the hedgeside would often happen upon her pram with the two prize-winning babies inside it, parked beside a convenient stile; but they noticed that Pru had now provided the pram with a red rear lamp. Once, when I had got up very early to go duck-flighting down by the river, I met her pushing her pram from the direction of Elmbury. She looked as fresh and dewy-eyed as the autumn morning itself; but when I took my hat off to her she modestly dropped her glance and gave me such a mere shadow of a vestal smile as Lucretia herself would not have been ashamed of. I was not at all surprised to meet her coming from Elmbury, because we were all aware by now of the identity of her new young man. No narrow nationalist was Pru. She was courting Pierre, the friend and partner of 'Enery, Pierre the French-Canadian with the wonderful side-whiskers and the sleek oily black hair.

Autumn drifted imperceptibly towards winter. For a week or two the hill was as many-coloured as Joseph's coat, then gradually as if they ran together on a palette the greens and reds and yellows blended into brown. Mr Chorlton, enjoying a respite from his gout, went pike-fishing in the river, caught nothing, lost all his tackle in a sunken chain belonging to the dredgers, and produced an apt quotation from Martial to fit the case: *Ecce redit sporta piscator inani.* Sir Gerald perfected (so he said) his razor-blade mowing-machine and proceeded to invent an improved model. He also added another society to the hundred or so to which he already belonged: he became a Baconian, to the vast annoyance of Mr Chorlton, who was often to be heard arguing with him very fiercely in the village street: 'I think perhaps the most insane part of the whole extraordinary heresy is your monstrous assumption that Bacon could possibly have created Bottom . . .'

George and Susan went nutting in the hazel-brakes and people said 'Ah' in a significant way, because we have a queer superstition about what happens when young couples go nutting together. The devoted pair, who daily discovered new enchantments in each other's company, now went to the Saturday night hops in the Village Hall for the sole purpose, it seemed, of slipping out together after the first dance; from that time onwards they were seen no more. Come snow, frost, rain or hail, it was all the same to them: 'Sure you won't get cold?' said George solicitously. 'It won't be so cold as sprout-picking,' Susan whispered back. There was also at this time a perpetual whispering among the Frolick Virgins, rather like the ceaseless and sibilant murmur of wind in aspen trees, and we got the impression that something highly dramatic was likely to happen soon in connexion with George and Susan: they were going, said the Frolick Virgins, to Elope.

Pistol, Bardolph and Nym, assisted by 'Enery and Pierre, discovered a new racket, and drove round to all the game-keepers in the district offering fancy prices for various sorts of vermin. They had a typewritten tariff which ran like this:

Grey Squirrels	4/6
Moorhens and Coots	2/9
Crows and Magpies	2/-
Jays a Bob	

and at the bottom of it was a rather furtive-looking scrawl in pencil:

Rabbits, partridges, pheasants by negotiation.

It was assumed that the squirrels, moorhens, crows, jays, etc, would appear later under the style of *chicken en casserole* in the more expensive London restaurants. Death, observed Mr Chorlton, is a great leveller.

As Christmas approached, the black market enjoyed its seasonal heyday and Nym sold a rabbit to a visitor from Birmingham for seven and sixpence. Later this record was beaten by Pistol, who came into the Horse and Harrow smiling happily and carrying an old sack which heaved in a familiar way (as if it were a lung breathing) and which contained, we knew, his fitcher ferret.

'Two rabbits' – he said – 'how much do you think I had for two rabbits, from a swell in a motey-car? How much?'

We said we couldn't guess. Pistol opened his hand to show us three ten-shilling notes. '"How much, mister?" the swell says; so I takes a chance and asks him fifteen bob: meaning for the two, see. But not a bit of it. "That's apiece?" he says. So "Let's 'andle," says I—' Pistol grinned and scratched his palm. '"Let's 'andle," says I, and he pays up, and I slings the rabbits all bloody on to his back seat and off he drives pleased as Punch.'

A week or two later 'Those Spivs', as Vicky angrily called them, went into the mistletoe trade; and we were rather surprised to learn that George Daniels was associated with them in this – he had bought a pair of climbing-irons with which he climbed up the trees to cut down the mistltooe boughs. We supposed that he went in for this dangerous pastime because he found peace boring, having been dropped so often out of the sky during the war. But Mrs Merrythought, when she heard of the climbing-irons, was filled with alarm for the safety of her girls, and especially of Susan. '*Men,*' she said darkly. 'They get up to anything.' And she had the windowsills of the land girls' bedrooms strung with barbed wire.

General Bouverie held his Opening Meet and needless to say failed to kill a fox; but he made up for this omission at his pheasant-shoot, when he completely filled the yellow wagon with slaughtered birds and also shot a record bag of woodcock. He was a strict and regular churchgoer, and he was heard to remark after the service on Sunday: 'I always notice that the woodcock arrive in these parts round about the time when the First Lesson is about Shadrak, Mishak and Abednego.'

So November went out, in a first flurry of snow, and as always happened at that time of year the world seemed to narrow about us. The village became a microcosmos, and within a circle which contracted as the days shortened our own affairs became proportionately larger, as if we saw them through a magnifying-glass. A poachers' hare-hunt across the General's fields, told at the Horse and Harrow, became an Odyssey. When Joe Trentfield killed his pig it was a drama watched by half the village. Dick Tovey was a priest with his sacrificial knife, and the pig's squeals filled the universe. Neighbours' quarrels were magnified into little wars; and every ordinary courting couple became Romeo and Juliet. And then suddenly the case of William Hart blazed up again, and loomed over all.

The Siege

We had heard that William had made a good recovery from his illness and was able to hobble as far as his drive-gates. His friends who called on him reported that he had broached a new cask of home-made wine (it was parsnip, very strong and very old, the same brew which had once robbed the Rector of his power of locomotion and laid him flat on his back on the roadside for the whole parish to see) and they added that he was rapidly drinking his way to the bottom of it. Perhaps it was this parsnip wine which fortified him and lent him its lustihood on the fourth of December, when at noon precisely, it being then ten weeks after Michaelmas Day, some minor official of the WAEC, accompanied by a valuer, arrived to complete the formalities of taking over his farm.

There was a very dirty and stinking pond, a disused drinking-place for cows, just outside William's farmyard; and having manoeuvred the official to the edge of the pond and having presumably surprised him off his guard, old William pushed him in.

We did not hear about this until the following morning, when Dai Roberts Postman, our village Mercury, brought round the news with the letters. Later in the morning I went to see Mr Chorlton and we discussed what to do next. It was apparent that something had gone wrong, because only a few days earlier Mr Chorlton had heard from Halliday that the Minister had promised 'sympathetic consideration' of William's case. The House was in the middle of some controversial legislation, with fierce debates and all-night sittings, and Halliday wrote that he was desperately busy. He wouldn't be down at Brensham until the recess, but then he hoped to give himself the pleasure of meeting old William and seeing if he was really as 'fierce and free as the weeds'. Also, said Halliday, he was going to hold a political meeting in the village on December 21st, under the chairmanship of Blacksmith Briggs; he hoped we'd all go and heckle him.

Certainly something had gone wrong. 'But it's a far cry,' Mr Chorlton pointed out, 'from the Whitehall desk to the local office. Perhaps an official goes on holiday or falls sick or instructions are misunderstood or a document goes astray; such things happen even in the best regulated bureaucracies. Meanwhile the Fate spins her inexorable thread.' We both, I think, felt by now that the case of William Hart was moving towards an inevitable climax and that we were helpless to alter the destined course of events. However we went down to the Post Office and sent a long telegram to Halliday; and then we dropped in for a drink at the Adam and Eve, where we learned that William, anticipating further developments, had begun to barricade himself in. He had driven his yellow wagon sideways against the garden gate and covered the top of it with a spider's web of barbed wire. The baker, paying his daily visit, had tossed the loaves to Pru across this obstacle. 'We'll take extra today,' said Pru calmly, 'in case we're besieged.'

'*I wun't go willing,*' I remembered William saying. '*They'll have to fetch I.*'

At six o'clock that evening a wire came from Halliday: 'Making urgent inquiries.' But by then it was already too late. The official had returned with two companions. They had driven their car down the drive, where they were halted by the formidable barricade, which was now reinforced with a huge pile of prickly hedge-trimmings. Glancing up at the farmhouse, they had found themselves face to face with a shotgun, which was poking out of a bedroom window and behind which they caught a glimpse of William's unblinking blue eyes. They had retired hastily, and in the course of backing their car down the drive had had the misfortune to bog themselves in a deep ditch. Our local garage-man had pulled them out, and they had driven away with the intention, he understood, of reporting their alarming experience to the police superintendent.

No, said Mr Chorlton, we could do nothing more. Things had gone too far for our intervention. Clotho, Lachesis and Atropos had the business in hand. Already, no doubt, there was a summons out against William for assault, to say nothing of being in possession of a firearm with intent to endanger life. 'I suppose,' he said, 'that in the end they'll have him certified; for surely the State must either do that or admit itself to be insane – which, of course, is unthinkable.'

Two days later we heard again from Halliday. He enclosed copies of his Private Notice Question and the Minister's reply. 'The case of William Hart had been given careful consideration in view of his age and alleged infirmity. There had, unfortunately, been a regrettable development within the past forty-eight hours. An assault had apparently been committed upon one of the Ministry's servants, and the Minister would point out that if Mr Hart had been as infirm as he was represented to be it seemed unlikely that he could have thrown the official into a pond. (Laughter.)'

'So, you see, I can't do much more,' wrote Halliday. 'Our poor old farmer seems to have taken the law into his own hands (demonstrating, incidentally, the strength of Samson, whereas I had pitched a tale that he was on his death-bed) and I'm afraid he'll have to suffer the consequences. But if you think of any way in which I can still be useful, let me know.'

The Stirrup-cup

Conscious and confident of its tremendous power, the State sometimes chooses to exercise that power in a way that seems almost leisurely. I have often thought that the very slowness of these processes makes them more terrifying than any swift retribution would be. It is the leisureliness of a huge and mighty animal which bestirs itself and yawns and with the utmost deliberation stretches out its deadly paw. There is no immediate response to your gesture of defiance; your ringing challenge echoes and dies away in a horrible silence, your fierce blows expend themselves uselessly like the fists of a maniac hammering on the walls of his padded cell. Nothing happens; but the challenge is noted, the blows are counted, all you have said and done is set down against the hour of reckoning.

So it was in the case of William. The officials drove away, and we all said: 'Tomorrow they will be back, and they will bring the police with them.' Mr Chorlton, who had taken the trouble to acquaint himself with the law, asserted that if necessary even the military could be called in to evict old William. Soldiers! It didn't seem possible, we said, in England. But the officials did not return on the morrow, nor on the next day, nor the next; and the only policeman who went to William's farm was our own Constable Banks, who climbed painfully over a prickly hedge – he was still suffering from boils – to deliver a summons for Common Assault. He saw no gun, he said, and found William in a normal frame of mind. He was offered, but did not accept, a glass of parsnip wine. Ten days passed, and still nothing happened; except that William continued to consider himself in a state of siege, and strengthened the fortifications outside his front door.

On the tenth day I happened to pass by his farm, on my way back from a walk over the hill. There is a field-path, an old right-of-way, which leads round the edge of the Home Ground and within a few yards of the back of the farmhouse. At the stile into the Home Ground I found young Jerry, armed with his catapult. I inquired what he was doing and he said he was a sentry; but if I was a Friend, I could go by. I asked him what enemies he expected and he said cheerfully: 'The police. They were here this morning but Grandad frightened them away.' So that was that, I thought. We had come nearly to the end of The Case of William Hart.

I left Jerry at the stile, where he strutted to and fro very confidently, reminding me of David and planting in my mind the gravest doubts concerning the accuracy of the Book of Kings. *Dieu est toujours pour les gros bataillons!* I thought.

I went on and came to the place where the path skirted the farmhouse and buildings. The garden was a brown thicket, for the first frosts had stripped the foliage from the riotous multitude of flowers and vegetables; but beside the back door there was still a bed of orange-tawny chrysanthemums with drooping heads nearly as big as dinner-plates. Only William, surely, could grow such flowers! I saw Pru, as demure and composed and unconcerned as ever, hanging out the washing on the line; and I waved to her, but I hadn't the heart to stop and talk. Then I happened to glance up at the house, and at one of the bedroom windows I caught my last glimpse of William.

His face was as brown as old shoe leather and as wrinkled as a russet apple in the New Year. His beard and eyebrows, in striking contrast, were snow-white, a wild lock like Whistler's swirled up from his forehead, his beard jutted out in a jaunty fashion, the moustache and the bushy eyebrows likewise had an upward curl. His eyes, old as he was, were as clear and blue as the Germander speedwell. And he was laughing.

He had a pint mug in his hand, and now he raised it ceremonially and drank my health. Still laughing, he picked up the gun off his knees and patted its butt. Then he filled the glass again and held it out at arm's-length like one who takes his last farewell drink before a journey; and as I went on my way he waved his hand to me in what seems now to have been a valedictory wave.

PART FOUR

THE WIND

Joe's Dream – William Hart is Dead – Like Wind I Go – The Funeral – Carminative Drinks – Runaways' Eyes May Wink – Age, libertate Decembri – The Last Untidy Corner – Epilogue

Joe's Dream

NEXT morning I had to drive into Elmbury and I stopped at the Horse and Harrow on the way, to make some arrangements about a cricket-meeting. It was about ten o'clock, and Joe Trentfield was sweeping out his bar. He stood at the open door and insisted on telling me in elaborate detail the peculiar dream he had dreamed the night before. Joe was much given to dreaming and he thoroughly enjoyed it, for there was never anything horrific about the phantasies which ornamented rather than troubled his repose. They were benign, extravagant and absurd, so that even in his sleep he sometimes chuckled at them, and his nights were almost as merry as his days.

On this occasion he had dreamed that he was standing in the middle of the Summer Leasow, which is our big common field in the bend of the river, with his gun under his arm, waiting for duck. Mrs Trentfield, rather unsuitably dressed in the huge flowery hat she had worn at her wedding, stood at his side. There was a turbulent sunset ('like a whacking great poached egg,' said Joe) out of which flew in successive formations a procession of strange and heraldic beasts. First there came lions, golden and formalized, making much the same pattern against the clouds as they make on the Royal Standard. They were followed by a phalanx of spotted leopards which wafted themselves through the air in a very dignified fashion by means of an undulating movement of their paws. White horses succeeded them, rising and falling like the wooden horses on roundabouts at the Fair; at the heels of these came rampant tigers, and a squadron of unicorns brought up the rear. This unusual spectacle by no means daunted the stout heart of Joe Trentfield, nor did it occasion him any great surprise. He did, however, observe thoughtfully to Mrs Trentfield: 'They're flying south. We shall get some rough weather.' Then he woke up.

When he had finished telling me his dream his wife's voice, from within the bedroom upstairs, commented that it was all them chitterlings on top of a bellyful of cider. Joe grinned tolerantly. 'Maybe,' he said, 'but all the same it *is* blowing hard.' The gilded weathercock on the spire of the church was pointing nor'-west; and from the north-west out of a grey sky the wind came whistling up the village street, tearing at the boughs of the big apple tree beside the inn and blowing into fantastical shapes the remarkable assortment of family washing which Mrs Trentfield had hung out in the yard the night before. An outsize blouse bulged as if Mrs Trentfield's vast bosom still inhabited it; stockings, pair by pair, danced jigs and minuets; Joe's long-legged winter combinations imitated the grotesque contortions of a fat man hanging from the gibbet; suspenders dangling from a pair of corsets had captured a pale-blue brassière which like a mackerel on a handline frantically flapped and wriggled;

wind-filled bloomers achieved voluptuous shapes resembling the jaunty and generous behinds of their owners, Mimi and Meg. Joe, who had an eye for such things, placed his hands on his hips and laughed heartily; and when a pair of pink knickers became detached from the line and sailed away over the garden fence he laughed the louder. The wind whisked away his deep guffaw and sped it up the street in the wake of the knickers, which came to rest at the feet of Dai Roberts Postman, who was delivering letters next door.

Dai Roberts picked them up, handling them with obvious distaste and embarrassment, for he was a puritanical man who believed that the cause of morals, as well as that of comfort, was best served by flannel next the skin. As he did so a sound other than Joe's laughter made him tilt back his head and stare upwards. It was a queer sound, a sort of breathless clamour, as if a pack of hounds was hunting up there in the heels of the north wind. I craned my neck, and at last I saw a small cloud the size of a man's hand, dark against the grey mass of clouds, which even as I watched it became teased out into a long skein like a ball of wool unwinding or the swift streak of an approaching line-squall, and then suddenly resolved itself into a pattern of flapping wings. Grey geese! – two score of them in the first ragged V, and a bigger lot behind stretching wing-tip to wing-tip half-way across the horizon. Their honking filled the air, a crazy wild cry out of Spitzbergen or the Siberian waste, the untamed voices of creatures inexpressibly free. It was an alien sound in our placid English countryside, and I felt a kind of pricking at the back of my neck as I listened to it. Dai Roberts too sensed the strangeness and the wildness of it; he waved and shouted. But now the vanguard was vanishing towards the south, the main body was passing overhead, the last stragglers were coming up over the church spire. Joe declared that they formed much the same pattern in the sky as the heraldic creatures in his dream; the geese rode on the wind's back as easily and swiftly as those phenomenal leopards! He was filled with awe at the strange coincidence, and being assured now that his dream had contained a prophecy, he announced in a loud voice to his wife within the bedroom:

'They're flying south, my dear. We shall get some rough weather.'

William Hart is Dead

Joe asked me into the bar for a half-pint of beer; and because of the strong wind he closed the front door. A moment later Mimi's pink knickers and the morning letters came tumbling together into the wire letter-box. Dai's sing-song voice came after them. He is something more than a postman, for he bears every day from house to house the latest tidings, scandal or gossip.

'Mr Trentfield,' he said, 'I haf some sad news for you. Old William Hart is dead.'

When he said that I had a queer feeling that Brensham would never be quite the same again; it was as if the whole landscape was altered, as if Brensham Hill itself had suddenly disappeared during the night.

Dai spoke through the letter-flap, for he had a strong prejudice against public houses and it was his stern boast that he had never set foot in one. He went on:

'Died in his chair he did early this morning with a glass they do say in his hand.'

'Old William,' said Joe. 'Well, well.'

'And as soon as it was light the police came to his farm, and surrounded the house, because they believed he was desperate and armed, do you see; and all the time he was lying there dead to shame them.'

'Well, well!' said Joe again.

'And the boy Jerry shot at them with a catapult,' Dai went on. 'Truncheons they had brought to deal with a maniac who carried a shotgun; and a little boy with a catapult they did find.' He paused to take breath and continued: 'Natural causes the doctor says it was. No inquest will there be. Better part of a jugful of wine he had drunk before he died. Empty to the last drop they do say the glass was in his hand!'

'It would be,' said Joe, nodding his head in grave approval of this demonstration of the fitness of things. 'Aye, it would be empty.' Dai withdrew his mouth from the letter-slit and the flap went back with a loud click. As he took Mimi's crumpled knickers and the letters out of the box Joe shook his head and sighed.

'That's a queer ending,' he said, 'to the case of William Hart.'

'Perhaps in a way the best ending,' I said. I was thinking of Mr Chorlton's dreadful prophecy: 'I suppose that in the end they'll have him certified.'

'Aye. He had a good innings,' went on Joe. 'He must 'a' bin nearly eighty. 'Tis ten years at least since we saw him in this bar.' I followed his glance as he looked towards the chimney-corner by the fireplace which had been William's favourite seat, and as if it were yesterday I could remember the wild old man sitting there. I saw him with a red-hot poker in his hand warming up a pot of the spiced ale which always set him singing. The ale fizzed into brown froth round the poker till it had a great mushroom head in it overhanging the rim of the pot. William raised it to his lips and drank deep, and the foam flecked his white moustache and beard. Then while he beat time with the blackening poker he began to sing. Surely nobody had ever possessed such powerful lungs as he! When he sang it was like a tornado blowing through the bar. You had an impulse to pick up your glass off the counter lest it should be swept away by that torrent of sound.

'What a man!' said Joe reflectively. It was curious how often people said 'What a man!' when they spoke of William. He shrugged his shoulders. I suppose if you keep a pub your bar becomes increasingly populated by ghosts as the years go by, although there are always new customers, young and vigorous, elbowing them out of the way. The memory of William Hart, I thought, would surely be one of those late-lingering and obstinate ones which wouldn't readily give way to the youngsters and which would never again take any notice (William when alive had never taken much notice) of 'Time, Gentlemen, Please!' It was difficult, even now, to imagine him lying dead. Life in him had been like a yeast, ever fermenting and renewing itself and furiously working again.

Joe picked up his broom and began energetically to sweep out the bar, as if he would sweep the ghost of William out of the way. For a moment or two he swept in silence, then as the rising wind howled in the crooked chimney he paused on the broom and glanced out of the window at the dark threatening sky where the clouds surged like waves in a rough sea.

''Tis William Hart's own weather,' he said oddly. 'You could almost think him to be up there in the wind.'

Like Wind I Go

For three days after William Hart's death the boisterous wind barged about Brensham with the aimless mischief of a cart-horse colt. It thundered through the orchards and gave the plum trees a rough and ready pruning. It plucked the thatch from cottages and the hats from people's heads. It tugged at sleeves and fluttered skirts, and somehow when it did so it seemed to tug at the spirit and flutter the heart as well. It was a rollicking, uproarious, antic wind, which reminded us all, as it had reminded Joe Trentfield, of the free spirit of William Hart.

And indeed one felt, somehow, as one went about Brensham during those three days, a strange sort of restlessness, wildness, excitement, what you will. If there was grief and anger blowing about in the wind, there was laughter and song as well, and something else which I cannot explain, something which I can only describe as a turbulence of the spirit as well as of the air. Dai Roberts felt it, when he went about his rounds singing *Land of My Fathers* at the top of his voice and composing, he told me, a poem of forty stanzas about the Pentecost in the manner of the great bard Taliesin. Mr Chorlton felt it when his hat went spinning down the village street and, forgetting his gout, he pursued and fielded it as smartly as he'd fielded many a ball when he played cricket for Somerset forty years ago. Jeremy Briggs the blacksmith felt it, when he stood at the door of his smithy and remarked to me that his bellows, compared with the wind, were as puny as the Labour Government, and discoursed of a revolution after his own simple heart which should be as fierce and brave and cleansing as the gale.

Odd things happened which matched our turbulent mood. The wind toppled over one of the dredger-cranes which was engaged in destroying Sammy Hunt's osier-bed, and as it fell into the river Sammy performed a war-dance of delight upon the bank. Then in accordance with the tradition of his sea service, which will not let even an enemy drown, he took out his boat and rescued the crane's operator who had fallen in with it.

And late one afternoon, as I was walking, I was startled to hear the sound of singing, coming, it seemed, out of the very sky. I looked up, and nearly at the top of a sixty-foot aspen tree I saw George Daniels, hanging on for dear life and hacking away with his knife at a misletoe bough to which he had already attached a rope. The tall tree creaked and groaned, and the swaying motion, accompanied by the rush of air, must have reminded George of the time when he parachuted down to fight the Germans at Bruneval.

'*Singing yi-yi-yippy-yippy-yi!*'

yelled George.

'They'll be wearing their red berets when they come!
They'll be wearing their red berets,
They'll be wearing their red berets,
They'll be wearing their red berets when they come!'

But just as he cut through the mistletoe bough an extra strong gust interrupted the song, and for a moment he was compelled to cling to the rough stem of the aspen with both his hands and both his knees. The tree leaned so far with the wind that its branches grated against those of another tree; then as it slowly righted itself George lowered the mistletoe to the ground, steering it neatly between the branches, to where Pierre and 'Enery stood ready to receive it. (Their lorry, I now saw, was parked by the side of the lane.) 'I've had enough of this hushabye-baby stuff!' shouted George; and quickly followed the mistletoe bough, digging his climbing-irons into the bark and hugging the rough aspen-trunk as tightly, I'm sure, as he'd ever hugged the slim waist of Susan.

Then Jaky Jones, who was busy making William's coffin, brought back a strange report from the farmhouse where he had been to do his necessary business. He told me this story as he planed a piece of wood in his workshop and grumbled at its twisted grain and the rough knots in it. ('Lord knows what old William would say!') I must tell it here in my own way, for I cannot attempt to sustain for long the individual manner of Jaky, every paragraph peppered with 'Matey' and 'How's your father'. Jaky, it seems, when he came downstairs from William's room, found the three daughters, Betty, Joan and Pru, 'looking a bit queer' and when he saw the bottle on the table he realized that they'd been at William's home-made wine. This bottle was labelled 'Sloe gin'; no doubt they had thought it a ladylike, respectable and almost teetotal drink, and being unaccustomed to drinking had taken too much. Without speaking, they beckoned to him and led him along a passage towards the still-room. At the end of the passage Joan opened the door, stood back, and said simply: 'Look.'

It was an astonishing sight. The small still-room was filled, from floor to ceiling, with casks and bottles. The casks occupied the whole of the floor-space and were stacked three deep; Jaky said they made him think of Gunpowder Plot. The bottles took up four long shelves, and he reckoned there must be twenty dozen at least. All were carefully labelled, and there were almost as many sorts as there were bottles. *Elderberry*, *Elderflower*, *Dandelion*, *Mead*, *Mangel-Wurzel*, *Nettle*, *Parsnip*, *Carrot*, *Potato*, *Raspberry*, *Gooseberry*, *Rhubarb*, *Raisin*, *Blackcurrant Extra Strong* . . .

Listening to Jaky, I could well imagine that Guy Fawkes' well-stocked cellar had contained nothing half so dangerous. What pranks and riots and fights and foolishness were confined like genii in those two hundred-odd bottles! What devilry lay dormant in those piled-up casks! What concentrated mischief grew daily more potent as it fermented privily in that little dark room! The place, said Jaky, was like an arsenal and the stupendous thought that troubled him was this: *The old gentleman had really intended to drink the lot!*

Back in the kitchen, Joan poured Jaky out a glass of sloe gin; she also refilled her own and her sisters' glasses. The effect of the drink was so palpably beneficial that nobody saw any harm in having another; and after that it became almost a sacred duty to have a third. By this time Betty's eyes had a curious dreamy look, while Joan's cheeks were the colour of a ripe Ribstone Pippin.

''Tis sad but certain,' said Joan in a far-away voice, 'that we couldn't drink all that wine ourselves, not if we lived to be a hundred.'

Betty nodded gravely.

'Not if we lived to be as old as 'Thuselah,' she declared.

''Thuselah, 'Thuselah,' repeated Pru solemnly; and suddenly giggled.

'The thing that's worrying me,' said Joan, 'is what in the world shall we do with it all?'

'Listen!' said Betty. 'Please do listen! I've got an idea.' She paused and took a deep breath, for she was already, Jaky thought, beginning to find it difficult to put things into words. Then she made a momentous statement.

'I think the village should have it,' she said. 'The whole village. After the funeral. You know he always liked people being happy.'

'Oh, Betty,' said Joan, 'I think it's a *beautiful* idea!'

'Oh, Betty, how *clever* you are,' agreed Pru.

'We'll have it taken down to the Horse and Harrow,' Betty went on. 'They'll be glad of it, because they're always short of beer. And everybody in the village can drink a health to poor old Dad! Think of it, the village all crowded elbow-to-elbow in the bar, and Joe says, "Ladies and gentlemen, here's to William Hart, God Bless Him, and—"'

At this point Betty's moving speech was suddenly interrupted by a loud crash. The indecorous wind had blown down a chimney-pot from the roof of the farmhouse, and as it crashed on to the gravel path in front of the window Pru remembered her two babies in the pram outside and with a squeak of alarm ran out to make sure that they had come to no harm. Betty and Joan ran out after her; and Jaky followed.

The babies were sleeping peacefully (and indeed they were so used by now to moving accidents by flood and field that they would probably have taken no notice of an earthquake!); but as the three sisters stood arm in arm beside the pram the fresh air began to affect them, they swayed slightly, and suddenly a gust of wind seemed to blow them together. Each leaning inwards, they formed a pyramidal pattern, like a camera tripod, said Jaky, or the piled rifles of soldiers; and if one had let go they would all have fallen down. Thus they hung on to each other with their heads almost touching and their legs forming the base of the pyramid; and as a turbulent eddy surged about them, Joan gasped, half-crying, half-laughing:

'Oh, Betty, listen, listen—'

'The wind!' cried Betty.

'Boisterous he was.'

'He always loved a wind. Often he'd laugh and shout when it was blowing.'

And suddenly, said Jaky ('for to tell the truth, Matey, the sloe gin was beginning to work on me too!') – suddenly it seemed as if the air was full of voices. It chuckled, sang, shouted, bellowed, hollered its joy like old William taking leave of the pub or for that matter like old William taking leave of the world.

The Funeral

On the twenty-first of December, the day of the funeral, when they carried William down to the churchyard in his own yellow wagon, the wind blew harder than ever. It had been William's wish that he should make that last journey in the great wain; and George Daniels with Susan's help had washed and scrubbed the flawless paint and groomed the old horse and polished the head-brasses till they glittered. The words 'W. Hart, Wainwright' on the side of the wagon looked as clear and fresh as on the day when William had stencilled them.

Almost everybody in the village, and some people from far away, turned up at the funeral. The Fitchers and Gormleys were there in full strength, dressed in their best clothes, and wonderfully sober; but they would be drunk later, we knew, for their grief was deep and genuine and they would be constrained to drown it. Halliday arrived with Vicky at the last moment, having just driven down from London; he seemed very upset, and blamed himself, he said, for not acting quickly enough. But we all felt that nothing which Halliday or anybody else could have done would have altered the course of events; it was destined and somehow fitting that William should have died when he did.

While the coffin was being lowered into the grave which Jaky Jones had dug for it the wind reached its crescendo. Mr Chorlton whispered to me: '*He is made one with Nature: there is heard His voice in all her music,*' and just then a flock of geese with a wild cry went over towards the south.

After the funeral Pru in her mouselike way padded to and fro among the people in the churchyard inviting them in a soft meek voice to go to the Horse and Harrow in the evening to drink William's health in his own home-made wine. Her step-sisters, Betty and Joan, invited some more. As a matter of fact, because we live so close to the Welsh border, it is not at all unusual in our parts to hold a kind of wake after a funeral; and nobody except perhaps the Hallidays was unduly surprised.

So in the afternoon the yellow wagon, driven by George Daniels, made its second journey down to the village, this time filled with bottles and casks. Joe Trentfield had gone up to the farm to help with the loading; and he, with Susan, Betty, Joan and Pru, rode in the wagon sitting on top of the casks. It is said that some of the bottles exploded as they were loaded into the wagon, and that the party drove down the hill to the accompaniment of a violent cannonade; but nobody minded, because as Betty remarked it simply showed how powerful the stuff was – and what were a few bottles lost among so many?

It is said, too, that as the party were loading up outside the farmhouse the cork blew out of a bottle of parsnip wine; and rather than waste it they invited various passers-by whom they encountered in the lane to have a drink with them. Among these were a group of Fitchers and Gormleys, and the Frolick Virgins, bicycling up the hill to their afternoon work, and Dai Roberts coming back from his round. Now Dai Roberts is a strict teetotaller, and it seems unlikely that he would have accepted any of the wine. Nevertheless I assure you that I saw him going down the village street in the late afternoon, pedalling as fast as he could with the wind behind him, and singing very loudly indeed a song so cheerful that he would normally have considered it Profane – the merry little song called *Sospan*

Fach. Moreover, a party of Fitchers and Gormleys were certainly involved in a fight later in the day – the cause of the trouble, I understand, was an allegation that the recently-married Gormley youth had beaten his Fitcher wife – and for half an hour at least a rout of these gypsies ran up and down the village crying to each other their customary insults of 'Hatchet!' 'Gallows-birds', 'Wife-stealers!' – and 'What's in the salmon-nets today?'

As for the Frolick Virgins, they certainly did no sprout-picking; for General Bouverie and his hounds suddenly appeared in the neighbourhood in pursuit of their usual phantom fox which nobody had actually seen and land girls tearing after the hounds on their bicycles while General Bouverie clattered down the village street shouting 'Fishcakes and Haemorrhoids!' and demanding of all and sundry: 'Have you seen my fox, damn and blast you?'

At about half past five I called for Mr Chorlton and we walked down to the Horse and Harrow to drink a toast to William Hart as we'd promised to do. Sir Gerald told us that he would come down later; he was kneeling on the floor, surrounded by hundreds of razor blades, giving the final touches, he said, to the Improved Model of his patent mowing-machine.

There was a fitful moon, and by its light the antic aspect of Brensham was enhanced and exaggerated. The bare branches of the goblin trees, tossed by the gale, seemed to grope about the roofs of the queer-shaped huddled cottages and their twigs tapped at the windows beneath the shaggy thatch. The hanging sign of the Adam and Eve squeaked like a banshee as it swung to and fro. On the wind from time to time, now faint, now loud, came the harsh and terrible and nerve-tickling cry of the wild geese. Crack-brained Brensham! Any strange thing might happen here, I thought – in weather like this, what might not happen? I was aware of the adventurous wind blowing away at the very topgallants of my spirit, and as recklessly as any drunken pirate's my heart cried: 'Let it blow!'

Carminative Drinks

When we got to the Horse and Harrow Joe was busy tapping the casks of wine, and Mrs Trentfield, Mimi and Meg were decorating the bar ready for Christmas with sprigs of holly and a great bunch of mistletoe which bore such a crop of berries that it made you think of a rich dowager overdressed with pearls. The Frolick Virgins were there already, with about half a dozen of their young men, and everybody kissed everybody else under the mistletoe a great many times. I asked where Susan and George had got to, and Wistaria said 'Hush! It's a great secret. You'll know later,' and all the Frolick Virgins giggled and began whispering together like a flock of agitated starlings.

Soon Alfie Perks and Sammy Hunt arrived, and Briggs dressed up in his black Sunday suit with his thick gold watch chain and a red rosette in his buttonhole because he was going to take the chair later at Halliday's meeting. Then Halliday himself turned up, with Vicky looking unusually wind-swept, and Jaky Jones with his bowler hat on the back of his head. As the bar filled up, Betty, Joan and Pru began to pour out the wine and to hand round the glasses. At last when there were about thirty people in the bar, Betty nodded to Joe Trentfield and he climbed ponderously on to the counter and calling for a silence in his sergeant-major's voice asked everybody to drink a silent toast to William Hart.

So we drank to old William in the wine which his own hands had so skilfully concocted. The brew, I think, was

Raisin Wine Extra Strong, but whatever it was, Lord, it was cockle-warming stuff! 'Like a brazier glowing in your vitals!' said Jeremy Briggs. Pru, like Hebe, refilled our glasses, it seemed, before we realized that we had emptied them, and so we drank again. Mr Chorlton, smacking his lips, announced that the wine was Extremely Carminative, adding that one of his schoolboys in an examination paper had defined Carminative as 'something that makes you sing'.

'Bless me,' said Mr Chorlton, 'if we have a few more glasses of this we shall begin to prove that he was right!'

As Betty filled my glass again I happened to hear a curious aside spoken by her to Joan.

'Do you think Pru ought to have another?' she asked doubtfully.

'The Nurse said I must never touch a drop when I was having our Ivy,' whispered Joan, and I realized that Pru was in disgrace again. 'She said it might bring me on else.'

Betty gave way, however, and filled Pru's glass. Meanwhile we were all, I think, beginning to feel the effect of the heart-warming drinks. Sammy Hunt was fairly launched on his story about the Engine-Room Mutiny ('There were little yellow men all round me, and I felled them one by one with a clip behind the ear'), Joe Trentfield uttered from time to time his deep chuckle which was really very much the same noise as the *Minnehaha Laughing Water* of the tank filling when the plug was pulled, and Halliday, with reckless empiricism, had changed from Raisin Extra Strong to Plum Jerkum 'just to see what it tasted like'. 'Please do remember,' said Vicky in alarm, 'that you've got another meeting in Elmbury after your meeting here.' But Halliday only laughed and said the wine would make him talk better.

Betty came round again, holding the bottle rather unsteadily, and pressed us all to have 'just one more'.

'But not for Pru,' she said firmly.

'Oh, Joan, *please*' – and Pru's enormous china-blue eyes looked as if they were about to fill with tears.

It was impossible, for long, to resist the pathetic stare of Pru, as half the young men in Brensham had discovered. So Betty relented, and indeed she was feeling so benevolent by now that she would, I am sure, have bestowed the whole bottle upon anybody who had asked for it. Pru, as a matter of fact, was the only person in the room who looked completely composed. She took her drink, in her quiet mouse-like way, as she took life – as it came.

It was about this time (though one tended to lose count of time) that Halliday, Vicky, Briggs and a few more went off to the political meeting; but their places were taken by new arrivals, and half Brensham was packed elbow-to-elbow in Joe's little bar. Among the new arrivals was Sir Gerald, who made a spectacular entrance, for both his hands, were swathed in blood-stained bandages. '*Now does he feel his secret murders sticking on his hands*,' said Mr Chorlton. 'What the devil have you been up to, Gerald?' Sir Gerald gave us a wan smile. Something had gone wrong with the Improved Model, he said. In some mysterious way the razor-toothed blades of the machine had 'sprung back and sort of snapped at him'. He added with pride that the machine had nevertheless demonstrated its cutting power in a remarkable fashion: if he had not been wearing stout gloves he would certainly have lost his fingers.

I was in no mood for politics so I didn't go to the meeting which Halliday, elevated by a mixture of Raisin Wine and Plum Jerkum, addressed for nearly an hour. I don't know what he talked about (save that Vicky remarked later that if there had been a reporter present he would have lost his chance of an Under-Secretaryship) and I don't know what resolutions were passed nor what terrible threats against the

Tories were uttered by Jeremy Briggs as he stamped about on the platform in his Sunday suit and gold watch chain. I only know this, that a dozen reliable witnesses affirm that as they passed the Village Hall about eight o'clock they heard the sound of singing. And the words of the song with which, it seemed, the meeting was being wound up were the words which Brensham men had sung in their pubs for generations but which nobody, I am sure, had ever before sung at a political meeting.

Roll Me Over, came the chorus, borne up the street from the Village Hall on the wings of the north wind, *Roll me Over – in the clover – Roll me Over, Lay me Down, and do it agen!*

Runaways' Eyes May Wink

Now I shall find it difficult to write coherently of the remaining events which happened on Brensham's craziest evening, the evening of December the Twenty-First which, as Alfie Perks remarked, quoting an old rhyme, was

> St Thomas's grey, St Thomas's grey,
> The longest night and the shortest day.

First of all the crowd came back from the meeting, a sudden rout swirling into the tight-packed bar, and they told us that there were trees down all the way along the Elmbury road and there was another blocking the lane at the top of the village, so that the Hallidays could neither return to their house nor go on to the meeting at Elmbury. 'Tory Plot,' said Halliday with a sideways grin at his wife, who surprised us all by grinning back; she did not, as a rule, think that Tory Plots were anything to make fun of. Halliday added with obvious satisfaction that the telephone-lines were down too and it was impossible to get through to Elmbury. It gave him the greatest pleasure, I think, to picture his Agent anxiously biting his nails, and the little bespectacled Secretary running about in a flap in the horrible cobwebby Tolpuddle Memorial Hall. How much more pleasant to stay in the Horse and Harrow and drink William's cockle-warming wine than to stand before the dusty carafe of water with the glass upside down on top of it and face the persistent heckling of the unspeakable man with the pimply red face and the rainbow-striped Old School Tie!

'It can't be helped,' said Halliday cheerfully. 'There's no way of getting to Elmbury so that's that. You cannot legislate against the wind.' And as if this rather curious phrase pleased him, he repeated it slowly, and I realized that he was more than a little drunk. It occurred to me that it was probably years since he had been drunk if indeed he had ever been drunk before in his life and that he was obviously enjoying the unfamiliar sensation. Once again he repeated that stray wisp of a sentence which seemed to be related to nothing in particular – 'You cannot legislate against the wind. By God,' he said, 'I like that. It's the sort of thing a Frenchman might have said, Danton himself might have said, when the mobs were marching to the *Marseillaise*!'

Meanwhile Vicky in her precise way was explaining to Joe about the fallen trees. 'So, you see,' she ended, 'we can't go on to Elmbury and we can't go back home.'

'Well, you be proper buggered!' said Joe, roaring with laughter because nobody's minor misfortune ever failed to delight him. 'You'll have to stay the night here.'

Just then the door opened and there entered, in procession, Pistol, Bardolph, Nym, 'Enery and Pierre, followed by George Daniels and Susan. Through the open door we could see 'Enery's old lorry piled high with mistletoe. While Pru, who remained perfectly calm and self-possessed, speaking only when she was spoken to in her small prim voice, poured them out glasses of wine, Pistol told us a long story about how with George's help they had collected nearly half a ton of mistletoe, and how a man they knew in Birmingham had offered to buy it for seventeen pounds a hundredweight. 'So "Let's 'andle," says I, and we done the deal.'

Then Wistaria climbed on to the counter and announced dramatically that George and Susan were going to run away together and get married. George, it seemed, had made enough money out of his share of the mistletoe-deal to furnish a cottage, and they were going to buy a tractor and set up in a little business. ('Ploughing by Contract,' said Susan proudly.) So we all drank their health and wished them luck, and when they drove off with 'Enery in the lorry to Birmingham, where Susan said she had a married sister living (though nobody really believed this) the Frolick Virgins all rushed out and cheered them away as if they had indeed been setting out on their honeymoon.

'St Thomas's grey, St Thomas's grey,' cried Alfie Perks in valediction, 'the *longest night* and the shortest day!'

Pru, whose pram I nearly fell over when I went out to see George and Susan drive away, took advantage of a moment when her sisters weren't looking to slip out through the door. Light-hating, dark-loving, 'negatively phototropic' as Mr Chorlton put it, she wheeled away her babies into the windy darkness; and shortly afterwards Pierre crept out after her. Perhaps it was Pru's last chance, for we were told that she was going to live with her step-sister Betty, who had declared a firm resolve to 'keep her out of mischief in future'. 'This,' quoted Mr Chorlton, 'will be the decay of lust and late-walking throughout the realm!'

Age, libertate Decembri

Meanwhile Betty and Joan and Mimi and Meg still went about through the crowded room like almsgivers dispensing old William's particular brand of happiness to anybody who happened to have an empty glass. In retrospect the wine seems to have had a peculiar lightning property of illuminating certain incidents with vivid unforgettable flashes, while others have disappeared for ever into the darkness of oblivion. Of these disconnected flashes my memory of the evening is made up.

I remember, for instance, watching Halliday sitting in a corner with Pistol, Bardolph and Nym while they vied with each other in telling him stories about the campaigns they'd fought against Germans and Italians and Arabs and Afghans and fuzzy-wuzzies of various kinds. On Halliday's face, as he listened to these fantastic tales, there was – I swear – a look of real envy. This was the kind of things which he would have liked to have done himself! And when Bardolph held up his hand to demonstrate that he'd lost two fingers at Mons, and Pistol pulled up his trouser-leg to show the long scar which he said was due to the thrust of an assegai, what matter if I was aware that Bardolph had once put his hand under a circular-saw and that Pistol had spiked himself when he climbed over a fence to escape from an angry keeper? For the moment at any rate they were veterans of Agincourt:

Then will he strip his sleeve and show his scars
And say, these wounds I had on Crispin's Day,

and as I watched them I had the same sense of the proximity of Shakespeare and of the continuity and immortality of his people as I had had before when I talked to Jaky Jones and saw suddenly, peering out from under his bowler hat, the grim clown who dug Ophelia's grave.

I remember, in another vivid flash, a strange speech by Betty (or was it Joan ?) when she declared that she could never forgive herself for telling her father, on some occasion long ago, that his home-made wine was like the Devil inside him, making him bawl and holler. Too late, said Betty, she realized that she had been wrong; for she herself felt now as if she were filled, not with devils but with a whole choir of chanting angels; and to everybody's astonishment, in a rather quavering voice, she began to sing.

That set everybody singing. Mimi strummed on the piano, and we sang such a medley and mixture of songs as not even Brensham, surely, had ever sung before: a mixture half-Christian and half-Pagan like ourselves, for there were carols and folk-songs and soldiers' songs in the mixture, we sang impartially of Good King Wenceslas and Tom Pearce's Grey Mare, and the rats of exceptional size in the quartermaster's stores and of some unspecified person who would be wearing silk pyjamas when she came; of shepherds watching their flocks and of the wonderful Wizard of Oz; of Billy Boy and his charming Nancy Grey ('*She lies as close to me As the bark is to the tree!*'), of Mademoiselle from Armentières and John Peel. Alfie sang about the red poppies and Joe sang his imitation of the grunting pig, and the Frolick Virgins sang a song of their own invention, a very mournful song, about picking sprouts. And Sammy, of course, bellowed in his deep sailor's voice about the girl who had a dark and a rolling eye,

> '*And her hair hung down in ringalets,*
> *She was a nice girl and a decent girl,*
> *But one of the rakish kind!*'

And then suddenly, without being conscious that we were doing so, we found ourselves singing one by one all the songs which old William used to sing when he sat in the corner-seat by the fireplace and beat time with the poker. It was as if, said Alfie Perks, he stood close to us and prompted us; for there was no need for anybody to suggest a song, as soon as we'd finished one we were on with the next, as if the same thoughts ran through all our minds at the same moment.

We were still singing *Roll Me Over* when the company in twos and threes began to go home; and for hours afterwards, it seemed, people were singing in the streets, little snatches of song were blowing about Brensham on the wind. William's home-made wine was a carminative drink indeed!

The Last Untidy Corner

At last there were only about half a dozen of us left sitting round the sweet-smelling cherry-log fire which Joe always built up with architectural skill so that it made a bright pyramid of flame. Then Sammy put on his duffel-coat, slung the hood over his bald head, and remarked that it was time he went home to see if his house was still there or whether it had sunk under the river. Jaky Jones pushed his bowler hat still farther on to the back of his head, gave a sardonic shrug, and said, 'The Missus'll be lying in wait for me, else. And then it's Matey, look out!' They went home together, and Sammy called back to us through the door: 'The wind's going uphill, you can feel the sharp edge of it.' 'Feels like snow,' Jaky added. ''Ow's your father!' The five of us, Mr Chorlton and Sir Gerald, the Hallidays and I, still sat in front of the fire while Joe washed up the glasses. We had lost all sense of time.

Mr Chorlton glanced from Halliday to Vicky, and said:

'Well, you've seen us at our most disorderly now. Crack-brained Brensham at its best or worst. We're one of the last untidy corners in your tidy England. Do you still want to tidy us up?'

Vicky shook her head slowly.

'No, Diogenes . . .' That was her pet name for him now, Diogenes in his tub. 'No, I don't, but in some way or other I want to fit you in.'

'*Can you?*' Mr Chorlton leaned forward. 'Can you so arrange this planned and orderly world which you dream of so that there is still a place in it for the rebellious, the eccentric, the unruly – for people like William Hart? In such a world will we not all have to be good and bad in the same ways, all possessing the same moral stature, or being at any rate neatly graded – "From the left, in two ranks, size!" Can you fit in, let us say, people like Sammy Hunt who likes rivers to be crooked, or the odd-job-man (or do you call him a self-employed person now?) like Jaky Jones? Or even such an amorous individualist as Pru?'

Halliday was silent, wrinkling his forehead and staring into the fire as if he saw two conflicting dreams there and was trying to sort them out. Mr Chorlton went on:

'In the story of your England, will the huge shadow of Falstaff ever fall across the page? And the smaller, sneaking, troublesome shadows of Pistol, Bardolph and Nym? Or will you quietly eliminate them as Spivs and Drones? Will the people in that tale possess humours in the Elizabethan sense? Will ginger still taste hot i' the mouth to them? Will your standard of living, as you call it, have regard to fun, without which living is hardly worthwhile? Or will fun itself be something which has to be organized or controlled under a Minister of Popular Recreation with twenty psychologists and half a hundred censors on his staff?' He paused. 'Let

William Hart, for a moment, be the yardstick by which we judge your world. Have you room in it for these strange flowers that blossom in unexpected places, and give colour to the scene, like poppies in corn or wild weeds in a well-kept garden? Those people who, however headstrong and wrong-headed, nevertheless reaffirm in their lives the ancient freedom and dignity of man? Because if not, I warn you, though your great machines serve you like slaves, though your citizens have only to press a button to obtain all the ease and comfort and all the pleasure and knowledge they desire, then it will all be meaningless, it will taste like dust and ashes upon the tongue. So I ask you again: Can you fit in the William Harts?'

'I don't know,' said Halliday gravely. 'I don't know.' He looked up suddenly from the fire. 'But by God we'll try!'

Mr Chorlton smiled. 'Well, good luck to you! It's time I hobbled home.' He got up painfully; his joints were old and stiff. 'But one last word before I go. I'm going to say something now which is far more subversive than anything you've said or even thought of—' He smiled at Vicky. 'A more dangerous proposition than ever my female Cobbett has dared to put forward. It's simply this: *The ideal citizen is not the ideal man.* Norman Douglas, I think, was the person who said it. The ideal citizen is not the ideal man.'

We said goodnight to Vicky, Joe took her out into the kitchen to find a candle, while Sir Gerald opened the door and a few snowflakes came drifting in with the wind. My last memory of the evening is a rather odd one. Halliday as he put his glass down on the counter caught sight of the statue of the Long Man among the snuff-tins and suddenly leaned across and picked it up and set it on the counter in front of him. For a moment he stood smiling at it; and then he repeated once more that stray phrase which had pleased him earlier in the evening. 'You cannot legislate against the wind.' I don't know what he meant by it, nor whether he really knew himself. But I thought, as I looked at the little figure, that there was a great tearing wind of laughter and mischief blowing there, like the gale which had swept William Hart through life; and that was a wind which never blew in Westminster. You couldn't legislate against that!

Then Vicky came back with the candle, and Halliday put his arm round her, and they went through the kitchen and up the creaking stairs. Just as I followed Mr Chorlton out, Mrs Trentfield bustled into the bar for a final tidying-up, saw the Long Man on the counter, and observed cheerfully as she put him back behind the snuff-tins:

'Well, we do See Life, don't we?'

Epilogue

Three or four weeks later I walked down to the churchyard with Mr Chorlton to see the memorial headstone which, we heard, had been put up on William Hart's grave. It was a still sad day in January, and the village after its brief Saturnalia had gone back to the humdrum routine of sprout-picking. On the way to the churchyard we passed Alfie Perks' smallholding and recognized as we went by the patched breeks of Jaky Jones, the sombre backside of Count Pniack, and the behinds of the five Frolick Virgins bent over the sprout plants. Alfie in his gumboots went *plop, squelch, plop, squelch* through the mud. No, you certainly wouldn't suspect my people of their turbulence and their wildness and their dreams!

As we approached the lych-gate we met Pru coming out. As usual she was pushing her pram, in which the two tough little babies were happily sucking the paint off a couple of wooden toys which William Hart had carved long ago. The one baby licked the bowler hat of Jaky Jones, the other was chewing the feet of Joe Trentfield. Pru gave us a modestly downcast glance and a small, grave smile.

We walked across the cut grass to the grave. Betty, Joan and Pru, we understood, had together composed the wording on their father's headstone after days of cogitation and argument. The task could not have been an easy one; for the virtues and vices of William Hart were large ones, which might be chronicled in a whole book but could not baldly be set forth on a stone tablet. But in the end they hadn't made a bad job of it: and with a strict regard for truth and an admirable ecomony of words they had paid their modest tribute to William. 'Well . . . I wonder,' said Mr Chorlton, and we stood before the tombstone and read the lettering on the new stone. It said, briefly and simply:

HERE LIES
WILLIAM HART
HE WAS SAID TO BE A
DESCENDANT
OF THE
POET
SHAKESPEARE

R.I.P.

John Moore
The other two books in his famous Brensham trilogy